A BOBWHITE KILLING

T0159029

A
BOBWHITE
KILLING

Jan Dunlap

NORTH STAR PRESS OF ST. CLOUD, INC.
St. Cloud, Minnesota

First Edition, June 1, 2010

Printed in the United States of America

Published by
North Star Press of St. Cloud, Inc.
P.O. Box 451
St. Cloud, Minnesota 56302

www.northstarpress.com

info@northstarpress.com

CHAPTER ONE

W hat do I love about birding weekend trips? The camaraderie. A bunch of birders together with the same objective for a short thirty-odd hours: see as many birds as possible in a specific area. Sometimes I know a few of the other people; sometimes I get to meet all new folks. Kind of like a group blind date: I never know who I'm going to end up with. Maybe I'll get Cameron Diaz. Maybe I'll get stuck with the class clown. But, unlike a blind date, when I go on a birding weekend, I can always count on one thing: everyone there will want to talk about birds. Birds they've seen. Birds they hope to see. Birds they thought they saw, but couldn't confirm.

Okay, so maybe it's not the most diverse range of topics in the world. For a birder, though, it's a slice of heaven.

So I go on these weekends, follow the trip leader around, do a lot of driving, walking, and talking, and see birds. Usually, the leader has already scouted the area, which gives everyone a head start on finding the birds the group is targeting. Even on the weekends that don't produce all the birds I hope for, though, I still get to trade leads for hot new birding spots or try out other birders' new scopes or cameras. As far as I'm concerned, birding weekends are always win-win situations.

Except, maybe, for those rare weekends when the leader turns out to be a dud.

Or dead.

Yeah, that definitely puts a damper on a birding weekend.

GOING ON THE BIRDING WEEKEND trip to Fillmore County was one of those last-minute decisions I occasionally make when I'm desperate to get away. And believe me, I was desperate. If I had to listen one more time to my sister, Lily, gush about how wonderful her fiancé (a.k.a. the man formerly known as my best friend), Alan, was, I was either going to stuff a sock in her mouth or recount for her the lurid details about the droves of girls Alan used to "entertain" in our college dorm room.

Not that he actually did any of that, but Lily wouldn't know.

However, since I also figured that would probably get me a vicious shin-kicking from my tiny, but older, and very mean (sometimes), sister, I decided the smartest alternative was just to get out of town—and out of Lily's kicking range—for a few days.

Fillmore County, here I come.

Fortunately for me, there was room for one more person on the trip. With Luce, my girlfriend, booked to cook for an executive conference over the weekend, I was going to be flying solo anyway. I called up the BW—that's Birding Weekend—leader, took the slot, threw a change of clothes into my duffel bag, grabbed my binoculars and tripod, and put the rubber on the road.

By eight in the evening, I was in Fillmore County, signing my name at the front desk of the Inn & Suites in Spring Valley, where the weekend group was staying. According to the hotel clerk, I was the last one to check in. The BW leader had left a packet of information for me at the desk, and I scanned the materials while the clerk ran my credit card through the hotel register. Ten people were signed up for the weekend, and I was happy to see that one of them was my longtime birding buddy Tom Hightower. So at least it wasn't going to be a total blind date weekend. Worst case, if there was a class clown on the trip, I could always escape by grabbing Tom and taking off for birding on our own.

The clerk handed me a room key and I turned around, almost knocking over the woman who had come up behind me. I caught her shoulders to steady her and glanced down at her face.

And froze.

Only one person in the world had that particular shade of emerald in her eyes.

"Hello, Bob," she said. "It's been a long time."

I waited for my ability to speak to kick back in. "Shana Lewis," I finally managed to get out. "What are you doing here?"

She took a step towards me and stood on tiptoe to brush a kiss on my cheek. I caught a whiff of White Shoulders, the same scent she'd worn eighteen years ago, when I'd been crazy about her. I was sixteen and she was a junior in college; we bumped into each other looking for gulls at Black Dog Lake one Christmas. The following summer, we birded together regularly around the Twin Cities, and I fantasized about her falling in love with me.

Which she never did.

Instead, she graduated with honors from the University of Minnesota and took off immediately for California, where she earned a doctorate in the reconstruction of ecological communities. Last I'd heard, she was somewhere in South America working for the Nature Conservancy, which didn't surprise me in the least. When Shana Lewis set her mind to something, nothing could shut her down.

I remembered that well from the birding we did together. Just like I never forgot those emerald eyes of hers, either.

"It's Shana *O'Keefe*, Bob. Jack and I got married five years ago."

"No kidding? I hadn't heard." I figured I should let go of her shoulders, but my hands and brain had spontaneously disconnected the moment I recognized her. I still couldn't believe I was talking to Shana Lewis again after all these years. The idea that she was married to Jack O'Keefe—our BW trip leader—blew me away even more.

Not that Jack wasn't a great guy. He was. I'd known him for about ten years, in fact, but our birding trails hadn't crossed in a long time. Seeing Jack listed as the weekend's leader was one of the other reasons I'd decided to sign up at the last minute besides escaping Lily's gush fest. Jack was an extraordinary birder, and if he put a bird—even an uncommon one—on the list for a weekend, I could just about be guaranteed I'd see it. In fact, it was the uncommon one he'd listed that had tipped the scales for me in favor of joining the group, rather than taking off on my own bird chase.

Jack listed a Northern Bobwhite.

Which I've never seen in Fillmore County.

Let alone in the state of Minnesota. Especially since wild Northern Bobwhites were declared "extirpated"—locally extinct—back in 2004.

But if Jack O'Keefe said he'd find a Bobwhite, I believed him. And when he did locate the bird, I was going to be right there with him.

Along with his wife, the former Shana Lewis, my one-time summer love.

Talk about a surprise blind date.

"I'd ask you what you've been up to, but I read your posts on the MOU list serve all the time," Shana laughed. "It's nice to know your enthusiasm for birding hasn't dimmed at all since you were sixteen." She took a step back and looked me over from head to toe, and my hands finally responded to my brain's signals and slid gently off her shoulders. "Though I think you've gotten taller, Bob."

"Older, too," I smiled. A sudden wave of memory took me back eighteen years. I'd tried to kiss the twenty-year-old Shana and she'd fended me off, saying I was too young for her.

Looking down into those bright green eyes now, I couldn't help but think, *Not anymore.*

And then I gave myself a mental head slap. What was I thinking? I wasn't some lovesick teenager. I didn't want Shana Lewis. Or Shana O'Keefe. I was in love with Luce Nilsson. Hell, I'd even been on the verge of asking her to marry me before the Lily and Alan tsunami hit town. I was still going to propose, but now I wanted to wait till my sister was off center stage. Heaven forbid that Luce and I try to horn in on Lily's wedding of the century extravaganza. I wouldn't live to my wedding.

Suddenly seeing Shana again, though, was like I'd slipped into a time warp. Just hearing her voice was enough to send me back to that summer we spent together. I could still see her ponytail, her halter top over tight faded jeans filled out so perfectly behind. And regardless of my feelings for Luce, Shana's signature White Shoulders and green eyes were still potent stuff eighteen years later.

"So, what's it like to be married to Jack O'Keefe?" I asked her, deliberately focusing myself on the present. "I hear he's the man to watch in this state. Between the family fortune and his political connections, he seems to be calling the shots right now when it comes to shaping new environmental legislation." I stuck my room key in my pocket. "Not that I mind. I'm in Jack's camp all the way when it comes to preserving outdoor spaces."

"Hey, Bob!"

I looked past Shana to see Jack O'Keefe, tanned and fit, heading into the lobby. In three strides, he was across the room, extending his hand for me to shake.

"It's been a while, Jack," I said, taking his hand. His grip was firm, and he looked at least a decade younger than his fifty-eight years.

"And a lot of time out of the field, unfortunately. Taking care of business hasn't been leaving me much time for birding," Jack explained. "Even with Chuck minding the family store, I'm still spreading myself thin with developing these new eco-communities down here."

Chuck was Jack's son from his first marriage. I used to run into the pair of them on birding trips shortly after the first Mrs. O'Keefe passed away.

"Eco-communities?" I asked.

Jack planted a kiss on Shana's cheek and draped his arm over her shoulders. "Tomorrow, Bob, I'll tell you all about it while we're birding. Drive with us, and we can catch up in between stops. For now, I'm bushed. I've been out scouting all day, and I promised Shana we'd make it an early night. See you in the morning."

And that's the last I ever heard from Jack O'Keefe.

I did, however, see him again.

It was early the next morning when our birding group arrived at the Green Hills youth camp to try to locate a Yellow-billed Cuckoo on the property. Jack wasn't with us, leaving word with Shana that he'd headed out before dawn to draw a bead on the bird and would meet up with us at the camp. Spotting a small grove of trees that looked like it might be a good habitat for the Cuckoo, I walked down the slope from the gravel parking area and discovered an old covered wagon partially tucked into the grove.

Skirting around the rear end of the wagon, I found Jack sitting with his back to the buckboard. I noticed that he didn't have his binoculars with him. He did have something else, though.

Judging from the blood soaking the front of his jacket, he had at least a couple of bullets in him.

CHAPTER TWO

Do you see anything?" my buddy Tom Hightower asked as he rounded the corner of the old wagon, then stopped in his tracks. "Oh, my God."

I looked up at him from where I was kneeling next to Jack, checking for a non-existent pulse. "Don't let the rest of them come back here," I told him, pointing with my chin towards the other side of the wagon, where I could hear more birders starting to approach. "They don't want to see this."

Tom nodded, pulled out his cell phone, and dialed 911 as he went back around the wagon to steer away the rest of our group.

I sat back on my haunches and looked at the dead man in front of me. Jack's eyes were open and his mouth grim. His neck didn't feel stone-cold to me when I'd checked for a pulse, so I figured he hadn't been dead all that long.

Not that that made much of a difference in the big picture.

Whether you're dead for a short time or a long time, you're still dead.

"No! NO!"

I looked up to see Shana stumbling towards me, her face white with shock, her green eyes huge in her face.

And then, maybe because of my crouched position, I noticed something else that was huge.

Her belly.

Shana was pregnant.

As in, really pregnant.

I was speechless. How could I have missed that belly last night in the lobby or this morning at coffee before our group set out for the day? From what I could see now, that belly was going to beat Shana to Jack's corpse by at least a minute or two. The woman was huge.

Then my eyes caught the flapping of the oversized windbreaker Shana was wearing.

Mystery solved. That windbreaker could have been hiding a whale underneath it and no one would have been the wiser.

A whale? Make that a whole pod of them. I mean, seriously, I had never seen any woman's pregant belly as large as this.

Luckily for Shana, Tom was a lot faster to come to her aid than I was. Before she could trip on the uneven ground, he appeared behind her and put his arm around her shoulders, guiding her carefully closer to me and the body of her husband.

The stark look of loss on her face reminded me of what she was seeing: her husband filled with bullet holes. "Shana, you don't need to see this. Tom, take her back to the cars."

"No," she choked out, sobbing. "I need to be with him." She shot me a steely look that I vaguely recognized from a long time ago, and her voice sharpened. "Don't argue with me, Bob."

"No problem," I replied. I took another look at her swollen belly. If I thought Shana Lewis had been stubborn, I wasn't about to test it out with a super-sized Shana O'Keefe. Upsetting very pregnant ladies was definitely not on my list of things I really wanted to do today.

Tom helped her sit down on the ground next to me, and she immediately leaned into me, shaking and crying. I put my arms around her and held her close. "I'm so sorry, Shana," I said, squeezing her shoulder. "He was dead when I found him. I couldn't do anything for him."

She nodded into my shirt front and sniffed.

"Well, I guess that explains why he didn't meet us for coffee and rolls this morning."

I looked up to see silver-haired Bernie Schmieg, another familiar birder from our group, standing near the corner of the wagon. She was squinting at Jack through her glasses. "What'd you do, Jack? Spill some coffee on your jacket? Shana, honey, the drycleaners can get that out. It won't stain."

"Jack's dead, Bernie," Tom told her. "I don't think the coat is an issue now."

Bernie shot me a glance. "He's dead?"

I nodded.

Bernie turned as white as her hair and promptly passed out.

"Oh, crap," I said, still holding a sobbing Shana and the whales against my side.

Shana and the whales. It sounded like a band from the 1970s.

"I'll get her," Tom offered.

He knelt beside Bernie and lightly slapped her cheeks, then propped her up against the old wagon's front wheel. Tom's a registered nurse who worked the night shift at a nursing facility, so I knew that Bernie was in good hands. A couple moments later, he helped her stand up and guided her back to where the other birders, I assumed, were waiting for the police to arrive.

Shana whispered something into my shoulder, but I didn't catch it.

"I'm sorry, what did you say?"

"I know who killed him," she whispered again, this time louder and clearer.

A chill raced up my spine. I looked down so I could see her face.

"Who? Who killed Jack, Shana?"

Her emerald eyes bored into mine through a wall of tears.

"I did, Bob. It's all my fault. I killed my husband."

CHAPTER
THREE

N o, I thought, *you didn't. I don't think you can take the credit for this one, Shana.*

Before I could say anything aloud, though, the sound of sirens flared and came to an abrupt halt, and Shana fell sobbing against my chest again.

"I don't have any tissues," I said, more to myself than to Shana. As a high school counselor, I always had tissues within reach in my office. Dealing with the drama of teenage girls daily, tissues were my stock in trade.

But I wasn't in my office. School was out for the summer, and I'd come to Fillmore County to find a Bobwhite, not the murdered husband of a long-ago summer crush. A summer crush who looked like she could give birth to triplets at any moment. And here I thought that going birding for the weekend was going to be a relief from the burgeoning production of my sister's upcoming wedding. Now it looked like I'd landed in the middle of the first night of a B-rated television mini-series—one that not only featured a murder, but an impending birth. The fact was, weddings are over in a day, but murder cases can drag on for weeks.

I didn't even want to think about how long labor could go on.

Wait a minute.

"What did you say?" I asked the sobbing Shana. I lifted her chin off my chest and looked her in the eyes. "You didn't kill Jack. You told us he left early to find the Cuckoo, and you've been with the rest of us since coffee at the hotel. Whoever did this—whoever shot Jack—was here at the camp with Jack not that long ago. This isn't your fault, Shana."

Before she could answer me, three uniformed officers rounded the corner of the wagon and started barking orders at us.

"Step away from the body, please," said the woman wearing the sheriff's jacket.

"Don't go anywhere," the deputy instructed us. "We'll need statements."

"I need an ambulance," the third officer said into his walkie-talkie.

I helped Shana to stand up, and we moved away to give the officers room.

"I already checked for a pulse," I told the sheriff as she bent to drop her hand on Jack's neck. "He's dead."

"And you are?"

"Bob White. I'm one of the birding group that Jack's . . . that Jack was going to be leading today." I tilted my head to indicate Shana, who stood next to me, her arms wrapped around her expansive stomach. "This is Shana O'Keefe. The dead man is her husband, Jack O'Keefe."

The sheriff gave us both a quick once-over with her hard eyes. "And you were comforting the widow, I take it?"

I could feel the blood rushing to my cheeks, though my rusty beard probably hid it from the sheriff.

"They're both old friends," I said, bristling at her innuendo. "Actually, I was trying to keep Shana away."

"Didn't look like you were being very successful, Mr. White." She tapped her shoulder patch. "I'm Sheriff Paulsen. This is my county. And it looks to me like we're going to need to talk. The three of us."

Oh, boy. I was really excited about that idea. Especially since the sheriff seemed to be spinning her own version of what had happened.

"You got to talk to me, too!"

We all turned to see Bernie poking her head around the corner of the wagon. She'd obviously made a full recovery from her faint and managed to escape Tom's supervision. Her cheeks were flushed, but she was clearly eager to be included in our upcoming chat with the sheriff.

"They've been with me all morning," Bernie offered. "Me and the other birders. We had coffee at the hotel about 6:00 a.m.. Then we split up into three cars to come over here, but we stopped at the sewage ponds to see if we could spot any ducks, but all we saw were some turtles. Believe me, it's a slow day for birdwatching when you got a bunch of birders standing on the side of the road talking about turtles."

"Bernie," I said, trying to catch her attention. Judging from the deepening frown on Sheriff Paulsen's face, I was pretty sure Bernie wasn't scoring any points with her morning play-by-play. Turtles were obviously not high on the sheriff's list of suspects at the moment. But Bernie was on a roll.

"Anyway, then we drove over here, and after we parked, Bob and Tom took off in this direction, and Shana and I were still up the hill when Tom came to tell us about Jack." She paused to take a breath. "Besides, everyone knows that Bob wouldn't kill anyone. He's the sweetest man I've ever met. He just seems to find bodies a lot."

Thanks, Bernie. Not exactly what I would have shared at that particular moment, but hey—what are friends for, right?

Sheriff Paulsen's dark eyes locked back on mine. "Is that right?"

I started to shake my head and put my hand out in a qualifying kind of gesture.

"Absolutely!" Bernie gushed. "The first two times he found bodies, they were already dead, and the last time, he was right there when a man was shot. Right there! I know because I was right there, too. And then when that sweet little girl student of his got shot—"

"Bernie!" Geez Louise, she was making me sound like a walking death trap. I'd be lucky if I didn't get handcuffs slapped on me right then and there and hauled off to jail without even getting my Miranda rights read to me. In my peripheral vision, I could have sworn that I saw the two deputies getting ready to pull their guns.

Bob White, sensitive high school counselor and closet homicidal maniac. *Thank you again, Bernie.*

"Sounds like we've got even more to talk about," Sheriff Paulsen said, as the ambulance crew finally made it down the slope and hunkered down around Jack's body. Right behind them were the other six people who'd signed up for a weekend of birding with leader Jack O'Keefe. Standing just beyond the old wagon in a tight clump, they could almost have passed for a small brood of abandoned chicks, their faces ashen and lined with strain.

"You know, I'd kill for a cup of coffee right about now," Bernie announced. Then she pointed up at a bird in a tree behind the covered wagon. "Yellow-billed Cuckoo."

All of us, including the sheriff looked up.

"Ow," Shana moaned.

"What is it?" I almost grabbed one of the paramedics away from Jack's body. If Shana was going into labor, there was no way I was going to coach her through it.

"My back hurt when I looked at the Cuckoo," she complained, rubbing her knuckles against the small of her back. "Although, to be completely honest, it hurts when I do anything these days."

Great. Just what I wanted to hear. The pregnant lady was in constant pain. "I think you should go with the paramedics, Shana. Get checked out. Make sure you—and the baby—are okay."

"I'm fine, Bob," she assured me, even while tears continued to track silently down her face. "And I'm not having a baby."

I looked at her in complete disbelief, and she smiled, her eyes regaining some of their sparkle.

"I'm having twins."

Okay, so I was right. She did have a whole pod in there.

Holy shit.

CHAPTER FOUR

I t was one o'clock in the afternoon, and four of us were trying to eat a late lunch at the old-fashioned A&W drive-in across the street from the Inn & Suites in Spring Valley. Despite my considerable apprehension about her delicate condition, Shana hadn't gone into any kind of premature labor or distress during our visit with the sheriff, and while she still looked a little pale around the gills, I could see her old stubbornness kicking in.

"I'm going to find out what happened," she vowed over her mostly untouched burger basket. Her gorgeous eyes were red-rimmed from crying. "My children are not going to grow up with their father's murder unsolved. I swear it."

"I'm sure the sheriff isn't about to let this slide, Shana," Tom assured her. "She had everyone in the county down there at the station running around. I bet you she's already got leads to follow, and by tonight, she'll have a suspect in custody."

"I hope you're right, Tom." She gave him a watery but grateful smile. "Thanks for the vote of confidence."

"Ah, about the children," I tentatively began.

Three pairs of eyes swung to mine.

I swallowed. "How pregnant are you, Shana?"

Her green eyes lightened. "Well, let me see," she looked down at her imposing belly and patted the top of its mound. "I'd say I'm definitely pregnant."

I rolled my eyes, while Bernie chuckled. "Could you make this any harder for me?" I asked Shana, feeling the heat in my cheeks.

"I'm due in two months, Bob," she relented. "Is that what you want to know?"

I nodded. "That would be exactly what I wanted to know. And you're not at risk here, or anything like that?"

She shook her head. "No, I'm not going to pop them out any second, if that's what you're worried about."

"That's exactly what I was worried about." I looked at the ceiling of the diner. "Thank you, God."

"So now what?" Tom asked, tossing his napkin into his empty basket.

"I know," Bernie said. "Let's go to Lanesboro. It's just down the road. The sheriff said she wants us to stick close for a day or two, but she didn't say we had to stay here in Spring Valley." She polished off her last French fry after swiping it through a puddle of catsup in her basket. "I know the others went on out to bird some more, but I just don't think I have the energy to hike another mile or two. Besides, Lanesboro has all those cute little shops. They even have a hat emporium." She pushed her chair back from the table. "And a winery. Something for everybody."

She looked apologetically at Shana. "No wine for you, though."

"Actually, I think I want to lie down for a while," Shana said. "I have some more calls to make . . . arrangements."

"Well, of course, honey!" Bernie reached across the table to pat Shana's hand where it lay on the plastic red-checkered tablecloth, clutching a damp tissue. "Come on. I'll walk back with you and sit with you while you lie down. You boys just entertain yourselves for the rest of the afternoon. We can talk again at dinner."

Tom and I watched the two women walk out the door, Shana obviously waddling now, with Bernie virtually clucking at her like a mother hen.

"Do you think she's going to sit on Shana and stuff her under her feathers?" Tom asked.

"I doubt it," I replied. "Even if she wanted to, there's no way Bernie could stuff that much Shana under anything. It's hard to believe she's only got twins in there."

"Twins that aren't going to meet their father," Tom added sadly. "Shana's quite a trooper, isn't she?"

I took a final gulp of water from my glass and tried not to think about Shana's babies growing up without a dad. "Yes, Tom, she is." And then I decided I couldn't think about Shana, her babies, or Jack anymore right now. "So, how shall we spend our afternoon, birding buddy of mine?"

He didn't hesitate. "We look for that Bobwhite, Bob White. And I know just where to start."

TWENTY MINUTES LATER, I was pretty sure that, despite his confidence, Tom didn't have a clue where to start, because he was driving east from Spring Valley instead of south. Back in 2003, the last confirmed sighting of a wild Northern Bobwhite in Minnesota had occurred in Beaver Creek Wildlife Management Area, less than three miles from the Iowa border. When we'd stuffed ourselves into Tom's ancient Honda, I'd assumed that was where we were heading.

"Okay, I give up," I said. "Where are we going?"

We passed a mileage sign to Lanesboro.

"It's the hat emporium, isn't it? Darn that Bernie, she hit your hot button, Tom."

Tom laughed as he took a left, and we headed north on County Road 80 to the little burg of Wykoff. The scenery was pleasant—the rolling hills and scattered tree groves of Fillmore County. More than 150 years ago, the area just past Wykoff had a big swath of upland deciduous forest, filled with four types of oak tree, elm, basswood, ash, maple, hornbeam, aspen, and birch. Nowadays, farms have appropriated much of that space, but some pretty pockets of the old forest still remain and can be seen along some of the lesser-traveled back roads.

Like we were doing now.

My head hit the roof of the car as Tom's Honda sailed up out of a surprise pothole.

"Sorry. My shocks aren't as good as they used to be," he apologized.

"Tom, your shocks haven't been good since I've known you, which is about a decade."

He patted the dashboard lovingly. "Yeah, but this is the birdmobile. Nothing stops this baby when I'm on the chase."

"And exactly what are we chasing again?"

Tom pulled a crumpled note from his shirt pocket and handed it to me, all the while keeping his eyes on the road to avoid another pothole. "I heard Jack giving directions to the Bobwhites yesterday afternoon when I was checking into the Inn & Suites. He was on his cell phone in the lobby with a Frank somebody, and I jotted down what I heard him saying."

I looked at the directions on the paper. Wykoff to Fountain, then to County Road 11. There was a turn at Mahoney Creek into some brush prairie.

A Bobwhite Killing

It was possible, I conceded. Northern Bobwhites liked grasslands with scattered trees. Maybe there was a small enclave of the birds in north-central Fillmore. It would be a surprise, but possible.

And wasn't that one of the reasons I loved birding? A person took all the cues, all the clues, about the bird sought, then figure out where it might be—kind of like being a detective, in a way. Sure, it's always nice when the hunt turns out to be easy, and the bird's right where I expected, but on the other hand, it's a thrill when a bird is found where I DON'T expect it.

Tom pulled off the road into a turn-out that seemed to be well-used. But not by birders.

Instead, there were four cars parked, each one with a small trailer attached. In the distance, I could hear the unmistakable roar of the gunning engine of an ATV—All Terrain Vehicle.

We got out of the car and looked across the prairie that rolled up to a wooded area. Dirt trails snaked through the open expanses and disappeared into the trees. While we watched, two ATVs came tearing up over a rise and launched themselves into the air, the riders practically standing upright on their machines as they soared about fifty feet until they hit the ground again. Then, earth spewing up around them, the vehicles spun through a short gully and tore into the woods.

"Are you sure you heard Jack correctly, Tom? This is ATV country, not a happy haunt of a timid little quail."

Tom looked as confused as I felt. "I'm sure I got it right. I even asked him when he finished his call. He said it was Bobwhite property."

I drummed my fingers on the hood of the Honda and surveyed the wasted land gouged by the wheels of innumerable ATVs.

"Not anymore," I concluded. "I'd say it looks more like a three-ring circus. Those riders were flying through the air like trapeze artists. Find them a couple of big jungle cats to roar at a lion-tamer with a chair, and they'll be open for business." I shook my head in disappointment. "No, I'm afraid what we've got ourselves here is nothing but a wild goose chase."

I took another look across the prairie. About a hundred years ago, maybe even fifty years ago, Bobolinks, Meadowlarks, and Bobwhites probably covered the area. Once homesteaders began to shape the land to their needs, though, the native flora and fauna were gradually displaced, yielding to cultivated acres of farmland. Then, as family farming operations died out, much of the land was left neglected, victim to the ravages of disrupted ecological cycles and careless human abuse. Now, where lush grasses used to grow, thrill-seeking ATV operators spun their wheels in the dust that had become their unsanctioned playground. Without a doubt, Bobwhites had lost their right-of-way.

Not that I have a problem, per se, with folks who ride ATVs. I understand how much you can enjoy a hobby—I'm a serious birder, for crying out loud. What I have a problem with, though, is when some of those hobbyists enjoy their hobby to the point of going off the designated trails, and in doing so, damage wild land, not to mention natural habitat and entire ecological systems. There's more than a quarter of a million ATVs registered in Minnesota, and it seems that a lot of those vehicles are regularly violating state laws that protect our natural resources. I've still got a few pals who work for the Department of Natural Resources, and they say that enforcing trail regulations for ATVs is the biggest headache they've got. Up at Spider Lake Recreation Area in the north-central part of the state, the DNR has poured almost half a million dollars into trying to repair and restore the wetlands, lakeshores and hillsides that have been ruined by trespassing ATVs. What really burns me, though, is when I see riders ripping through agricultural ditches during nesting season because I know it's destroying prime pheasant nursery spots.

Which was what I was seeing happening right here. I wasn't sure if these lands were public or private, but either way, serious damage was being done.

I turned back to Tom. "Let's head south. We can make a run through Forestville/Mystery Cave State Park and still make it back to the Inn & Suites in time for dinner. I saw a posting yesterday in my email about some Acadian and Willow Flycatchers down there. At least then we'd have something to show for today."

Something besides an ATV track, a murdered trip leader, and his grieving pregnant wife.

For some reason, Shana's odd confession to me right before the sheriff had shown up this morning suddenly popped into my head. She said she'd killed Jack, but that was impossible.

Wasn't it?

CHAPTER
FIVE

Tom put the car in gear, and we started back towards the tiny town of Fountain.

Out my side window, I spotted a Red-shouldered Hawk gliding over the rolling plains and hills covered in a profusion of June's green growth. No ATVs here rutting the slopes or trashing the wetlands. The scene was good enough for a postcard. "Gliding along in Fillmore County," it could read. "Wish you were here."

For a moment or two, I could almost forget I'd started the day with discovering Jack's body. But I couldn't stay distracted very long.

"Do you know anything about Shana and Jack?" I casually asked Tom. "Before yesterday I didn't even know they'd gotten married. It's been years since I've seen either of them."

"You mean besides the political stuff that Jack's involved in?"

"Yeah."

Tom rolled his window down and a wave of fresh air blew through the car.

"Not much. It seems like Shana stays out of the spotlight—you never see her in pictures in the papers or on television with Jack. I guess they keep their relationship pretty private. And I expect, with her being pregnant, they liked keeping it that way." He threw me a glance. "I remember when they got married, though. A bunch of the nurses at work were sure that Shana was a gold-digger. I think they had a problem with the twenty-year difference in Shana and Jack's ages. Personally, I don't see what the big deal is. Lots of men marry younger women. Lots of women marry older men. I mean, geez, Jack had been a widower a long time, and if he and Shana could be happy together, why not?"

The hawk put in another appearance, gliding across the road ahead of us.

"Red-shouldered," Tom said.

"Yeah, I know. I saw it a minute ago, too." I watched it skim the earth and then lift skywards, a small rodent trapped in its claws. "Late lunch."

"Shana's not a predator, Bob. Besides, Jack was nobody's fool. Just look at the corporations and politicians he's taken on in the last couple years. Ever since Minnesota passed the Clean Water, Land and Legacy Amendment in 2008, Jack O'Keefe has been knocking heads together in St. Paul to make sure conservation legislation gets passed and implemented. From what I understand, he's just about abandoned the family business to devote all his time to the environment."

Tom slowed down to read a mile marker, then turned right onto the next road.

"I almost forgot—there's a seepage meadow up here on Rice Creek that I birded last year about this time," he explained. "I found some Upland Sandpipers there. Since we're in the neighborhood, we might as well check it out. You know, now that I think about it, I bet Jack got so involved with conservation because of Shana. She went to grad school in ecology or something."

"Yeah, I know," I said again. I didn't tell him how well I knew it, either. I didn't think he needed to hear about my teenage crush and how I nursed a broken heart during my senior year in high school because the older woman of my dreams had tossed me over to go dredging through muck in a graduate program.

Me or muck, Shana?

Gee, when I put it that way, it almost hurt all over again. Except for the fact that I'd finally arrived at the brilliant insight years later that she'd never considered me anything near a romantic candidate, thinking she chose muck over me might really put a dent in my self-esteem.

Good thing I'm a tough old bird, huh?

Of course, having Luce in my life probably made Shana's early rejection of me a lot more manageable now.

Actually, having Luce in my life made everything more manageable now. Except for Tom's driving.

I bumped my head again on the roof of the car as he hit another pothole.

"Sorry," he said. "These roads aren't too well maintained, are they?"

"I think we're on a cattle trail, Tom, not a road."

"Oh no, this is the road. Look up ahead."

Sure enough, there was an open wetland situated on what looked to be an old streambed about a hundred yards in front of us. It was bordered on one side by a stand of forest, with a few old oaks scattered across the surrounding hillocks. I noticed some wire fencing along the forest side, with a few "No trespassing" signs hanging along the edges.

Tom parked the car and we got out to walk closer to the meadow. Once we got within forty yards of the wetland, we saw two Upland Sandpipers poking their long bills into the soggy earth. Hoping to not disturb them, we skirted the meadow and slid in close to the forest where a portion of the fencing had been torn down. Then I had the weirdest sensation, like someone was watching me.

Behind me, brush moved.

A lot of brush.

I slowly turned around and there, about twenty feet away, was a cat.

A big jungle cat.

A tiger, in fact.

Oh joy. I'd apparently found the missing part of the circus, but unfortunately, I'd forgotten to bring my chair and whip.

Hello, kitty.

CHAPTER SIX

"D on't move," Tom breathed behind me.

What? Did he think I was going to tap dance? I wasn't exactly Fred Astaire on a good day, let alone when I was facing a six-hundred pound tiger. Besides, I'd come to the conclusion at the same instant I'd locked eyes with the beast that I was probably never going to move again.

Except through the digestive tract of a charismatic megafauna.

That's ecological-speak for a big animal that environmental activists liked to use as a poster child for conservation programs.

Only usually, poster children weren't prowling around near a seepage meadow in southeastern Minnesota where they could eat birders for an afternoon pick-me-up.

Fortunately, though, I didn't have the time to imagine myself as an hors d'oeuvre because the tiger jumped straight at me.

And then, as I sucked in what I knew would be my last breath, my death froze mid-air. I thought it was that slowing of time thing that happened sometimes in car accidents when a person saw the truck bearing down and watched kind of in hyperspeed as it sped into the crash. But the huge cat didn't slowly spread deadly claws and open a gaping, toothed maw. No. Instead it dropped to the ground, unconscious.

"Yes! Works like a charm!" came from somewhere to my right.

Or maybe it was to my left. I don't know. It could have been God himself calling down from heaven at that point. I was still stuck in that last long gasp, unable to check it out. Then, when it penetrated my petrified brain that I really wasn't eaten, I was hanging my head between my knees so I wouldn't pass out or throw up. Or both.

But there was one thing I was sure of—I'd never look at a box of Frosted Flakes in the same way again. Tony the Tiger had just taken on a whole new dimension of meaning in my eyes.

"Thought I recognized that red head of yours," my savior announced.

I took a deep breath, straightened up and turned around.

Crazy Eddie Edvarg, my old DNR pal, was standing next to Tom, who was looking more than a little shocky himself. He jovially thumped Tom on the back. "Scared you, huh? That big old cat was just having some fun with you. He gets fed plenty, but he misses the hunt. Instinct, you know."

Tom nodded slowly. "Yeah, right," he croaked. "Instinct."

"Let me take a wild stab here," I said, my heart returning to its normal rhythm.

Eddie laughed. "Wild stab. Funny, Bob."

I slid him my not-funny-at-all look. "You're not the one who just thought he was going to be lunch." I waved my hand at the edge of the woods. "You're doing some kind of electronics job." I glanced back at the tiger that was sprawled in the tall grasses behind me. "And judging from the jolt that cat must have taken, I'd say you've got one heck of a powerful invisible electric fence installed here."

Eddie tapped the tip of his nose. "Got it in one, Bob. I just finished getting it online earlier this week. When Kami called me up—that's the owner here, Kami Marsden—to tell me she was having trouble with her old security system, I hustled on down here to check it out. You sure don't want glitches when you've got a tiger for a house pet." He nodded at the now snoring big cat. "I was tracking Nigel today with my remote sensors when I saw your vehicle turning into the meadow. I didn't think there'd be a problem with the invisible fence, but Kami's had some sections of both the wire and electronic fencing randomly go down this week, so I thought I'd play it safe. Especially since this portion of the fencing hasn't been functioning properly since very early this morning."

He held up a black, palm-sized box in his hand.

"It's a manual control for Nigel's collar," he explained. "If the electric fencing was down, I could shock him to sleep myself. But I didn't have to. The new program I installed on the fence worked like a charm—it zapped Nigel as soon as he hit the new perimeter, which is ten feet inside the wire fence."

"Inside the fence?"

"Of course. You think a wire fence could keep Nigel in?" Eddie snorted. "We're talking about six hundred and fifty pounds of Bengal tiger here, Bob. The wire fence is to keep people out. The invisible fence is to keep Nigel in."

He scanned the ground around us until he saw what he was apparently looking for, some ten yards away partially hidden behind an oak tree.

"Looks like we had some more vandalism last night," he said, pointing to the section of wire fencing that peeked out from one side of the tree. "I just checked this perimeter yesterday, and it was solid. All I can figure is that somebody's got a death wish if they're trying to break into Kami's sanctuary."

Tom pointed to the wire fencing that ran the length of the meadow and disappeared over the rolling hills. "So this is a wildlife sanctuary? I never had a clue it was anything but private property."

"Not wildlife sanctuary," Eddie said. "Exotic animal sanctuary. There's a difference."

Eddie tucked the control box into the breast pocket of his trademark flannel shirt. I noticed that his white beard was growing back to its customary Santa-shape after having been close-cropped the last time I'd seen him.

"And I'm not surprised you didn't know about it," he continued. "Kami's a pretty private person. She's had this place a good twenty years now and never had any problems with her animals getting loose till the last couple of weeks. I think she's always figured if she was going to keep exotic animals here, she'd best keep a low profile. Better that way for both her and her animals."

On the other side of the fence, Nigel started to stir. I automatically backed up a few more steps.

"He can't hurt you, Bob. The fence—the invisible electric one—is solid. It's a big improvement over the old electrified fencing Kami was using on the other side of her property. That fencing was frying some very unlucky coyotes. She shut it down a while ago. We worked with a security equipment company out of St. Paul for the new system. Secure A-Man was the name. The owner is an old friend of Kami's." He chuckled into his beard. "Still, I bet they never considered they might be securing a tiger. "

He nodded at Nigel, who had flopped back on the ground. "Besides, he'll be groggy for a little while. I'll probably track him with the remotes for the rest of the afternoon just to be sure he's shaking off the shock okay. You boys done here?"

"Yup," Tom and I both answered. I guessed neither one of us was too excited about sticking around until Nigel woke up. Not that I doubted the security of Eddie's fence—my old buddy knew his stuff when it came to electronics.

I've just never been a cat person.

Especially when they weigh over three times more than I do.

My cell phone rang in my pocket. I took it out and flipped it open.

"Bob, you better get back here."

It was Bernie.

"Shana's stepson is here, and he's raising a real ruckus. Says he's calling the sheriff to arrest Shana for killing his dad." She paused a moment, and I could hear two voices yelling in the background. "I don't think he likes Shana, Bob."

From what I could make out of the shouting, I'd say Shana didn't like her stepson much, either, unless "bastard" was an O'Keefe family term of endearment.

"We're on our way," I told Bernie.

CHAPTER
SEVEN

By the time Tom and I arrived back at the Inn & Suites, the sheriff's car was parked in front of the lobby entrance. I came in through the automatic sliding door and started down the hallway before I remembered I didn't know which room was Shana's.

Then I realized I didn't need to know which room she was in, because I could hear the yelling almost all the way out to the lobby. Heck, they could probably hear the yelling all the way to the next county, for that matter. As it was, the door to her room was wide open and I almost had to fight my way through the crowd of our fellow birders that blocked the hallway.

"I want her arrested!"

Just inside the room, Chuck O'Keefe had his face inches from Sheriff Paulsen's. For his sake, I hope he'd used mouthwash because he'd need every bit of leverage he could get to make friends with that sheriff. After spending a good portion of the morning being thoroughly questioned by the lady lawman—make that lady law*woman*—I knew that Sheriff Paulsen was one tough cookie and wasn't about to let some man from the city tell her what needed to be done in "her" county. On top of that, she'd actually seemed to warm up to Shana after we'd settled into her squad car this morning for the ride to the police station to make our report.

"Sorry about the bumping," she'd apologized as we jolted onto the blacktop that led back to town. "Some of these county roads can do a real number on a car's suspension—even police cars that are practically built like tanks. You doing okay, Mrs. O'Keefe?"

Of course, that might just have been the sheriff trying to be nice to the pregnant lady. Once Sheriff Paulsen saw how awkward it was for Shana to climb into the cruiser's back seat, she'd probably figured she was going to have to get a car-sized can opener to get Shana back out. I wondered how quickly the Minneapolis police department could get a Jaws of Life to Fillmore County.

Seeing Paulsen stare down Chuck now, I had to admit that I was glad to have the sheriff on our side because I was fairly sure that if Chuck thought he could bully her into doing what he asked, he had another thing coming.

Or maybe even a pair of handcuffs, courtesy of Fillmore County's finest.

Shana, meanwhile, was standing on the opposite side of the room, her hands on her hips and her green eyes blazing with anger. A big bear of an older man I didn't recognize was patting her right shoulder, speaking hurriedly to her in an obvious attempt to calm her down.

Good luck with that. Even when she was an average-sized, nonpregnant woman, Shana had had the tenacity of a king-sized bulldog when challenged about anything. Don't even ask me about the time she insisted we could find a Mississippi Kite near Caledonia, down in the southeastern corner of Minnesota. Since those birds rarely make it north of the Iowa border to nest, I laughed when Shana told me she'd seen one in Houston County the summer before we met. Determined to prove it to me, she'd dragged me down to Caledonia three weekends in a row that following June to look for the bird—three miserably cold, rainy weekends. And sure enough, she found the Kite on our third try, not even a mile from where she'd located it the previous summer. Being the generous, gracious man I am—was, even back then at age sixteen—I conceded that she had been right and vowed to never again question her birding prowess. Shana, on the other hand, was not generous or gracious—she rubbed it in all summer long that she had been right and I had been proven wrong. If I learned nothing else about Shana from that experience, it was that I'd better be willing to take the consequences if I challenged her integrity.

The way Chuck was doing right now in a hotel room at the Inn & Suites.

"She killed my father!" he shouted, his finger pointing at Shana.

"No, she didn't," Sheriff Paulsen stated unequivocally. "She wasn't anywhere near your father at the time of his death, Mr. O'Keefe. She's got witnesses and an airtight alibi."

"She didn't have to be near him!" Chuck yelled. "She'd get someone else to do it. Do you think she's stupid? Believe me, she's not. She's had this one planned since the day she met my father. Marry the rich old guy, give him some great new cause to distract him, and then stick in the knife when he's not looking. Oh, and that doesn't even include the pregnancy part. Now she's got heirs to claim the family fortune. "

For a second, I thought Shana was going to leap over the bed—big belly or not—and go straight for Chuck's throat, but just as she moved forward, the man behind her grabbed both of her arms and held her back. It didn't stop her from shouting at Chuck, though.

"You bastard! As long as Jack was married to the company, you were happy. But you could never forgive him for finding something else to care about when he met me, could you? Especially since you saw me first. Don't think I don't know it, Chuck. You were so jealous of Jack and me that it ate you up. And now you want me to be punished for it."

She turned briefly to the man holding her arms. "Let me go, Ben. I'm not going to touch Chuck."

He did as she asked, but seemed reluctant to let her get too far out of his arms' reach.

Shana raked her hand through her chin-length black hair, dragging in a long deep breath. From where I stood in the room's doorway, I could tell that some of the fire in her eyes had gone out as she looked back at Chuck.

"If you want to know the truth, Chuck, I do hold myself responsible for Jack's death. But it has nothing to do with the family fortune." Her eyes shifted to the sheriff. "Now will you please get my stepson out of here?"

I moved aside as Paulsen pulled Chuck out of the room and down the hallway. Behind me, Bernie was shooing the other birders off into their own rooms, promising everyone a full report later at dinner at the A&W. I turned to leave, too, but Shana called my name.

"Bob, please don't go."

The tenacious bulldog had disappeared, and in its place was a very tired, very pale Shana. She indicated the man next to her. "I want you to meet Ben Graham. He's an old friend of Jack's and the mayor of Spring Valley. Ben, this is Bob White. He's a birding pal from way back."

I stepped further into the room and shook the man's hand.

"I'm sorry to be meeting you under these circumstances, Mr. White. I've known Jack my whole life. We grew up together. It's a terrible day for all of us."

I nodded in agreement and stole a glance at Shana, who'd practically collapsed into the armchair in the corner of the room. "I'm sorry for your loss, Mr. Mayor. Jack was a great guy."

"Yes, he was," Graham replied, sorrow thick in his voice. "And call me Big Ben. Please. Everybody around here does." He rubbed a huge hand over his forehead and closed his eyes briefly. "Sheriff Paulsen called me about noon with the news, and I tried to get over here for Shana as soon as I could. Unfortunately, Chuck beat me to it."

"He hates me," Shana said, her eyes fixed on the flat white ceiling. "From the moment I met Jack, Chuck started hating me. I'd just finished speaking at a fund-raising dinner for the Nature Conservancy at the Hilton in downtown Minneapolis, and Chuck was an attendee. He suggested we go downstairs to the bar in the lobby for an after-dinner drink. I was done shaking hands and begging for money for the night, so I said sure. We took the escalator down, and then, just as he pulled out a chair for me at a table in the bar, Jack walked in. He'd been at a board meeting in one of the hotel's other ballrooms. Chuck invited him to join us and . . . four months later, I quit my job with the Conservancy to move back to Minneapolis and marry Jack."

"You gave Jack another chance at life, Shana," Graham assured her, sitting down on the end of the bed. It creaked under his weight. He reached over to pat her jean-covered knee. "He was dying a slow death grieving before he met you."

Shana gave a brittle laugh. "I don't know how good a chance at life is when it ends up killing you." She glanced briefly at Graham and then me. "Jack got involved with the eco-communities because I was involved with them. We knew what we were doing was pushing a hot button in the state. We knew that Jack was making enemies. But we never imagined it would come to murder."

"You don't know that, Shana," Graham pointed out. "At this point, no one knows anything for sure. But the sheriff will find out, believe me. Sheriff Paulsen's a good woman and an even better sheriff."

The mayor stood up then and grabbed his suitcoat from where he'd apparently tossed it on the bed when he'd arrived. He leaned over to drop a kiss on Shana's forehead and turned to me. "Can you stay with her for a while? I think she needs a friend of her own right now more than she needs a friend of Jack's."

I took the hand he offered and shook it. "Of course. And if there's anything else I can do, let me know."

Graham left the room and shut the door behind him. I figured it was time to shift into grief counselor mode, but when I turned to Shana, she wasn't on the verge of more tears as I had expected.

Instead, she smiled apologetically.

"Sorry, Bob," she said. "You came to get a Bobwhite, and instead you landed in the middle of a soap opera. Welcome to a nasty part of my world."

I walked over to the bed and perched on the end of it, my hands on my knees.

"You want to talk about any of this?" I asked her. "I'm an experienced counselor, you know. Though I have to say that most of the time, the extent of my counseling involves badgering students to quit cutting classes or mouthing off to teachers. Insanely jealous stepsons don't usually figure into the mix, you know."

"Wow," she noted. "You really do have it easy, don't you?"

"My momma didn't raise no fool," I assured her. "Of course, I haven't told you about the zombies, wannabe vampires, and unrelenting egotists that brighten my day, either. And, believe me, a teenage girl in her first crush or dump is pretty intense. No job comes without risk, Shana. In fact, I'm lucky to be walking around with most of my brain cells still intact despite daily exposure to what often becomes mind-numbing routine, not to mention outright lunacy. And that's on a good day."

I caught a hint of amusement in Shana's eyes as she let out a sigh.

"Enough about me," I said. "How did Chuck get wind so fast of his dad's death? He sure hightailed it down here."

Shana rubbed her fingers against her temples. "I'm afraid that's my fault, actually. I called him on my cell this morning, just after we got to the police station. I thought he should know. I didn't want him hearing it from anyone else. I had no idea he was going to come to Spring Valley, let alone insist that the sheriff arrest me for . . . for . . ." She shook her head, hastily wiping away the tears that were collecting in her eyes.

Without thinking, I reached out and patted her knee in comfort. "Shana."

"Just give me a moment, Bob," she said, taking a deep breath. She wiped her eyes once more and then picked up where she'd left off.

"I guess it was a good thing that Ben rode over with the sheriff. Chuck has always respected Ben and his friendship with his father. He's known him practically his whole life. I think Ben's being here was probably the only thing keeping Chuck from going totally ballistic."

I blinked at her. "What I just witnessed wasn't totally ballistic? I thought Chuck was going to bite off Sheriff Paulsen's head for an appetizer before he tore you apart for the main course."

A loud knocking came from the other side of Shana's room door.

"It's probably Bernie," Shana said. "She's been so sweet, trying to take care of me." For a moment, she studied my face. "And she thinks the world of you, Bob. That you can do no wrong."

"Yeah, right," I laughed. "That's why she couldn't wait to tell Sheriff Paulsen this morning about my Angel of Doom persona." I got up from the bed. "I'll get it."

But when I opened it, it wasn't Bernie in the hallway. Instead, a hundred lights flashed in my face as voices shouted over each other to be heard. A crowd of people pressed toward me and I had the distinct impression of cameras and microphones being pointed in my general direction.

"Mrs. O'Keefe!"

"Who found the body?"

"Is it true that you and your husband were having marital difficulties?"

I slammed the door shut.

"It wasn't Bernie," I told Shana, who had covered her face with her hands. "A pack of vultures, maybe, but definitely not Bernie."

I could see one emerald eye peeking at me through Shana's fingers.

"You don't want to get involved with this, Bob. I should have realized the press would be all over it as soon as they heard. They love Jack." She closed her eyes and lightly placed her hands on the mound of her belly. "Loved Jack."

Now it was my turn to study Shana. If she'd slept at all while I'd been birding with Tom, it wasn't obvious. She had gray shadows beneath her eyes and her lips were tightly pressed together. I could feel the tension radiating from her all the way across the room.

The woman needed a break.

I walked over to the large window behind her and slid open the pane, then removed the screen. Setting my hip on the window sill, I angled my legs through the open space and stepped outside the building. As I'd figured, there were a bunch of cars and television vans in the parking lot, but no people. I turned back and held out a hand for Shana. With a little careful maneuvering, I was sure we could get her out through the window.

"Let's blow this pop stand, honey. We've got birds to chase."

CHAPTER EIGHT

Since we still had hours of daylight left, I headed south and east for the part of Mystery Cave State Park that straddled Forestville and Carimona Townships. Earlier in the week, I'd seen postings on the MOU net of three different flycatchers and five different sparrows in the area, and I was hoping that would be enough to keep us occupied for a few hours while the media cleared out of Spring Valley. Once we got out of town, Shana called Bernie and told her to let everyone know that she'd gone into seclusion and would make a formal statement to the press the next morning. She also told Bernie that she was with me, not to worry, and that we'd be back in time for dinner.

"Meadowlark," I said, pointing to the birds sitting on the wire fences near the road. "Both Eastern and Western Meadowlarks, I'd guess."

Shana nodded. Since Eastern and Western Meadowlarks look identical, I'd have to stop the car to listen to their two distinct songs—one a slurred whistle, the other strong like a flute—to make a positive identification. Knowing that Shana and I had both heard meadowlarks plenty of times, though, I decided to keep driving. Besides, the birds would probably take flight as soon as I stopped the car on the side of the road. That happened to me all the time: I see a bird—one I've been looking for—while I'm driving, but when I stop to make the identification, it takes off.

Kind of like the way I felt that summer when I finally admitted to myself that Shana was exactly the kind of woman I wanted in my life, only to have her take off for college again and then on to grad school in California.

"Bobolink," she said, pointing towards a dark-breasted bird rising out of a young hayfield. "Horned Lark," she added almost immediately.

"Geez, Shana, leave some for me," I pretended to complain. "It's no fun if you get all the birds."

"Girls just want to have fun, Bob," she replied, a touch of lightness in her voice.

Which, unfortunately, immediately faded away.

"I didn't think anyone else knew." Shana's voice was barely audible in the car. "I wasn't even sure myself until last night."

"Sure about what?" I asked.

"Jack was having an affair."

I almost drove off the road.

"What are you talking about?" I glanced over at her after I straightened the wheels back onto the pavement. "Are you nuts?"

There was no way on earth that Jack had been cheating on Shana. The man wasn't blind, or stupid. Not only was she twenty years his junior, but she was smart, beautiful, charming and funny. Not to mention pregnant with his twins. What man could possibly be married to Shana and still wander into another woman's bed? Granted, I wasn't privy to the details of their relationship, but last night when Jack had shepherded Shana out of the lobby, I could have sworn he wasn't thinking about going to sleep when they got to their room. I'm no marriage expert, but I've seen enough body language in my counseling career to know what physical attraction looks like, and that's exactly what I had seen last night in the hotel hallway between Jack and Shana.

"You heard that reporter in the hall back at the hotel, didn't you?" I guessed. "Just before I shut the door. Come on, Shana, you can't think that. Jack was crazy about you. I saw it last night—he was practically glowing."

"It's the woman who glows when she's pregnant, Bob, not the man."

"On no," I corrected her. "Jack was glowing. Trust me. I could feel the watts from across the room."

"Then how do you explain my husband being out all night last night?" she challenged me. "And, by the way, it wasn't the first time, either. It's been happening a lot the last month—overnight trips he needed to take down here to Fillmore County. Alone. Come on, Bob," she echoed me. "Minneapolis is barely two hours away, but Jack couldn't make the drive home after his eco-community planning sessions in Spring Valley? Meetings that wrapped up by 10:00 p.m.? Give me a break."

She turned away from me to look out her side window. "They say the wife is always the last to know, but not this wife. My momma didn't raise no fool, either."

Since I had no idea what to say to that, I said nothing. Not only were crazed stepsons beyond my counseling repertoire, but so were cheated-on wives.

Make that pregnant cheated-on wives.

Definitely a rarity in my line of work.

Not that I was looking to add it to my list, that's for sure.

We drove another mile in silence before I saw two Turkey Vultures circling over a distant field. It reminded me of the media people who'd tried to storm Shana's room. Talk about insensitive. She'd found her husband murdered this morning, and they were already trying to cook up sensational headlines about a marriage gone bad. I thought some more about Shana's accusation about Jack, but I still couldn't believe it.

"So you don't know it for a fact, do you?" By the time I realized I was thinking out loud, it was too late: Shana heard the question.

"No, Bob, Jack didn't give me the details."

I stole a glance at her while I drove. She had covered her eyes with her hands again.

"But I was suspicious enough that when our last cell phone bill came to the house, I checked for numbers I didn't recognize," she finally confessed. "I found one that he was calling a lot. And then, one night, while Jack was sleeping, I took his phone and called the number to see what name popped up."

Shana's hands dropped to her lap. "It was Kami Marsden."

The name rang a bell, but I couldn't place it right away. Then it hit me.

"The exotic animal sanctuary person?"

Shana gave me a piercing look. "Do you know her?"

"No, but Tom and I were just birding on the edge of her land this afternoon," I explained. "That's where I was when Bernie called me to mount up and ride to your rescue from Chuck. You think she and Jack were having an affair?"

"The pieces fit," Shana said without enthusiasm. She shifted in the seat, readjusting her seatbelt to ride lower across her abdomen. "His frequent calls to her number. The overnight trips he insisted he had to take alone to Spring Valley for 'meetings.' His being gone last night—all night."

I pulled onto the entrance road into the park. "Yeah—I've been meaning to ask you about that, by the way. This morning at coffee you didn't say Jack had been gone all night. You told us that he'd left ahead of everyone to scout the area for the cuckoos."

For a second or two, she didn't reply. When she did, I could hear the embarrassment in her voice.

"What do you think I was going to say? 'Okay, everybody, Jack spent the night with his lover so we'll just meet up with him at the youth camp.'"

"You have a point," I conceded. I thought I heard Shana sniffle.

Smooth move, counselor. Make the lady cry some more.

I parked my SUV at the trailhead and grabbed my binoculars from where they were laying behind the driver's seat. Then I reached across Shana, popped open the glove compartment, and pulled out the extra set of binos I kept there. I handed them to her silently and got out of the car.

Knowing how my last conversational attempt had bombed, I was more than happy that the mother-to-be wasn't in the mood for talking as we struck out on a path into the woods. That's one of the nice things about birding with someone else, actually—if you don't feel like talking, or you have nothing to say, you don't have to feel awkward about it. You can just walk and walk and listen and look for birds. You get fresh air, exercise, and the pleasure of someone else's company. If you want to talk, you can. If you don't, that's okay, too. And if you want the people you're birding with to shut up because they like talking and you don't, you can just ask them to be quiet so you can hear the birds. Very civilized and polite. And, as in my case, keeping quiet to listen for birds also prevents you from opening your mouth just so you can stick your foot in it.

Isn't birding a great hobby?

"There it is," Shana said in a low voice, pointing into the trees.

I lifted my binoculars to examine the little flycatcher she'd spotted sitting about two-thirds up into the canopy of the forest. He had the distinctive long wings of the Acadian Flycatcher, and when he opened his bill to sing, we heard the short burst of his *peet-suh* song.

"I thought you said you were going to leave some of the birds for me," I grumbled.

Shana dropped her binoculars back down and continued to watch the bird. "I never said that. You just assumed it."

Just like I assumed any man married to Shana would never look twice at another woman.

Although, to be honest, it would probably take two looks to see all of Shana at this point in her pregnancy.

Keep mouth shut, foot out, I reminded myself.

"White."

I practically jumped out of my skin. I grabbed my chest and spun around.

"Geez, Stan, you're going to give me a heart attack yet," I told the man who had materialized directly behind me. As I would have expected, he was dressed entirely in camouflage. "Can't you just, like, announce your approach with snapping some twigs like a normal human being or banging a gong or something?"

Although, I have to admit, if Scary Stan Miller acted like a normal person, I'd probably never recognize him in the field. As it was, he had a habit of totally blending into his surroundings; if he stood out like every other birder I know, I'd never guess in a million years that it was him. Stan being normal would be an aberration.

"Shana."

"Stan."

My long-time birding rival tipped his sunglasses down and looked at Shana over the wire rims. "Where's Jack?"

Stan had obviously missed the big news today while he was birding. That surprised me, since Stan usually seemed to know everything about everything and usually before it even happened.

I shook my head, trying to think of a simple way to let Stan know what had happened without upsetting Shana again.

"He's dead," she said, beating me to it. "Somebody shot him this morning at the Green Hills Youth Camp."

Stan considered that for a moment, as motionless and inscrutable as ever. Then he cocked his head a fraction of an inch and pointed at the flycatcher above us. "Acadian."

"We know," I told him. "Shana spotted it."

"Come here," he said, then turned off the trail and almost disappeared into the woods.

"You're supposed to stay on the trails, Stan," I reminded him. "You know, be considerate of the natural habitat and leave no footprints behind." I held a lowslung branch back for Shana as we followed him through the trees and thick undergrowth until we came to a spot where several fallen trunks had made a natural woodpile.

"Okay, I get it. This is your secret camp. We stumbled on your lair. Sorry, Stan. It won't happen again."

Stan stopped on the far side of the woodpile.

I checked the branches above me. Had Stan found a rarity back here? I'd heard rumors that a Worm-eating Warbler had been seen in Fillmore County a year ago, but no one ever produced any photographs of it. Not that a lack of a photo of it would keep Stan from finding one here. If the Worm-eating Warbler were around, Stan would find it. Stan had skills. Actually, Stan had skills I didn't even want to know about, thanks to his former life as a government agent.

Suffice it to say, he hadn't been stamping applications at a driver's license bureau.

A foul odor hit my nose.

"Ah, geez, Stan. You got a skunk in that woodpile? I do not want to smell like skunk for the rest of the day."

From the other side of the fallen logs, Shana looked up at me, her face drained of color. "It's not a skunk, Bob. It's Billy Mason."

"Dead," Stan added.

It took a second for me to follow what Shana and Stan were saying. For a second there, I thought maybe Billy Mason was the name of some rot gut liquor, and Stan had found a broken crate of it stinking up the clearing. Now that I understood, my stomach started north. I put my hand out to lean against the tree next to me, waiting for my head to clear and my gut to settle. "Who's Billy Mason?" I asked Shana.

Her eyes were bleak. "He's Jack's administrative assistant."

"Not any more," Stan noted.

I threw a glare at Stan. "Thanks for the employment update," I told him. "Did you call this in?"

"Yes."

"When?"

"Ten minutes ago. Before I heard you two."

I swiped a line of sweat off my forehead and my feeling of nausea passed. "Any ideas what happened?"

"Shot. Single round. Dead center."

I couldn't believe it. For the first time in my life, Scary Stan gave me more information than I wanted to hear. "Thanks, I think."

Stan shrugged. "Whatever."

Shana, meanwhile, had lumbered her bulk back around the tree pile to sit on a rock near me. I studied her profile. I could feel two questions bubbling up inside me, and though I tried, I couldn't keep the stupid one from slipping out first.

"How come you don't throw up?"

She shifted on the rock to look at me.

"I thought pregnant women threw up," I tried to explain myself, as if stupid really had a logical explanation. "I mean, you see two dead bodies today and you hardly miss a beat. I'm not pregnant, and I can barely keep food down."

"You're an idiot," Stan said.

"He's not an idiot," Shana corrected him. "Misinformed, maybe, but not an idiot."

"Thanks, I think," I said again.

"It's just the first trimester, Bob," Shana continued. "A lot of women have nausea then. I did then, too, but not after that. I honestly don't know why I'm handling this as well as I am. Either I'm in deep shock or I saw enough grisly animal—and other—remains when I worked in the jungles for the Nature Conservancy. I guess I developed a really strong stomach."

"Other . . . remains?" I choked.

"Don't ask," Stan warned me.

It suddenly occurred to me that Shana and Stan seemed to know each other better than just as birders passing in the woods. I shelved it for later, though, since my second question was already half-way out of my mouth.

"You don't seem surprised to see Jack's assistant, Shana. Why is that?"

She briefly turned away from me and glanced at Stan. Her eyes dropped to the leaf debris that littered the ground. "He was at the Spring Valley Inn last night with the rest of us. Jack had invited him to come along for the weekend. Then, last night, about one o'clock in the morning, when I realized Jack was still gone, I asked Billy to drive up to Kami's to see if Jack's car was there."

She looked back towards me then. "I had to know, Bob. Then, this morning, when Billy didn't show up for coffee, I figured that Jack had caught him snooping around at Kami's and sent him home to Minneapolis. I never imagined that . . . something . . . had happened . . . to Billy."

And then she broke down into sobs.

"Smooth move, White," Stan said in his usual flat tone. "Make the woman cry." He took a step towards the forest.

"Hold it right there, buddy," I told him. Don't you dare disappear on me. If you leave me holding the bag on this one, I swear to God I'll sic Lily on you."

Stan visibly flinched, and I rolled on.

"If you thought she was merciless when she gave you the boot back in March, you have no idea what misery a bride-to-be can bring down on anyone who threatens to steal her spotlight, deliberately or not. I need to be so far below the radar on this one," I nodded in the direction of Billy's body, "that I'm underground. Got it?"

Apparently, he did. Stan's relationship with my sister hadn't lasted long, but Lily had obviously made a lasting impression on him. Or at least, the caliber of her anger had.

He returned my glare for only a moment.

"Go," he told me. "You were never here."

I pulled Shana to her feet and headed back to the trail.

Two bodies in one day.

Great.

Whoever thinks birding is dull has never been birding with me.

CHAPTER
NINE

Not a single media van was in sight when I pulled into the parking lot at the hotel just before six o'clock. After hightailing it out of Mystery Cave State Park, I offered to go back to the motel, but Shana didn't want to. Not yet. Instead, we'd driven southwest to Beaver Creek Wildlife Management Area, hoping to scope out the area where I suspected there might still be some wild Bobwhites. Unfortunately, though, despite our best efforts, we couldn't find any of the little quail, which was no great surprise, since Northern Bobwhites in the wild were notorious for their shyness. Shana and I did spot a few of the sparrows we wanted—we saw Vesper and Savannah Sparrows in the young hay fields lining the road, along with Field Sparrows in the taller grasses near stands of trees. In Beaver Creek, we also picked out a Willow Flycatcher and an Indigo Bunting, so the afternoon had produced decent results for us.

Decent as far as birds went, that is.

As far as bodies . . . not so good.

I was pretty sure, however, that the reason the media vans were gone had less to do with our earlier vanishing act than it had to do with the radio reports we'd listened to on our way back to the hotel. Not only had the announcement of Stan's discovery of Billy's body interrupted a Minnesota Twins ballgame broadcast, but somebody else was now topping the news: exotic animal sanctuary owner Kami Marsden.

According to the radio report, Kami had been brought into the local police station for questioning in relation to Jack's murder . . . and Billy's.

"Sources inside the sheriff's office tell us that no arrest has been made at this point, and that it is still too early in the investigation to name suspects," the reporter on the radio commented. "Yet the confirmed presence early this morning on Marsden's property of vehicles belonging to both murder victims is a clear indication that she will continue to be a prime subject in this investigation."

"How can anyone possibly know for a fact that Jack and Billy were there?" Shana argued, confusion and disbelief in her voice. "Does she have cameras mounted on her garage? An orbiting satellite transmitting surveillance? What?"

Eddie's face popped into my head.

Damn.

Eddie had gotten it all on tape.

Or disk.

Or whatever technology he was using these days to perform his electronics magic.

He'd said he had monitors tracking Nigel. I bet some of those monitors were motion sensors, and they'd triggered cameras that must have caught the cars on Kami's land.

"The lady was having some issues with her tiger," I told Shana. "When Tom and I were out there birding today, I ran into a good friend of mine who's a surveillance expert. He's helping her find the bugs in her perimeter fence. Apparently Nigel's been getting some free passes off the sanctuary without her knowledge, and she's literally trying to close the gap."

Shana's green eyes caught mine when I glanced over at her in the passenger seat.

"Who's Nigel? Your friend?"

I shook my head as I turned into the hotel parking lot. "Nigel's the tiger. Eddie Edvarg is my friend. I call him Crazy Eddie because he's independently wealthy, but he still likes to work. We met one summer on a DNR job. Me and Eddie, that is, not me and Nigel. I had that pleasure this afternoon." I pulled into a parking space. "Eddie's an ace at tracking anything that moves."

"I should have sent him after Jack, then. Not Billy," Shana said, her voice filled with misery.

Not again, I groaned inwardly. I could practically hear the waterworks cranking up. I was going to have to start carrying a sponge with Shana around. Maybe a bucket.

Maybe a shopvac.

"Where have you two been?"

Yes! Saved by the Bernie.

She must have been watching for us from just inside the hotel doors because I swear I had barely turned off the ignition before she was pulling Shana's car door open and wrapping her in an ample-bosomed hug. "I've been so worried about you, honey!"

"I'm all right, really, Bernie," Shana insisted, wheezing a little from Bernie's mothering embrace. "I needed to get away for a little bit, and Bob obliged me."

"Got some birds, too," I added, walking into the hotel.

"Well, you missed a ton of excitement around here," Bernie said, releasing Shana, only to hold her at arm's length for inspection. "You need some sleep and a good meal. But not in that order. We're all going to dinner across the street in five minutes."

"Yes, Mom," I told her.

Bernie pretended to slug me in the shoulder. "It's a good thing you're so handsome, or I'd toss you to the wolves in a minute," she said. "But since I happen to need a young man to escort me to dinner tonight, you're in luck. Now go clean up. I'm starving."

And with that, she steered Shana through the lobby and down the hall to her hotel room, leaving me at the registration desk. I checked for messages—there was one—and then went to my own room to do as I had been told.

I'd no sooner unlocked my door, though, than my cell phone rang.

"I swear, I let you out of my sight for twenty-four hours and you're in trouble. What am I going to do with you?"

It was Luce, and even though she was trying to joke with me, I could hear the concern in her voice. Obviously, bad news had traveled at its usual warp speed and found its way straight to my girlfriend.

"Hello to you, too. I'm assuming you're talking about Jack O'Keefe's murder."

"Please tell me you didn't find his body this morning. The radio reports are saying he was found by the group of birders he was leading, and I know that a group is more than one, but I have a really bad feeling that, if there was a body found, you were the one in the group to find it first."

"What can I say? You know I'm really good at finding things."

"Birds, yes! Bodies . . . that's not so much a skill as . . . really creepy!" Luce's voice came out of the cell phone loud and clear. "Okay, the first time I can understand—it was a fluke. You stumbled on a scam that was tied up with Boreal Owls. A totally random chance. And the second time? You were taking your mother birding. Not your fault that a homicide victim floats up in the marsh. But Bobby, this time you're with a bunch of talented birders. Why do you have to be the one person to find the body? Why couldn't someone else do it for a change?"

I looked at the phone in my hand. For the first time in the years I'd known Luce, I thought she sounded distraught, if not on the verge of actual hysteria. But Luce Nilsson never got distraught.

And then I realized what was going on.

"It's Lily, isn't it? She's getting to you," I concluded. "I told you it was a mistake to agree to be her maid of honor. What has she got you doing now? Looking at dinner mints stamped with their silhouettes?"

"Dinner mints I could handle," Luce said, some of the tension leaving her voice. "It's the horrible DJs I helped her audition this afternoon for the wedding reception. If I hear one more oily 'This one's for you, baby,' I'm going to lock myself in a closet and never come out."

"It's just another month, Luce. You can hang in there."

"Easy for you to say. You're out of town. And you don't have to be a part of the show until the wedding day." She paused a moment. "I wish I were the best man."

"No, you don't. Believe me, you don't want to go to the stag party I'm planning for Alan. Heck, *I* don't want to go to the stag party I'm planning for Alan," I laughed.

"So what's going on?" Luce asked, abruptly changing the subject. "Do you have to stick around in Spring Valley a few days, or are you coming home tomorrow?"

It dawned on me I hadn't thought ahead to the next day yet. In reality, there was no reason I couldn't go back to my townhouse in Savage after breakfast in the morning. For that matter, I could probably check in with the sheriff and leave right now, since I didn't have anything more to contribute to the investigation than the statement I'd given after I'd found Jack's body.

But for some reason, I found myself hedging with Luce.

"I'm not sure," I told her. "I think I need to stick around another day, maybe two. You know, see if there's anything I can help with. Birding-related stuff. I mean, Jack was here for birding, and now there's a group of birders here with no leader, so maybe I can help out."

There was a beat of silence in our conversation.

I noticed I hadn't mentioned Shana.

Luce sighed. "Okay. I suppose I can manage a few more days of wedding madness without you. I've got a full night at work tonight with the conference, anyway, so maybe tomorrow I'll just turn off my cell phone, barricade the door, and pretend I'm nobody's maid of honor."

"That's the woman I know and love," I assured her. "You were scaring me there with that panicky bit."

Luce laughed. "Yeah, it scared me too. Look, gorgeous, do me a favor. Don't find any bodies tomorrow when you're birding, okay? I want you back home where I can keep an eye on you and you can keep me from killing your sister before she gets married."

"Roger on that," I told her. "No bodies tomorrow, I promise."

We said our good-byes and I closed the phone. I hadn't lied to Luce: if at all humanly possible, I was not going to find a body tomorrow. Then again, I hadn't been completely honest with her, either.

I hadn't told her that my dead body tally for today had already risen to two.

Nor had I told her about a certain emerald-eyed woman who was not only a blast from my past, but also a suddenly betrayed and beleaguered widow I just couldn't walk away from.

At least not tonight.

I shook my head in self-disgust. What was I doing? I loved Luce, and she deserved the whole truth. She trusted me.

So why did I have the distinct impression that if I had told Luce both of those things, the body tally would have risen to three?

Jack.

Billy.

Bob.

It sounded like the name of a country & western artist.

Throw in a truck, a broken heart, and a good bird dog and we'd have a hit on our hands.

Instead of a murder case.

Chapter Ten

I was back in the lobby, waiting for Shana and Bernie, when I remembered that I'd picked up a message at the front desk earlier. I pulled it out of my jeans pocket and unfolded the note. Scanning the paper, I saw that it was signed by Eddie. Since the Spring Valley Inn & Suites was the only hotel in town, he'd apparently deduced where I was staying for the weekend. Like I said, the man can track anything that moves.

"Bob," the note read. "You should have told me about Jack. He was a good friend of Kami's. The sheriff was out asking questions, and I gave her the tapes. They don't help Kami at all. I'm going home. You know how I feel about the media."

I did know. Eddie was independently wealthy because he had won the lottery years ago. The resulting media glare had forced him and his wife to retreat to some far north woods property where they could live quietly and anonymously. Ever since, Eddie has avoided the press like the plague. I could definitely understand his heading home if Kami suddenly found herself in the bright eye of a media storm. I also knew, though, that Eddie would never leave a job undone, so I had to assume he'd finished mending Kami's electronic fence, which meant Nigel was safely corralled back home on the ranch.

In which case, maybe Tom and I could make another run up to that area first thing tomorrow morning, I thought, and try to do a wider search of the area for birds. It still puzzled me why Jack would have said there were Bobwhites up there when it obviously wasn't the kind of spot the birds preferred. Heck, with all the racket those ATVs made, I couldn't imagine any kind of creature—human or otherwise—who'd find a happy home there.

But Jack was way too good of a birder to make that kind of error.

Which could only mean he knew about a location we hadn't found yet. A spot where there were wild Northern Bobwhites.

And if he had found it, I didn't see any reason why I couldn't, too.

What's that old saying? "Pride goeth before a fall?"

According to my estimate, I'd already done that: taken a fall because of the pride. Okay, yes, technically, Nigel was only *one* tiger, and lions formed prides, not tigers, but he certainly humbled me when he leaped in my direction. And if it hadn't been for Eddie's electronic wizardry, that big cat would have been burping happily. Then, I believe, the proper phrase would be "The cat who got the canary."

Or, to be completely accurate, the Bob White.

Wait a minute.

Could there possibly be a connection here? Bobwhites and Jack. Jack and Kami. Kami and an exotic animal sanctuary near where Jack said there were Bobwhites.

Was Kami protecting Bobwhites along with Nigel?

Would a big cat not eat a canary?

Only in a Disney film. And since Kami's cat was far from an animated cartoon character, I had to believe that Nigel would as soon eat a Bobwhite as share sanctuary space with it. My free association technique might work great for helping high school students come up with solutions for relationship and classroom issues, but when it came to helping me locate a birding rarity, it wasn't exactly burning up the barn.

But it did make me wonder if Kami might know something about the Bobwhites Jack had mentioned to Tom. After all, Jack had put Bobwhites on our list for this birding weekend, and so far, I'd come up empty-handed in the places I'd looked. There had to be a place I was missing, and Kami surely knew this neck of the woods better than anybody else since she owned a large piece of it. Maybe I could chase her down first thing tomorrow and pick her brain about Bobwhites.

Unless she landed in jail on a murder charge before I could get to her.

That would be a problem.

I wondered what really happened to Jack O'Keefe. Thanks to Eddie's tape, there was no doubt that our birding leader had been at Kami's last night; according to Shana's admission that Jack never got home, it also meant that Kami may have been the last person to see him alive.

If she'd shot him, then she was definitely the last person to see him alive.

Then again, Jack wasn't the only man at Kami's last night: Eddie's tape proved that Billy was there, too. So what was going on, and who saw who doing what? And what reason would Kami have to kill Jack or Billy? If she and Jack had quarreled, murder was a pretty extreme measure for settling an argument. Not to mention how inconvenient it would have been for Kami to chase him down to the youth camp to do the deed. And how would that play out?

"Hey, Jack, I'm furious with you. Could you just walk down this slope and go behind the old covered wagon there? No reason. I just want to shoot a couple of bullets into your heart."

I don't think so.

Trying to factor in Billy, too, only made the whole mess worse. Did the sheriff think that after Kami killed Jack, she took off after Billy? Just because he'd been on her property? Valuing one's privacy, I could understand. But to murder for it? There again, the woman must have been pretty determined to do the deed if she'd followed Billy to Mystery Cave. Or did she have a standing appointment with Billy to kill him later?

"I'm going to be busy a little while offing Jack, so could we just meet at Mystery Cave in about an hour? By that big logpile off the main trail? You're an administrative aide, you understand how challenging schedules can be."

Right.

Heck, if she'd planned to kill the guy, she could have just fed him to Nigel and saved herself a bunch of time, if not gas money. As someone who does a lot of driving to go birding, I certainly appreciate the price of gas and the dent it can put in my budget—it's not like gas coupons grow on trees in Minnesota. The way the media was already painting Kami, though, she sounded less like an economizing driver and more like a serial killer on a shooting spree. True, I didn't know Kami, but I did know Jack, and I couldn't see him being involved with a woman who had a problem with violence.

For that matter, I couldn't see him involved with anyone but his wife. Especially when that wife was Shana.

But I was no sheriff either, and since the two men were on Kami's property shortly before their murders, that was enough of a link for Sheriff Paulsen to question Kami about both deaths. Obviously, I had a lot to learn about investigating murders because, from my perspective, the sheriff was making quite an assumption that the two deaths were linked to Kami. I mean, for all the sheriff knew, maybe Billy had taken off to spend the morning birding alone after doing his spying gig for Shana, and he'd just had the rotten bad luck to accidentally walk into a random bullet.

Happens all the time, right?

Not.

Which meant the deaths were linked. But whether Kami was the connection was still hard for me to swallow. Even Shana, who suspected that Jack and Kami were having an affair, immediately thought that Jack's death had something to do with the work he'd been doing with eco-communities. She told us all that Jack had made enemies.

Although, to be one hundred percent accurate, her first comment was that she had killed him.

At the time I'd chalked it up to hysteria, but now that I recalled her exact words, I felt a ripple of unease slide up my spine.

Shana had said, "It's all my fault."

All?

What was Shana not telling us?

CHAPTER ELEVEN

B ob!"

I turned my head to see Renee and Mac Ackerman, two members of our birding group, walk into the lobby. Since we were all going to be having dinner together at the A&W across the street, they plopped down on the sofa next to my armchair and began to tell me what I'd missed when Shana and I had slipped out the hotel window to escape the media circus.

"That Chuck O'Keefe sure hates Shana," Renee reported. "He kept yelling at the sheriff, saying that Shana was a manipulative schemer, and that he wasn't fooled by her innocent grieving widow act. He said she had more irons in the fire than anyone knew about, and he wasn't about to let her take OK Industries away from Jack's real family."

"OK Industries?"

"O'Keefe Industries, Bob," Mac clarified for me. "It's the family empire. They've got interests in just about every business in the state. Mills, real estate, grocery stores, banking."

"Jack O'Keefe came a long way from his humble origins, that's for sure," Renee added. "I told the reporters that when Jack was in high school, all the girls were in love with him." A distinct red blush colored her cheeks. "Including me."

Mac threw his arm around his smiling wife and hugged her close. "That was a long time ago."

"Yes, it was," Renee agreed, wiping away a tear that had crept into her eyes when she'd said Jack's name. "But it doesn't make it any easier to see someone you know . . . dead."

She sniffed and turned away to dig into her purse for a tissue.

"Yeah, if it hadn't been for that Ben Graham, I don't think the sheriff would have ever gotten Chuck to calm down, let alone leave the hotel. I guess he's an old pal of Jack's, and he's known Chuck since he was a baby," Mac continued. "Anyway, as soon as he told the reporters about Jack and Kami Marsden having an affair, they could have cared less about Chuck, I think. I guess a sex scandal beats an outraged stepson when you're looking for head-lines."

"Say that again?"

Mac looked at me for a moment in confusion. "I guess a sex scandal—

"

"No, not that part," I interrupted him. "The part about Jack and Kami Marsden."

"You mean about them having an affair?" Renee was back in the con-versation. "Apparently it was common knowledge down here in Spring Valley. The sheriff didn't seem surprised at all when Big Ben—he's the mayor, you know," she added for my benefit, "mentioned it. Of course, he didn't come right out at first and say 'affair.' He said they had a 'close, personal relation-ship,' but of course, everyone could figure out what he wasn't saying. And then the sheriff told the reporters that private affairs weren't her concern, but murder was, and that she would be talking with Kami later today. Which I guess she did, according to the radio."

Renee sniffed one last time into the tissue in her hand. "Poor Shana. I can't imagine how she must feel."

"Actually, I'm pretty hungry."

We all looked up to see Shana and Bernie standing at the edge of the lobby. Renee's cheeks blazed a brighter red in embarrassment, and Mac quickly rose from the sofa, pulling his wife up with him.

"I think we'll go on across the street and find a table," he said. "See you there."

Renee ducked her head and made a beeline for the hotel's front doors.

I watched Shana's green eyes follow Renee's back out the hotel entrance and had no clue what to say.

"Too bad Renee wasn't in such a rush this morning to get to coffee," Bernie commented as she and Shana crossed the lobby to me. "As I recall, we waited a good half-hour for her to get back from that twenty-four hour pharmacy with her allergy prescription. If it hadn't been for her, we could have gotten an earlier start on our birding. I mean, really, how could the woman forget her allergy medication at home when it's allergy season? Talk about being unprepared."

As I motioned for Shana to precede me through the hotel doors, her eyes caught mine, a hint of a smile playing around the corners of her full lips, and

A Bob White Killing

I immediately knew what she was thinking. Without a moment's hesitation, I could feel my memory flying back to the summer I was sixteen and Shana Lewis was the woman of my dreams . . .

"TALK ABOUT BEING UNPREPARED," I'd moaned, trying not to scratch at the million mosquito bites that were welling up all over my legs and arms.

"You didn't have to go into the swamp with me," Shana laughed. "I told you you weren't properly dressed, but you just couldn't stand the thought of me getting that Louisiana Waterthrush when you haven't been able to find it all summer, could you?" She pulled a tube of bite balm out of her backpack. "That competitive streak is going to get you into trouble, Bob, mark my words. Now turn around."

And then she proceeded to massage the whole tube into the backs of my stinging legs. For that one short moment, I thought I'd died and gone to heaven.

But not because the balm soothed the itching.

Because Shana, who was driving me crazier every time I was near her, had her hands on me.

Not that it meant anything more to her than having to take care of a stupid, careless, proud and overconfident young birder. After all, she had been the one wearing the long-sleeved bug shirt and pants that covered almost every inch of her beautiful, ivory skin in mosquito-proof protection.

I, on the other hand, had been the "What NOT to wear for birding in August" model. Dressed in a tee-shirt and shorts, I was every mosquito's fantasy feast—skin, skin, and more skin. I think it was a week before I could sit down without my legs tingling from the overwhelming need to itch. But even then, every time I thought about Shana touching me, I would have walked right back into that swamp had I been given the choice.

YEAH, I'D BEEN UNPREPARED BACK THEN.

Just like I was unprepared right now as the memory of that summer flooded over me, filling me with a yearning I couldn't begin to describe.

"Are you going to stand there all evening with your mouth open catching flies, or are we going to dinner?" Bernie called back to me from the other side of the hotel's entrance drive.

Only then did I realize I was frozen in the path of the hotel's sliding doors. Shana, standing on the far curb with Bernie, also looked back at me, smiling, and I kicked myself in the head for so easily losing my sense of time and place, not to mention control of my libido. A whiff of White Shoulders lingered with me in the doorway, and I shook my head to clear it.

How about some focus, here, buddy? I asked myself. *You want to help Shana, then get a grip, because the last thing she needs is a mutton-headed sixteen-year-old following her around.*

A scream of brakes rounded the corner of the hotel as a news van headed straight for Shana and Bernie.

I was wrong.

The last thing Shana needed was an unexpected visit from the media.

Then I realized that the cameraman hanging out the window on the passenger side of the van wasn't aiming his camera at Shana.

He was aiming it at me.

CHAPTER TWELVE

T urn away!" Shana shouted at me, but it was too late. The van roared off, the cameraman grinning as he waved good-bye.

I crossed the driveway to Shana and Bernie. "This is not a good thing, is it?"

"Not unless you don't mind having your personal life totally and completely appropriated by the media," Shana replied, a quiet resentment lacing her voice. "When I married Jack, he warned me that our marriage was going to be a bonanza for gossip-mongers, so I've spent the last five years ducking the press as much as possible so we could have a real marriage, and not an unending media event." She glanced in the direction of the disappearing van. "I'm afraid to even think about what's going to be leading the news on television tonight."

It took a second or two for me to catch Shana's meaning, but when I did, it wasn't pretty.

"Let me guess," I said. "Jack's murder is going to be at the top of the hour, with more details to follow. Details like you," I pointed at Shana, and then curved my finger toward my chest. "And me."

Shana nodded slowly in affirmation.

"Oh boy!" Bernie said, linking her arms through Shana's right elbow and my left. She turned us toward the street and started pulling us along. "I'm having dinner with two celebrities! Wait till I tell the girls back home. They'll be so jealous."

Jealous?

Oh, man.

I almost stumbled over my own feet. What if my face did show up on the evening news as the lovelier-than-ever Shana O'Keefe's brand-new companion? And what if Luce, the woman I loved, saw it?

Luce, the woman to whom I hadn't mentioned Shana O'Keefe.

"I think I just lost my appetite," I muttered.

"Nonsense," Bernie said. "What you need is a good meal to fortify you for the night ahead. We're going owling after dinner, aren't we? I know I'm looking forward to some evening walking. If we have to stick around till tomorrow like the sheriff asked, I don't see why we can't just pick up what was on our original weekend birding plan for tonight anyway." She gave Shana's arm an extra pat with her hand. "I know it's been an awful day for you, honey, but I can't think of a better way to get your mind off your troubles than to go birding."

And with that remark, our self-appointed mother hen hustled us across the two-lane road that separated the hotel from the restaurant and then ushered us into the old A&W drive-in. As soon as we walked in, Tom called to us from a table at the far end of the diner. I noted that Renee and Mac were seated with another couple from our birding group at the table next to ours and that everyone seemed fairly engrossed in reading through the menu.

Which, to be honest, wasn't going to take too long since the A&W specialized in burger baskets and not much else. Not exactly nouveau cuisine, if you know what I mean. But definitely familiar fare for birding weekend trip regulars. I'm sure I'm not the only Minnesota birder who can say he's eaten burgers in nearly every county in the great state of Minnesota.

Come to think of it, maybe the weekends should be renamed. "Birds and burgs" might work. Although then the trip leader better proofread the flyers carefully or we might be signing up for "birds and bugs" weekends.

Actually, I've been on some of those too. Trust me, when someone asks you to go birding in the Sax-Zim bog in July, say, "No." The birds might be good ones, but the mosquitoes can carry off small children.

Glancing at Renee and friends as I headed towards Tom and our table, it occurred to me that their intense menu perusal was more likely out of consideration for Shana's circumstances than any gastronomical curiosity. In fact, it seemed almost too obvious that the four birders were feverishly intent on not making eye contact with Shana as she passed their table.

Respect for a grieving widow was one thing, but the vibes I picked up from the group before I sat down next to Tom seemed distinctly different than sympathy.

Embarrassment?

Maybe. In the hotel lobby, Shana had walked in on the last part of Renee and Mac's "sex scandal" commentary, casting Shana in the role of the naive wife. Having already had that conversation with Shana myself, I knew how she felt about people's intrusive speculations, as well as her determination not to be labeled as the poor, pitiful wife who was caught unaware by her husband's infidelity. So, sure, maybe Renee was feeling a little residual discomfort from that earlier encounter in the hotel.

Yet embarrassment didn't quite fit the mood I felt emanating from the adjacent table. If I had to make a gut call on it, I would have said it was smugness, like they knew something the four of us at my table didn't.

And that got me to wondering what else had happened at the hotel after Shana and I had made our window exit. Between Chuck's accusations and Big Ben the Mayor's revelations, I figured Jack must have been cringing in his grave.

Well, maybe not in his grave, since he wasn't buried yet, but you get my point. The man's dirty laundry was being strung out on the line for the whole world to see, and he wasn't even around to throw a little bleach at it. It sure didn't look like his best friend the mayor was going to be of any help in salvaging Jack's reputation, either. In fact, based on Renee and Mac's report, it sounded like good old Big Ben had been all too ready to throw the choicest bits of gossip meat to the media pack.

A best friend like that, nobody needs.

Yet he'd shown up pretty quickly to offer Shana condolences and support.

A soft chuckle interrupted my thoughts, and I glanced at Shana sitting beside me. Tom was telling her about our afternoon encounter with Nigel and had managed not only to amuse her, but elicit a small laugh. The woman was holding up pretty darn well, I thought, especially in light of what she'd been through since sunrise this morning. But then again, the Shana I'd known was like that: a real trooper who didn't think twice about taking on the world or wading through mud for a chance to find a rarity.

Actually, Shana herself was the rarity.

No matter what the situation, it seemed like passion virtually spilled out of her, whether she was facing down a vengeful stepson or planning a future of research in exotic locations. The more I thought about it, the only time I'd ever seen her falter was this morning when she'd cried for Jack in my arms. And even that was passionate—I don't know that I'd ever seen such stark grief in a person's face as when Shana first saw Jack's frozen features. Yet here she was, sitting in a diner with Bernie, Tom and me, planning a night of owling to pass the time while Sheriff Paulsen tried to solve her husband's murder.

The fact was, Shana O'Keefe was a woman any man would be attracted to. If her raven-haired beauty didn't catch a guy's eye, her sheer vitality would. Heck, even here in the A&W, I noticed that the high school boys flipping the burgers were checking her out.

So why, I asked myself for the hundredth time, would Jack have cheated on her?

And why would Big Ben have been so eager to let the world know about it?

The waitress brought us the basket of onion rings that Tom had already ordered for us, but something didn't smell right to me.

Not the onion rings. They smelled great. I loved onion rings.

No, something else was beginning to stink.

Or, rather, someone.

And his name was Big Ben.

CHAPTER
THIRTEEN

I t was a nice night for owling. We'd picked a spot just about twenty minutes away from the hotel where a spread of old-growth forest offered plenty of roosting spots for owls. About five minutes into our walk through the woods, we spotted a Barred Owl perched at the entrance of a tree cavity. Since it was still dusky, we could just make out his dark eyes peering at us above his richly barred chest.

"Those black eyes always give me the creeps," Bernie whispered at my shoulder. "All the other owls have nice yellow eyes. They're like little night lights in their faces."

"Barn owls have dark eyes," Tom corrected her.

"Well, I've never seen one," Bernie replied. "But I'd guess it looks pretty spooky, too, sitting there in the dark with its black eyes glowing."

"But Barn Owls have the sweetest face shape, Bernie," Shana told her. "It's like a white heart. And because they're so light in color, they're easy to see even at night. I saw a lot of them in Central America while I was working for the Nature Conservancy. Some of the biologists there think that the Barn Owl population has dramatically increased in wet lowlands and highlands because so much of their native habitat is being destroyed by deforestation."

She paused when a low hooting call sounded through the trees.

"Sounds like a Great Horned Owl," I said. "I guess the deforestation hasn't pushed more Barn Owls our way yet."

Shana chuckled lightly. "Can you believe that Great Horned Owls are very rare in Central America?" Shana asked. "I think everyone in America lives within the calling distance of a Great Horned Owl, but it's a real find down there."

We walked a while longer, listening to the call of the Great Horned as it floated through the night. Shana's casual comments about her work in Central America reminded me that I knew little about the woman walking beside me in a Fillmore County forest on a balmy June evening. While Jack's involvement with conservation had been highly publicized in the last few years,

Shana's name had never surfaced. Yet her passion for her chosen field was clearly something she hadn't put aside when she'd left her job to marry Jack. Even when she referred to it in passing, as she'd just done, I could hear an excitement just below the surface of her voice. I could hear it because it was the same excitement that I always felt when I started talking about birds. For the first time since I'd seen her in the hotel lobby last night, I wondered what it had cost her personally to give up her globe-trotting research career to become Mrs. Jack O'Keefe.

Considering how she and her stepson had nearly come to blows this afternoon in her hotel room, I'd guess the price had been plenty high. And judging from Chuck's threats as he left Shana's room in Sheriff Paulsen's company, that price was only going to go higher. Not only did Jack's son want to blame his stepmother for his father's death, but he was bound and determined to let everyone know exactly what he thought of the second Mrs. O'Keefe.

And it wasn't a very complimentary picture.

"I'm beat," Bernie announced when the trail ahead of us started up a slight rise.

"I say we call it quits for the night."

"I second it," Tom said. He caught my eye and tipped his head in Shana's direction. "I think we could all pack it in, Bob."

I stole a quick look at Shana and agreed. Either the shadows were especially dark here, or the day had finally caught up with her, rimming her eyes with circles of fatigue.

"Last one back to the car is an extinct species," I announced.

The closer we got to the parking area, though, the louder the Horned Owl calls became. As we rounded the last bend of the trail, we saw the reason why. Standing next to her green Ranger with its "Owl Aboard" back tire cover was Karla Kinstler, a long-time birding pal of mine, who also happened to be the director of the Houston Nature Center and the world-renowned International Festival of Owls. As always, Karla wasn't alone. Perched on her wrist was Alice, the Great Horned Owl.

"Karla," I called to her as we approached.

She and Alice both swiveled their heads in my direction.

"Hey, Bob," she answered back. "I thought that was your car, especially since I don't know anybody else with a 'BRRDMAN' license plate. What are you doing down here in my neck of the woods?"

"Owling, my dear," I told her. I introduced her and Alice to my little crew. "Alice is an educational bird. She came to Karla when she was about eighteen months old. She was hit by a car, and her wing never healed properly to allow flight."

"He's talking about Alice, not me," Karla added, laughing. "Alice works with me at the Nature Center. We present programs."

"And Karla is also a world authority on Great Horned Owl vocalizations," I noted. "In fact, I bet some of what we just heard was you, not Alice."

Karla laughed again. "Guilty as charged. It was such a nice night, I thought Alice and I could both use a walk in the woods. I assume you heard some owls?"

I nodded, and Tom told her about the Barred Owl we'd seen.

"Really? I'm beginning to think we've got a little bump in the population of Barred Owls in Fillmore County this summer," Karla said. "Last night I found one up near Kami Marsden's place when I was leaving. Jack O'Keefe was there because he's leading a Birding Weekend in Fillmore this weekend, and I told him he should take his group out tomorrow night to find one."

For a second, I thought maybe I'd misheard her. I opened my mouth to ask her to repeat herself, but Shana beat me to it.

"You were at Kami's last night? What time?"

Karla cocked her head to consider Shana. "What was your last name again?" she asked.

"O'Keefe," Shana said.

"You're Jack's wife!" Karla gently rubbed her knuckle along Alice's feathered breast. "He said you were here birding with his group this weekend. I'm pleased to meet you. You really lit a fire under him, you know. He's doing great things for Minnesota with all his lobbying and support of the eco-communities. He's just the guy we needed at the Capitol to put some muscle into our conservation efforts."

Silence suddenly surrounded us.

Karla didn't know about Jack.

"Jack was found murdered this morning, Karla," I quietly told her. "He was shot at Green Hills Youth Camp."

Karla leaned back against her car. Alice's yellow eyes pinned each of us in turn.

"Oh no," Karla breathed. "I just saw him last night. We were talking about the plans for the eco-community we want to border Kami's land. Jack was so sure we could get the land-use permit approved and keep the ATV riders out of there, but this whole process of getting the zoning changed has been such a headache, and it's taken so much time and effort. All those late night meetings . . ." her voice trailed off. "Oh, Shana, I am so sorry. Jack was such a good man."

"Late night meetings?" Shana's voice cracked.

"For months now," Karla continued, "Kami and Jack have been hammering out zoning ordinances with the county. The ATV contingent kept showing up at the meetings, arguing and complaining that the land next to Kami's isn't suitable for anything besides a dirt track. I went to some of the sessions to offer moral support, but I usually just sat in the back, appalled at how nasty the fighting got. I thought this one guy—some big ATV fan—was going to slug it out with Jack right there one night. Those meetings really took a toll on Jack, I could tell. He usually just holed up at Kami's for the night, rather than drive back to the Cities."

I held up my hand for Karla to stop talking. "Wait a minute," I said. "Jack was down here for late meetings about the eco-communities?"

Karla nodded.

"Kami and Jack weren't . . . involved?"

Karla gave me a funny look, then shook her head vigorously. "I heard once that they were old high school sweethearts, but that was a long time ago." She turned to Shana, who was leaning against my car parked next to Karla's. "Jack was crazy about you, Shana. Don't ever think anything different."

An almost smothered sob slipped out of Shana's lips as Bernie wrapped her arms around her. Out of the corner of my eye, I could see Tom moving closer to Shana's other side, ready to catch her if she collapsed.

"Go back to last night again, Karla," I said, refocusing my attention on her. "When did you leave Kami's?"

Karla closed her eyes and took a deep breath. "It was late. After midnight, I think."

"Did you see any other cars on the road when you left? Was Jack still there?"

"Jack was still there." She shot a glance at Shana who was now being seated in my SUV by Tom. "They weren't involved, Bob. I know that for a fact. Kami and I are good friends, and she'd tell me." She hesitated. "Besides, Kami's involved with someone else, Bob. She keeps it quiet, and that's all I'm going to say about it."

I nodded in understanding. Nice to know somebody could keep something quiet in this county. Ever since I'd found Jack slumped over behind the covered wagon this morning, it seemed like the only thing everyone wanted to do was make noise—Chuck, Big Ben, the sheriff, the press, even Renee and her husband. I looked at Karla who was making a low hooting sound at Alice.

Okay, even Karla was making noise, albeit very softly.

"Now that I think about it, there was another car," she said. "I passed it south and west of Kami's farmhouse. It was by that seepage meadow on Rice Creek. I thought it was kind of late for someone to be out that way, but hey, I was out there."

"You had a reason," I reminded her. "You were talking with Kami and Jack. Did you say Rice Creek?" I asked as the name rang a bell inside my head. A bell with a very big tiger attached to it.

"Yup."

I watched Karla slowly stroke Alice's folded wing while my mind spun a little. Late last night, a car was in the vicinity of the seepage meadow.

The seepage meadow that abutted Kami's wildlife sanctuary.

The same seepage meadow where a portion of her fencing was found ripped and torn aside this afternoon while Nigel lay peacefully stunned in the grass, thanks to Crazy Eddie's electronic genius.

Aha. It wasn't going to take a genius to put this two and two together.

Somebody deliberately cut Kami's fence last night. Jack was nearby, at Kami's place, at approximately the same time. The next morning, Jack turned up dead barely ten miles away. Conclusion?

Unfortunately, I had no idea.

Okay, so math has never been my strong suit. I was going to have to find someone else to do the addition.

My cell phone chirped in my pocket.

I took it out and looked in the window to see who was calling, but it read "Caller unknown."

"White," I answered.

"Something you should know."

"Stan?"

"Jack cut off Ben. Chuck started it up again. On the sly. I tracked it."

"What are you talking about? I'm trying to figure out Jack and the fence here. I don't know anything about Jack and Ben. Or Chuck." I pulled the phone away from my ear and stared at it. I had an unlisted phone number. I'd never given it to Stan.

"Help Shana, White," his voice carried out of the phone. "She's a special lady." And then he hung up.

The little window on my phone glowed brightly in the full darkness as I stuck it back in my pocket. I could have sworn Stan's voice had softened just a fraction when he said Shana's name, but I must have been mistaken. Stan wasn't prone to empathy. He wasn't prone to speaking much, either. In fact, one of these days I was going to tell Stan to feel free to use compound sentences with me, something more like what normal people used to converse. Maybe I'd even get him to go wild and put together a whole paragraph. As it was, talking with Stan was like listening in on a secret code, but never having the secret decoder ring to make any sense of it.

"Everything okay?" Karla asked.

I made a quick list in my head: Jack was murdered, his assistant was dead, Chuck wanted to arrest Shana, Big Ben lied about Jack and Kami to the press, someone wanted to give Nigel a free pass out of the sanctuary, Chuck was apparently sliding money to Big Ben without his father's approval, and, within hours, my name was probably going to be linked with Shana's in the most talked-about murder case of the decade.

Oh. And one more thing: I had yet to find a Northern Bobwhite.

I gave Karla my best "everything is under control" smile. "Absolutely," I assured her, pulling open my car door. "It's just been a long day, you know?"

"You can say that again," Bernie piped up from the back seat. "I'm taking two aspirin when I get back to the hotel. I want to be sure I get a good night's sleep. We've still got birds to find this weekend, and tomorrow's another new day."

Oh, joy. Just what I needed—Little Orphan Annie had come home to roost in my back seat in the shape of Bernie Schmieg. If she started singing, I was walking back to the hotel.

"Good to see you, Karla." I waved good-bye as she and Alice got into her car and left the lot, then hopped into my own driver's seat. I stole a glance at Shana in the seat beside me and noticed she was trying to read a small piece of paper with the meager light from the overhead car lamp. "What's that?" I asked.

"I don't know," she replied. "It's so odd. It's a note on the hotel's stationery, and it's in Jack's handwriting. I found it on the bedspread in my hotel room after Ben left. You know, before we went out the window."

I vaguely remembered Big Ben picking up a jacket off Shana's bed when he'd left us alone in the room.

"I think it may have slipped out of one of Ben's pockets," Shana continued. "I know it wasn't there this morning when I went to meet everyone for coffee and rolls. I would have noticed a note on the bed." She studied the paper again before looking at me in complete confusion. "I forgot all about it until just now when I was digging around for another tissue in my pocket. I don't understand."

She handed me the note, and I held it up to the roof light to read it.

"Yeah," I said, "odd is one way to put it."

Especially since it read "BEN—KILL BOBWHITE?"

CHAPTER
FOURTEEN

I looked at the note again, hoping the magic wish fairy might have suddenly appeared and rewritten it to say "You won the lottery!" or "Beer is now free at your favorite liquor store!" But no, it still read "BEN—KILL BOBWHITE?"

"Okay. That's it," I groaned. "Someone stick a fork in me. I am so done."

And then the note disappeared. Only it wasn't the wish fairy making a belated appearance. Bernie was leaning over my shoulder, reading the note that was now clutched in her fingers.

"Ooh!" she gasped. "This explains everything!" Her eyes darted to my face, then Shana's. "Jack knew about you two! He was insanely jealous. He planned to kill Bob this weekend while we were birding."

"What about Bob and Shana?" Tom asked from the backseat.

"What?" Shana and I said at the same time.

"Well, it sounds good, doesn't it? Just like one of those movies of the week on the cable channel. Love triangles, betrayal, revenge, murder. I love those movies! I can hardly peel myself away to microwave popcorn even during the commercial breaks."

Bernie waved the note in excitement. "This clinches it. Jack must have sent this note to Ben after he checked into the hotel. He had it all planned out. He'd have Ben, his lifelong buddy, set up the hit on Bob because he was jealous of any of Shana's male friends—even though he had no reason to be because we all know that Shana would never cheat on Jack, and that she's crazy about him. Jack, though, is insecure because he's not getting any younger." She turned to Shana. "Sorry, honey, but it's the truth."

"Bernie—" I tried interrupting, but she was on a roll now.

"But since Big Ben runs the show around here, no one would ever suspect him of being part of a murder plot, so Jack figures it's the perfect crime. He asks Ben to kill Bob, and no one's the wiser."

"But I'm not the one who's dead," I reminded Bernie.

"Yeah," she admitted, frowning at the hotel stationery in her hand. "That sort of messes up my plotline. I guess those television writers really do have their work cut out for them, don't they?"

"What about Bob and Shana?" Tom asked again.

"Nothing!" I sputtered.

"We're old friends," Shana said. "That's all. I didn't even know Bob was going to be here this weekend till I saw him in the hotel lobby last night. Bob has nothing to do with Jack's murder. Bob has nothing to do with anything."

Gee, that sure told me where I stood in the grand scheme of things. I didn't know if I should be relieved or disappointed: not a killer, but definitely insignificant.

Shana wasn't finished, though. She plucked the note from Bernie's fingers. "I don't know what this is about," she said, waving the bit of paper in the air. "But I do know one thing: Jack would never, ever, even think about killing someone, no matter what that person did."

Stan's words suddenly came back to me. "But he'd stop funding him, wouldn't he?"

Shana's eyes caught mine. In the dim glow of the overhead light, I could see no green in them, only a dark reflection of confusion that slowly gave way to suspicion. "How did you know that?" she whispered.

"A little birdie told me," I answered. Then I wondered if she knew the other thing that little birdie had shared with me.

"But Chuck started the payments back up, Shana."

Her face visibly paled even in the semi-darkness of the front seat of the car. "Stan found them," she said, her voice flat. "That son-of-a-bitch."

"He likes you, Shana. He's trying to help. I think," I added.

"Not Stan," she ground out. "Chuck. He's the son-of-a-bitch. He was making payments to Ben behind Jack's back. That's why Stan was down here birding. He was supposed to meet Jack and me after dinner tonight to tell us what he'd found. Jack hired him to make a very discreet audit of OK Industries because Ben didn't seem to be hurting financially the way we thought he would after Jack cut him off."

She crumpled the note in her hand. "I asked Jack to bring Stan in. He's an old friend, and I trust him. Jack didn't want to think it was Chuck making the payments. That son-of-a-bitch," she repeated.

"You and Stan are old friends?" I asked, but Shana had already turned around in her seat to face Tom and Bernie.

"Jack and Ben grew up together," she explained to them. "Their families were close. When Ben went into politics, Jack supported him financially on a regular basis, because the Grahams didn't have any money, and because Jack believed in Ben's judgment." She rubbed her hand across her brow. "Until this spring. Then Ben started siding against Jack when it came to developing the eco-community here. It wasn't like he sided with anyone else—he just kept his considerable political clout—as you mentioned, Bernie—out of the discussion altogether." Shana shrugged. "So Jack stopped funding Ben."

"And now Jack's dead," Tom finished.

"But Big Ben's still getting money from OK, right, Bob?" Bernie pointed out. "Isn't that what you said?"

I nodded.

"Then Big Ben has nothing to complain about," she concluded. "He's still got the money coming in." She tapped the wadded note in Shana's hand. "So who knows what this is about, but it sounds to me like your stepson has some explaining to do, Shana."

I looked at the faces of my passengers. No one seemed able to comment on Bernie's remark, so I turned off the overhead light and put the car in gear.

"It's past my bedtime," I said. "We can think some more about this tomorrow, but right now, my pillow is calling me."

Unfortunately, so was someone else. I handed my ringing cell phone to Shana and told her to answer it for me.

She popped it open. "Hello."

After listening for a moment, she glanced at me and said into the receiver, "This is Shana O'Keefe."

Another moment passed with Shana listening. "He's driving," she told the caller.

Yet another moment went by with Shana on the phone. "I'll let him know," she said and ended the call. She laid the phone in the cup holder next to my seat. "That was your sister. She wants you to call her as soon as you stop driving."

Great.

Lily.

Like I really wanted to hear her rip into me about my latest birding-gone-bad weekend. I could already imagine what she had to say.

"I'm getting MARRIED, Bobby, and you find another body! What are you THINKING?!"

I'm thinking I'm going to drive to Arizona. No, make that Alaska. Hell, I'd drive to China to avoid talking with Lily tonight. Maybe by then she'd forget what she wanted to say to me.

Not in this lifetime, if I knew my sister.

"She also said to tell you that you looked terrible in the footage on tonight's newscast," Shana added. "And she said you can forget about renting a tux for her wedding because you're no longer invited. Somebody named Rick can be the best man."

CHAPTER FIFTEEN

T hat's a relief," I said into the silence that hung in the car after Shana passed along Lily's message. "I hate wearing a tux."

"Wait a minute," Bernie said from behind me. "Is that the same Rick I met birding with you back in May? The policeman with the diamond stud in his ear?"

"Yup. That's him."

"Now, I'd love to see him in a tux. He could moonlight as a male model if you ask me. Heck, I'd be happy to see him without the tux, if you know what I mean."

Tom groaned in the back seat.

"You're not serious," Shana said to me. "You wouldn't miss your sister's wedding."

I blew out a breath of exasperation. "No, Shana, I'm not going to skip out on Lily's wedding. Though God knows she might just drive half of her wedding party over the edge before the big day finally gets here. Luce is the maid of honor, and she's hanging on by a thread."

"Who's Luce?"

It suddenly dawned on me I hadn't mentioned Luce to Shana before this moment.

And then I wondered: why hadn't I?

"She's my girlfriend."

"She's his girfriend," said both Tom and Bernie at the same time the words came out of my mouth.

"Okaaay," Shana drew out. "It's obviously unanimous. Luce is your girl-friend."

"They met on a birding weekend," Bernie informed her. "I was there, in fact. I could tell something was going on right away. And that was years ago now. I keep telling Bob he ought to marry her pretty quick because she's not going to wait around forever."

"Bernie?" I caught her eyes in my rear-view mirror. "Do you mind?"

"Not at all, Bob," she replied. "Luce is such a sweet gal," she told Shana.

"Bernie!"

"I'm done!"

Silence filled the car again.

"There's got to be a reason for that note," Tom finally said, his voice breaking into the low hum of my tires on the county road.

I shook my head. "Whatever it is, I'm clueless. I only knew Jack from birding and I never met Big Ben until this afternoon. It's got to be another Bob White. Someone they both knew."

"Jack would never plot to kill someone," Shana repeated, exhaustion edging her voice. "That is *so* nonnegotiable."

Yet she had a note crumpled in her hand that suggested to Ben Graham that he kill Bob White. As I drove the last few miles back to the hotel, I spun around and around in my head everything I'd heard about the eco-communities Jack was working on. Had there been any big controversies, any confrontations, beyond the usual complaints of local residents when a new developer arrived in town and threatened to shake up the status quo? Was there another Bob White running around in Fillmore County, making so much noise he was courting a killer?

If there was, I sure didn't know him. Which should have allayed any fears I had about the mysterious note from Big Ben's pocket, but for some reason, I still felt vaguely uneasy about that little piece of paper in Shana's hand. It meant something to someone, all right, and I had a feeling we really needed to know what if we were going to make any sense of Jack's murder.

I pulled into the hotel parking lot and noted there were more cars than last night. Two cars had trailers behind them on which sat ATVs, their thick wheels muddied with dirt and leaves. I wondered where they'd been riding today, remembering the vehicles that Tom and I had watched flying through the air near Kami's land.

Near Kami's land.

I parked the car and turned to Tom in the back seat. But just as I was going to ask him to wait for me in the lobby, Bernie pointed out her window.

"I didn't know Mac rode an ATV," she said.

I followed the direction of her finger and saw Mac Ackerman on the other side of the parking lot, spotlighted beneath a lamppost. He had his hands in the engine of an ATV that was on a trailer attached to his car. The toolbox beside him must have been metal, since it looked shiny in the lamplight.

"When we went birding this morning, he must have left that trailer here in the lot, because I sure don't remember him towing one to the youth camp." Bernie climbed out of my SUV and shut the door behind her. "I don't know any birder who rides an ATV," she added.

Now that she mentioned it, I didn't either. That's not to say there might not be birders who enjoy driving All-Terrain Vehicles, just that I didn't know any.

"Well, we know one now," I told Bernie.

"You know, I don't think he's much of a birder," she confided in a hushed voice. "He wasn't exactly raring to go this morning, if you know what I mean. I noticed he drank three cups of coffee before we left the hotel this morning. Guess he'd had a rough night." She took another look at Mac tending his ATV. "I bet Renee put him up to coming birding with her. She's crazy about it. Or maybe she was just crazy about Jack."

She threw a glance towards Shana, but Shana and Tom were already inside the lobby doors.

"I saw the mooneyes Renee was making at Jack yesterday evening when we all had an ice cream at the A&W before you got here, Bob. I know Jack was a handsome man, but Renee just seemed to be noticing him a little too much, if you get my drift."

"They went to school together, Bernie," I told her. "Renee mentioned it to me before dinner tonight. She even said she'd had a crush on him, along with all the other girls in her class."

Bernie huffed and turned toward the lobby doors. "Well, that may be. But you can't hang on to old crushes forever. Life goes on, Bob, and you've got to go along with it. Take it from me, an old lady: life's way too short to hang on to the past. What's that saying I saw on a coffee mug? Oh, yeah—today's a gift, that's why it's called the 'present.' Pretty good advice, I'd say." She patted me on the arm. "Good night, good-looking."

And with that bit of wisdom, Bernie left me standing in the lobby. A moment later, Mac Ackerman came in, nodded at me, and started down the same hall Bernie had taken.

"About Mac," Tom said behind me.

I turned to face him and he waved me over to one of the sofas in the lobby. He'd gotten two bottles of water from somewhere and left them on the end table. I uncapped mine and took a swig. "What about Mac?"

"This afternoon, while you and Shana were gone birding, I saw Mac leave with his ATV. I asked Renee about it, and she said just what Bernie was saying: she's the birder in the family. Mac came along to keep her company, and she promised him he could have ATV time in the afternoon. Apparently that place where we saw all the riders this afternoon is a popular spot in Fillmore for ATV enthusiasts."

"Near Kami's land," I confirmed.

"Yeah. Are you thinking what I'm thinking?"

"If you mean that there's a connection between Kami's land and her fence being damaged and the ATV riders and Jack's murder, then yeah. That's what I'm thinking."

"You think Jack saw someone tearing out Kami's fence?" Tom asked.

"Maybe," I admitted. "But I can't figure out how that explains how Jack ended up at the youth camp with a couple bullets in his chest. Let's say some ATV guy wanted to make it look like that land was too dangerous for an eco-community, so that it would be left undeveloped and a great spot for riding. He tears down the fence to let out Nigel. He catches Jack watching and kills him so he won't get blamed for the fence. But that's miles away from the youth camp."

"The killer takes Jack there to stash the body where no one will find him?"

"Except that we do. First thing in the morning, too."

"Okay," Tom said. "So the killer didn't know there was going to be a birding group coming by. His mistake."

"Or, he wanted someone to find the body, and he knew there was a birding group coming by."

"Why would a killer want the murder discovered? Never mind," Tom immediately added, his hands up in surrender. "Let's not go there. For argument's sake, though, say that the killer did know we'd be birding today. That implies that either the killer is one of the birders on the weekend or that it was someone else who knew our schedule." Tom rolled his water bottle between his hands. "So who else knew we were going to be at the youth camp this morning?"

"I wouldn't be so quick to dismiss our motley crew of birders," I told him. "For all we know, Bernie's an amnesiac killer. Of course, she would have had to commandeer a bicycle to get from here to the camp to kill Jack, because she doesn't drive anymore, and then she would have had to pedal like mad to get back here before coffee, but stranger things have happened."

"Yeah, right," Tom said. "Like I said, somebody else had to know our schedule if leaving Jack at the camp was deliberate."

I took another slug of water and thought about it. Who knew that our group of birders would be at the camp this morning?

Let me list the names.

Kami. Jack was at her place last night; I assumed that meant that she knew his weekend plans. But why would she want to kill Jack? Karla had told us that Jack and Kami were working together on the eco-community and that there was no romantic relationship there, so a deadly lovers' quarrel didn't hold up.

Unless Karla was lying to protect Kami. She'd said they were good friends.

Big Ben, on the other hand, had eagerly announced that said relationship did exist, and he'd apparently been quite ready to toss Kami's name into the investigation. Why was that? Did Big Ben have something to gain by slandering Jack's good name? True, Jack had stopped funding Big Ben, so maybe the mayor was making a little post-mortem payback out of spite. Not what I'd call a friendly gesture, despite Shana's claim that Jack and Ben were old pals. Yet Ben hadn't been left in the financial lurch after all, according to Stan. Thanks to Chuck's sleight-of-hand, Ben had continued to feed at the OK trough. Whatever was behind Ben's comments about Jack and Kami, it wasn't money.

And whether or not Big Ben even knew Jack was in town was another unanswered question. I made a mental note to ask Shana if Jack had contacted Ben about being in Fillmore for the weekend.

Billy, Jack's assistant, would also have to be on a list of people who knew Jack's plans, but since Billy had also been murdered, I figured that was a dead end for consideration.

Literally.

Which left me with our motley crew again.

One of whom was Mac Ackerman, the ATV enthusiast who must have had a rough night because he needed three cups of coffee to get going this morning.

71

I shared my list with Tom.

"You forgot one," he pointed out to me. "Chuck O'Keefe. He's a birder, too, don't forget. I bet he knew his dad's plan for the weekend." He paused and stared at the water bottle in his hand. "And he sure doesn't like Shana, Bob. That's obvious. I also wonder how much of a rift there was between Jack and his son. I mean, Chuck was paying off Big Ben on the sly specifically because he knew his father would disapprove."

Tom's eyes met mine. "Murder is ugly enough without it staying in the family, if you know what I mean."

I nodded, mentally reminding myself that Tom probably didn't even know about the jealousy that Chuck harbored against his dad because of Shana. I tried to circle back to our original hunch. "But what does Chuck, or Big Ben, have to do with Kami's fence going down and ATV riders?"

"Beats me," Tom said. "I'm a birder, not a detective."

TWENTY MINUTES LATER, I sat on the end of my bed in my hotel room and dialed Sheriff Paulsen's direct line. She answered on the second ring.

"It's Bob White, Sheriff," I said. "I know it's late, but I wanted to pass along some information I learned this evening. Jack O'Keefe recently severed a financial relationship he had with Big Ben over a disagreement in county development policy. I don't know if it's any use to you, but I wanted to let you know."

The sheriff thanked me and said she'd look into it. "Are you heading home then?" she asked. "You sure don't have to stick around. I know where to find you if I need to talk with you."

"Can Shana leave?" The question popped out of my mouth without even thinking about it.

"Yes," Sheriff Paulsen said. "Although we're keeping the deceased's body here for an autopsy. I can't release it just yet."

I tried to decide what to do, but all I could come up with was to get some sleep. "I'll probably stick around to give Shana some moral support," I finally replied. "She doesn't have any family here."

"You mean, besides her stepson," she said and ended the call.

Yeah. Shana's stepson. Chuck O'Keefe. A real gem of a guy. Prince of the OK kingdom. For some reason, though, I wasn't expecting him to show up on a white horse in the morning to rescue his fair, albeit hugely pregnant, stepmother. In fact, seeing how furious Shana had been when I told her that Stan had caught Chuck's financial sleight-of-hand, I fully expected that the next time the two of them faced down, it was going to be less of a royal reunion and more like the shootout at the OK corral.

And I sure didn't want to be the one caught in the crossfire.

CHAPTER SIXTEEN

I couldn't fall asleep.

Physically, I was tired enough, but mentally, I was jumping through an endless chain of hoops. Why was Jack O'Keefe lying in a morgue tonight when he should have been in bed with his very pregnant wife? Shana seemed convinced that his death was the result of his work with the eco-communities, but murder for philosophical inclinations sounded pretty farfetched to me. On the other hand, money was always a good bet for a motive for murder, and Big Ben—childhood friend or not—sounded like a prime candidate for that one. Even though he was still on the dole from Chuck, maybe he figured his financial pipeline would run more abundantly without the elder O'-Keefe in the company picture.

And then there was Chuck. As we say in the counseling profession, he was a mess.

Actually, we don't say that. Usually, we say someone has "issues." In Chuck's case, we'd say he had a "truckload" of issues.

Like maybe a whole fleet of them.

None of which I had any interest in helping him resolve.

So sue me. I was on summer break. Besides, I counseled teenage kids, not kids that were thirty-something.

I got out of bed, pulled on my jeans, and walked down the hall to the lobby to see if there was anything edible in the sole vending machine that stood next to the emergency exit door. I dropped some quarters into the slot and punched the buttons for a bag of pretzels.

"Midnight snack?"

I glanced over my shoulder as I bent to retrieve the bag from the bottom of the machine. It was Renee Ackerman in a bright-blue sweatsuit.

"I have trouble sleeping during allergy season," she explained. "I have to get up and move around so I can clear the congestion from my sinuses. Otherwise, I just lay in bed snorting and clearing my throat." She dabbed at her nose with a tissue. "Sorry. Too much information, right?"

I waved a hand in easy dismissal. "Don't worry about it."

"So how long have you known Shana, Bob?"

The question caught me a little off-guard, but I covered my surprise at her bluntness by ripping open my pretzel bag and tossing a couple of the little twists into my mouth.

"Since I was in high school. We birded together a few times. I lost track of her once she left Minnesota to go to grad school."

"So you knew her long before Jack met her."

I wondered where this line of inquiry was going, and why.

"Yeah, I guess so."

She seemed to be waiting for me to ask her something, but I just kept chewing on my pretzels.

"Shana's a lot younger than Jack," Renee pointed out.

"Yeah, I guess so," I repeated.

I could have sworn I saw a spark of frustration flare in her eyes.

"I mean, Jack is—Jack was—a handsome, vibrant man any woman would want for a husband, but really, with Shana's looks, she'd hardly have to settle for an older man."

"Settle?"

This time, Renee heaved a very audible sigh of frustration. "I'm just saying that, if Shana were free, she could have her pick of young men."

I looked Renee straight in the eye. Was this the reason I'd picked up weird vibes from her at dinner? Had she been vilifying Shana to her fellow diners over the burger baskets?

"You're certainly not suggesting that Shana had anything to do with Jack's death, are you, Renee? Because if you are, you are not only way out of line, but certifiably crazy."

I turned on my heel to go back to my room.

"It's Ben's theory, not mine," she said behind me.

I stopped in the middle of the lobby and looked back at her. "Ben's theory? I thought he was touting Kami Marsden as a murderess, not Shana."

Renee walked over to stand in front of me. "The truth, Bob, is that Ben Graham will say anything to bask in the media spotlight. I've known him since I was a kid. We all grew up together here in Spring Valley—Ben, Jack, Kami and I. The Four Musketeers, you know?"

"No, I didn't know. And I really don't care, either," I bluntly informed her. "What I do care about is that Jack O'Keefe was killed this morning while he was supposed to be scouting birds, and that his death leaves an old friend of mine widowed and pregnant. That's what I care about."

Renee backed up a step, but didn't break eye contact with me. "I care about that, too, Bob. Like I said, Jack was a friend of mine from my childhood. That's why it surprised me so much when I heard Ben making insinuations about Shana's relationship with Jack. I've never in my whole life, heard Ben Graham even breathe a word of criticism about Jack or anything he was involved in. He worshipped Jack. In Ben's eyes, Jack could do no wrong. And he was here for Shana this afternoon, too."

I stuck another pretzel in my mouth and waited for her to finish.

"But I also know that Ben thrives on attention. Ever since he went into local politics, he craves sound bytes like it's a drug for him. If he thinks he'll get a few more minutes of air time by implying that Jack's wife might be less than devastated by his death, then he'll say it."

I chewed up the pretzel and swallowed it. "So, if you know this about Ben, why would you even listen to what he had to say about Shana?"

Renee crossed her arms over her bright-blue chest. "Because, once in a while, Ben turns out to be telling the truth. And it seems like it always used to be about the one thing you just couldn't believe possible."

"Such as?"

I noticed that she quickly checked around us to see if anyone else was within listening distance. Her actions reminded me of a high school student about to rat out a friend's bad choices. It was almost like she couldn't wait to share her inside information.

I was half expecting her to pull me aside, whisper in my ear, and then make me promise not to tell anyone.

I swear, some kids never do grow up. She and Chuck could start a club.

Apparently satisfied we were alone, Rene leaned toward me to give me the scoop. "When we were all twelve years old, Ben said he'd found an Indian arrowhead that was worth a thousand dollars. The three of us laughed at him, but sure enough, he had. It was in the local paper the next day. He'd been exploring by some bluffs near his uncle's farm and found these old arrowheads. His uncle took the arrowheads to a collector, and the guy said the arrowheads were not only authentic, but quite valuable."

That didn't surprise me. There were still plenty of areas in Minnesota where ongoing erosion exposed new finds on a fairly regular basis. Just south of the Twin Cities, in fact, there's a big park where elementary schools routinely take their students to find fossils of prehistoric flora. I know that when I went on that field trip in sixth grade, I got a whole new appreciation of what "ancient" meant. Before that, I thought my teacher, Mrs. Baumgarten, was ancient, but compared to the weathered piece of shale I picked up with a fossil embedded in it, I decided she was just "old."

Not that I shared that with her. I may have been a kid, but I knew enough not to tell my teacher she'd just made the leap from "ancient" to simply "old." Like I told Shana, my mama didn't raise no fool.

"So Ben found an artifact," I said to Renee. "Big deal."

"It was to us, Bob. This was a small town, you know. Believe me, not much happened here that warranted any media attention from the big cities. Getting his picture in the paper, along with a quick segment on the evening news from Rochester, was a huge event for Ben. We were all star-struck for a while."

I wadded up my empty pretzel bag and pitched it into the waste can near the vending machine. Renee yawned and patted her hand over her mouth.

"Sometimes I think that's when Ben developed his taste for fame," she added. "For weeks afterward, he kept telling us that one day he was going to find a gold mine in Fillmore and become famous. We were all pretty sure there was definitely no treasure hidden in these hills, but after the arrowhead story, we kept our doubts to ourselves." She glanced at the gold watch on her wrist and grimaced. "It's late. I'm going back to bed. Hopefully, I can get at least a few hours of sleep before we have to get up for birding in the morning. You're coming with us, aren't you?"

I covered a yawn of my own. "Yup. I don't get down here very often, so I still want to try finding that Northern Bobwhite that Jack promised us. I have a couple ideas about places to look."

"Great. I'll see you in the morning, then. Good night, Bob." She took a step in the direction of the hallway, then turned back.

"You know, Ben may not have found any gold in these hills, but he's sure famous enough around here. He and Jack both became celebrities in a way—Jack with the success of OK Industries and Ben with his little political kingdom. Funny how life turns out, isn't it?"

I nodded in agreement. "Good night, Renee." I watched her walk away down the hall.

She was right—life was a bag of surprises. If I could have a dollar for every time I failed to predict the future correctly, I'd be a rich man. I thought of all the students I'd counseled over the years and how, invariably, the class slacker turned into a prosperous businessman, the girl who wanted to become a lawyer ended up training to be a massage therapist, and the athlete who barely graduated buckled down to get a teaching degree.

As far as I could tell, my professional crystal ball was full of mud.

Actually, my personal crystal ball wasn't much better. If it had been, the last thing I would have done was sign up for Jack's weekend birding trip because it sure hadn't turned out fun at all.

Just deadly.

And then I registered what my eyes had noted on the back of Renee's bright blue sweatsuit as she'd returned to her room.

Words were emblazoned across the jacket: Secure A-Man.

Wasn't that the name of the security firm that had installed Kami's original electric fence?

And what were the odds that Renee just happened to have a jacket with that name on it, just when Kami was having a load of trouble with her perimeter security?

Another funny twist of life?

Not if my gut had anything to say about it. Even filled with late-night pretzels, I trusted my gut more than almost anything. Over the years, that instinct had served me well in counseling students and finding elusive birds all over Minnesota. Now I had to wonder if it was learning how to track down a killer.

Or at least a fence-cutter.

I rubbed my hand over my eyes. I needed to get some sleep if I was imagining that Renee Ackerman was trying to set loose a tiger in Fillmore County.

Maybe late-night snacking wasn't such a great idea after all. Good thing I didn't go for the bag of jalapeno cheese curls—I'd probably be hallucinating by now, thinking someone was out to kill me.

Of course, there was that note that Shana had . . .

I rolled my eyes in total exasperation with myself. I really needed to get some sleep.

CHAPTER
SEVENTEEN

By six o'clock in the morning, I was back in my SUV with Bernie riding shotgun beside me. Behind us in their car were Mac and Renee, along with Sonja and Anders Nyberg, the other couple who'd elected to finish the weekend's birding agenda despite the decidedly gloomy pall that Jack's murder had settled over the group like a dingy old blanket. Shana had opted to waddle over to the sheriff's office first thing to see how the investigation was going, and Tom had offered to accompany her. Depending on what they found out about any progress in the case, I'd make a decision about heading home or sticking around another day in Spring Valley.

"So did you call that sister of yours?" Bernie asked me as I pulled out of the parking lot.

I slid her a look. "Did anyone ever tell you you're nosy?"

"Oh, sure, lots of times," she cheerfully replied. "But I don't listen. It's my prerogative, you know. I'm an old biddy. Everybody knows that. So did you call her?"

I shook my head. "I'll see her when I get home. With any luck, the sheriff will make an arrest today and my name will fall right out of the headlines. That'll make everyone happy, Lily will forget all about it, and I'll still have to get measured for that tux."

"What about Luce?"

"What about her?"

"What did she think about you being on television with Shana?"

I followed the county road as it curved down out of town. "I don't know, Bernie. I didn't talk to her last night. And even though it's none of your bees' wax, Luce trusts me. She knows I love her. She's not going to worry about our relationship because I'm trying to help out an old friend who just lost her husband."

The car swung hard to the left as I rounded another curve and I noticed Bernie grip the dashboard.

"Okay," she said. "I get the message. I'll back off. You don't have to drive like Bo Duke to get me to shut my mouth."

"I'm not trying to drive like one of the Dukes of Hazzard," I told her, suddenly concerned. I checked my speed. For once, I was watching it, keeping my foot well off the accelerator, yet the car was steadily gaining momentum as the road wound downhill between some small bluffs. I tapped on the brakes.

Nothing happened.

I punched the brake pedal down.

Still nothing, and we were picking up more speed.

"Shit."

"What?" Bernie asked, still gripping the dash.

"My brakes are gone."

"Shit!" she agreed.

"Hold on!" I glanced in my rear view mirror to be sure that the Ackermans were a good distance behind me. Ahead of me, the road snaked past a small rough turn-out area before it took a sharp turn to the right. If I was going to do some fancy maneuvering, it had to be now.

I jerked on my emergency brake, sending the car into a spin. The tires screeched as they skidded across the pavement and into the turn-out. Gravel sprayed up around our windows and with a lurch, my SUV came to a bone-jarring stop, facing the direction we'd just traveled.

"Go, Bo," Bernie managed to say just before the air bags deployed and smacked us both square in the chest.

"Bernie!"

I released my seat belt and turned to help Bernie, who was looking dazed and frazzled behind her air bag, but all in one piece. "Are you all right?"

She nodded. "Is this the part where I jump out of the car window? You know I'm not exactly Daisy Duke material anymore," she added weakly.

I smiled at her reply. Not even faulty brakes were going to throw Bernie off her game. "You can be my Daisy anytime. Here, let me help you." I pushed her air bag out of the way and released her seatbelt.

"What the hell happened?" Mac shouted outside my window.

"Are you all right?" Renee was beside Bernie's door.

"My brakes quit on me," I told them. "But I think we're okay."

Renee carefully helped Bernie down from the SUV, while I stepped out on my side. Mac was bending down, hands on his knees, examining the wheel well of my left front tire.

A puddle of liquid was sitting under it.

"Brake fluid," Mac announced. "Somebody cut your brake line."

I looked at him in stunned silence.

"Somebody cut my brake line?" I repeated, doing my best idiot imitation.

"Yes, Bob, that's what I said," Mac grimly assured me.

"Why would someone do that?" I looked back at the roadside edge of the turn-out where Mac had left his own SUV. I could see the Nybergs in Mac's back seat, staring open-mouthed at our little accident scene. "I guess this means that Bernie and I are done birding for the morning. I'll call for a tow. You guys know where you're headed?"

Mac nodded. "Yeah, Renee knows the area. She's birded it with Jack a few times the last couple years."

From the other side of the car, Renee called out to me. "Bob, I think you'd better get an ambulance for Bernie. I think the air bag might have cracked one of her ribs."

I hustled around the back end of the SUV and found Bernie sitting on the ground, leaning against Renee and holding her arms wrapped tightly around her middle. Her face was drained of color and she was trying hard not to grimace with pain. "I'm on it," I told the women and pulled out my cell phone.

"Sorry, Bob," Bernie gritted out after I finished talking with the dispatcher.

"Hey, no problem, Daisy." I sat on my haunches beside her. "We'll get you fixed right up, Bernie. Don't you worry."

She reached out with one hand and grabbed my shirt to pull me down into her face. "I heard what Mac said," she whispered, almost nose-to-nose with me. "Someone's trying to hurt you, Bob." Her eyes filled with concern.

"Yeah," I said. "I got that."

"What are you going to do?"

I lifted a hand and gently patted her lined cheek. "I'm going to find out who, Daisy, and then I'm going to chase him down and make him apologize for hurting you. Nobody messes with a Duke and gets away with it."

She let go of my shirt, worry still clouding her eyes. "This isn't funny, Bob."

I leaned back and studied her. "No, it's not," I agreed. "I'm pretty sure my car insurance just went through the roof."

CHAPTER
EIGHTEEN

An hour later, I was back in the lobby of the hotel waiting for Shana and Tom to return from the sheriff's office. Bernie was on her way to the nearest medical facility for x-rays and a thorough physical examination, and my SUV was sitting in the parking lot of the local auto repair shop. Since it was Sunday, my SUV was down for the count until at least tomorrow morning, which meant I was going to be enjoying all of Spring Valley's ambiance and birding hotspots for another twenty-four hours or so. At least, I wanted to assume that I would be doing that.

After mulling over the fact that someone had deliberately sabotaged my car, and that Shana had a pesky little note in her possession that indicated Jack had asked Ben about killing me, however, I wasn't sure I should be assuming anything about my immediate, or long-range, future.

Maybe not setting up that IRA at work yet wasn't such a tragedy after all. If the next twenty-four hours were anything like the last, chances looked good that I wasn't going to have to do any worrying about funding my retirement, because I wasn't going to be around long enough to retire. Okay, I thought, mark that little task off the summer to-do list. One less thing to stress over, right?

Of course, stressing over getting killed wasn't going to improve my longevity, either. I needed some answers, and I needed them now.

Who cut my brake line and why?

Why did Jack write a note to Ben about killing me?

Could I get my deposit back on that tux I was going to rent for Lily's wedding?

A moment later, I saw Tom's car pass by the lobby doors, and then a minute after that, he and Shana walked into the lobby. They both looked grim.

"It's over," Tom announced. "They found the gun used to shoot Jack in the glove compartment of Billy's car. Sheriff Paulsen sent the bullets and gun to some lab to verify the match, but she's satisfied she can close the case."

Shana lowered herself to sit beside me on the lobby's sofa.

"I'm so sorry," I told her, taking her hands in mine. "I know you told me Billy was Jack's assistant, but you must have known him pretty well, too."

She nodded, her gaze on our joined hands. "I thought I did," she slowly said. "I can't believe he shot Jack. And I'm the one who sent him after Jack Friday night." She closed her eyes and sighed. "If I'd just left things alone, maybe Jack . . ."

"Don't do that to yourself, Shana," Tom warned, sitting down on her other side. It suddenly occurred to me that we could have been matching bookends with Shana playing the part of the Encyclopedia Britannica. All thirty-two volumes of it. "You can't play 'what ifs' here," he told her. "It'll eat you up, and I can't believe Jack would want that for you."

She lifted her eyes to meet his and I caught a weak smile flitter across her face. "Thanks for going with me, Tom. I really appreciate it."

To my astonishment, I watched a pink blush creep over Tom's cheeks. What the heck?

"What about Billy, though?" I asked, all at once feeling self-conscious about holding Shana's hands with Tom pressed against her other side. I released her fingers and leaned back against the sofa cushion. "Does the sheriff have any leads on who shot him?"

I saw Tom and Shana exchange a look.

"What?"

"This is where it gets weird, Bob," Tom said, his cheeks having resumed their natural coloring. "The medical examiner found a dart wound in Billy's back, up near the neck. The sheriff told us it was exactly like the puncture mark you'd expect to find in a large animal that had been shot with a dart from a tranquilizer gun. Apparently his killer shot him with the dart, then dragged him to the woodpile, where he finished him off with the bullet."

Yeah, bullets have a way of doing that. Especially when they end up in your chest. Dead center.

"Geez," I said. "Guess the killer didn't want to leave anything to chance, like maybe Billy waking up and walking away before he was really dead." I shook my head. "But if that was the case, why bother with the dart? Why not just shoot the guy with the bullet to begin with?"

A dart.

From a tranquilizer gun.

I realized what Shana and Tom hadn't told me yet.

"It's Kami, isn't it? She's got to have tranquilizer darts to use on Nigel if he gets out of her compound. Sheriff Paulsen has to know that."

Shana nodded. "The sheriff was going up to Kami's place when we left to bring her in for questioning. But I don't know that Kami killed Billy, Bob. Tom says that Kami was here yesterday afternoon with your friend Eddie when he stopped by the hotel to leave you his note. I'm sure that's one thing the sheriff needs to talk to Kami about: where she was and with whom early yesterday morning. If Eddie can back her up, then Kami has an alibi."

"But if Kami didn't kill Billy, then whoever did sure left a trail that leads straight to her door because of the dart." I drummed my fingers on my knee. "If you ask me, it sounds like somebody wants to frame Kami."

"And Billy," Shana suddenly added, her face lighting up with excitement. "I knew there was something wrong when the sheriff said that Billy shot Jack."

She pushed herself up from the couch and turned to face Tom and me, rubbing her hands along the sides of her extended belly. I could have sworn she looked even bigger this morning than she had yesterday.

"Billy hated guns," she explained. "He didn't even know how to shoot one. I know, because one day last month, Jack and I went to a shooting range, and Billy came along to brief Jack on some legislation while we drove to the range. Once we got there, Billy stayed in the lounge while we did some shooting. He told us that a good friend of his was killed in a gun accident when he was just a kid, and, because of that, Billy had sworn that he himself would never touch a gun, let alone learn to shoot one."

Shana paced away to the front desk, then back again to stand in front of us. "I'd bet the farm that Billy didn't kill Jack."

"So who did?" Tom asked her.

Shana threw her arms in the air. "I don't know!" Then her eyes locked on mine, like she suddenly saw me very clearly, and that surprised her. "What are you doing here? I thought you were taking the group birding this morning."

I debated how much to tell her. If she was already feeling guilty about sending Billy after Jack and finding them both dead the next day, she wasn't going to be too happy to hear about my close call and Bernie's injury.

"A change in plans," I finally said.

She narrowed her eyes at me, her hands massaging the top of her belly. "Where's Bernie?" she asked suspiciously.

"Where's your car?" Tom added. "I didn't see your BRRDMAN plates in the parking lot."

"Neither did I, White-man."

I looked over my shoulder towards the lobby doors. My best friend and soon-to-be brother-in-law was taking off his battered cowboy hat, mid-morning sunshine streaming in behind him.

I put my head in my hands and groaned.

"Take me now, Lord," I prayed.

Alan walked over to our little tableau and offered his hand to Shana.

"You must be Shana O'Keefe," he smiled at her warmly. "Alan Thunderhawk. I'm very sorry for your loss, Mrs. O'Keefe. Your husband was a good man doing good things for Minnesota."

Shana shook his hand briefly and thanked him for his sympathy. By then, Tom was on his feet, too, moving to stand beside Shana. He introduced himself to Alan.

"I know that name," Alan grinned. "You're the guy who calls Bob to get birdcall IDs over the phone. That's crazy, man. Kind of like remote bird watching, you know?"

"Alan," I said. "What are you doing here?"

He smacked his hat against his leg. "What, a man can't go for a drive on a beautiful Sunday morning without having a reason other than to enjoy God's good handiwork?"

I rolled my eyes. "Fillmore County isn't exactly in your neighborhood, Alan. Not when you live in Scott County, two hours away. And especially not before noon on a Sunday. Hell, I don't think you've seen a Sunday morning since we roomed together at Southwest State back in the nineties."

He inspected the band around his hat, carefully avoiding my eyes. "Not true. I saw a sunrise just last weekend. Of course, I'd been up all night, but, hey, I did see that sun come up. And it was pretty, too."

He smiled like a goof.

I groaned again, and then it hit me.

"Lily put you up to it, didn't she? I didn't call her back last night, so she sent you to ream me. Geez, Alan, I can take care of myself."

"You're the groom-to-be," Shana deduced. "You're marrying Bob's sister."

Alan turned his smile back on Shana. "Yes, ma'am, I am. And while I love that woman to distraction, I'm not letting her get away with firing my best man, here."

He faced me again. "Sorry, Bob, but you're not getting out of the biggest show on earth that easily."

"Ah," I replied, leaning back into the sofa cushion. "Now I get it. She's making you crazy with the wedding plans, too, isn't she? What did you do, volunteer out of the goodness of your heart to come track me down and drag me home just so she wouldn't have to worry about me instead of the color of the place cards at the rehearsal dinner?"

He tossed his hat down on the couch next to me. "Close. Very close. Let's just say the thought occurred to me that a little absence this morning might make the heart a whole lot fonder, not to mention restore some of my natural equanimity which has been sorely depleted as of late." He threw a glance at Shana, his eyes measuring her girth. "Do you need to sit down?" he politely asked her.

"No, I'm fine," she answered. "Thanks. So you're here to keep an eye on Bob for his sister?"

Alan nodded. "That's my story, and I'm sticking to it."

"You know, Bob, you don't have to stay on here in Spring Valley," Tom said. "Since Sheriff Paulsen says she's closing Jack's case, she said we can all go home."

"But I think she's wrong," Shana reminded him. "Billy didn't kill Jack."

"Then hire an investigator, Shana," Tom pressed. "A professional. Let him pursue it. You're not helping yourself or your babies hanging around here, wearing yourself out trying to make sense of this."

"Babies?"

"I'm expecting twins, Alan," Shana explained, then resumed her argument with Tom. "If I leave now, believe me, I'm going to be more miserable at home doing nothing and wondering what's happening than if I stayed here. Just another day or two. That's all. Then I promise I'll go back to the Cities."

"Actually, I can't go home today, anyway," I announced. "My car . . . well . . . it needs work. It's at the garage in town. Hopefully they can fix it first thing in the morning. But in the meantime, I'm stuck here in Spring Valley."

"What happened to your car? It was driving fine last night," Tom pointed out.

"Well, yeah. This morning I had some trouble."

"What kind of trouble?" Shana locked her eyes on mine. "Why do I get the feeling that you're not telling us something important?"

I returned her stare, wondering why all the women in my life seemed able to read my mind at whim. Lily had made a habit of it since we were kids; Luce had elevated it to a fine art. Now it seemed Shana had joined their club. At work, I prided myself on my repertoire of counseling faces; depending on the situation, I could do "Sympathy" or "Encouragement" or "Time to buck up and face the music, because you are so busted, kid" with just a quirk of my eyebrows. Yet no matter how many faces I could assume, I never seemed able to hide what I was really feeling from these three. Even that summer I was crazy about Shana, she could always read my mood and anticipate my reactions.

Oh, shit.

Shana had known I was in love with her.

Good thing I was already sitting down, because if I'd been standing, I would have found myself knocked on my butt.

Shana had known how I felt.

She'd never said a word about it, but she'd known. All these years I'd thought I'd hid my feelings that summer so cleverly, and she'd probably been thinking, "Aw, he's such a cute kid to have a crush on me."

Geez. Did I feel stupid.

Before I could really get a good case of total self-mortification going, though, Shana snapped me back to the present in all its glorious confusion. "Bernie was in the car with you. Is she all right?"

"Yeah, she's fine," I answered, maybe a little too quickly, since I could see Shana's eyes narrowing. "Well, she's a little shook up," I amended. "And her one rib might have gotten cracked when the airbag exploded, but—"

"WHAT?"

"Maybe you should sit down," Alan suggested to Shana again. "I have the distinct feeling this story isn't going to get any better. Am I right, Bob?"

I let out a long breath and looked at both Shana and Tom. "Someone cut my brake line. My brakes went out. I managed to spin out my car to stop it before we ended up tearing into a tree or going off the road. It could have been a lot worse."

For a moment, no one said anything.

"Yeah," Alan finally agreed. "You could have been dead. Then I would have to let Rick stand in as my best man. Nice save, White-man." Then he smacked me—hard—with his hat. "You idiot. What the hell is going on around here?"

CHAPTER
NINETEEN

J ack's note," Tom said.

Shana paled and sat down in the armchair across from me.

"What note?" Alan asked. "I swear to God, if someone doesn't tell me what's going on, I am going to get Lily on the phone right now to send that scary guy down here to make you all talk."

I made a grab for his hat, which he was waving in the air in front of my nose, and tossed it beside me on the couch. "Are you talking about Scary Stan?" I glanced at Shana to be sure she hadn't passed out. "How do you know Stan, Alan?"

He picked up his hat and sat where I had dropped it.

"He came by Lily's place last night. After apologizing profusely for stopping by unannounced, he said he needed to call you about something urgent, but he didn't have your cell number. When she asked what it was, he just told her to watch the news." I noticed he took a quick check on Shana, too. "He was kind of odd. It's like his eyes don't have any light in them, or something. I just had the feeling I wouldn't want to run into him in a dark alley, you know?"

Yeah, I knew. Stan had that effect on everyone, except, apparently, Lily. Lily didn't think he'd been odd at all when they'd been dating. She'd once told me he was "refreshing" because he didn't waste words.

I always thought he didn't "waste words" because he held the rest of humanity in utter contempt. Although if Stan had apologized "profusely" to Lily, as Alan had reported, then I guess my sister was the exception to his rule, too.

Go figure that one.

Anyway, that solved one mystery: how Scary Stan got my private cell phone number. It also told me who tipped Lily off to the newscast, which in turn revealed where I was temporarily seeking refuge from the Biggest Show on Earth, as Alan had termed it.

Thanks, Stan. I owe you big time for that one, buddy.

"So here's the deal," I told Alan. "Jack's dead. Billy, his assistant, is dead. The sheriff thinks that Billy shot Jack, but no one knows who shot Billy, though Kami's being questioned about it by the sheriff because of the tranquilizer dart. In the meantime, Shana found a note that Jack wrote to kill me, which she thinks came from Big Ben's pocket. Then this morning, my brakes failed and now Bernie's getting X-rayed."

"You forgot the part about Chuck cooking the books to slide money to Big Ben," Tom added to my report. He was sitting on the edge of the coffee table in front of Shana. "And that he's accusing Shana of planning the whole thing."

Alan rubbed his hand over his eyes. "I think I got lost at the dart part. So who shot the sheriff?"

"No one shot the sheriff," I said. "Kami uses the darts on Nigel when he gets loose."

Alan laid his head against the back of the couch. "I don't think I even want to know who Nigel is."

"He's a pussycat compared to Chuck," Tom said. "I'm sorry, Shana, but I think your stepson is a snake in the grass. He knew Jack stopped funding Big Ben, but he kept the payments rolling. So the question is, did Chuck pass the bucks to Ben because he wanted to spite his dad for ignoring OK Industries while he worked on the eco-communities, or did Chuck have another reason, like an under-the-table business deal with Ben? You said Ben and Chuck have been friends for a long time; maybe they'd started some kind of partnership on their own since Jack was devoting all his time to planning the eco-communities."

Alan snapped his fingers. "That's right! The eco-communities!"

The three of us looked at Alan.

"What about the eco-communities?" Shana asked.

Alan sat up straight and scooted forward on the sofa cushion. "It was on the news last night. The reporter said that Jack's untimely death was a real blow to the eco-community project down here because there has been so much opposition to getting the zoning approved."

A quiet tone of intensity crept into his voice. As a high school social studies teacher at Savage High, Alan was pretty low key, but I knew from our college days that if there was one thing that really gunned his jets, it was political activism. He was also a local news junkie, which meant he kept tabs on all kinds of issues around Minnesota.

"Just last week," he was saying now, "the state ATV recreational lobbying group asked for an injunction against Fillmore County to stop approval of the revised zoning that would pave the way for Jack's eco-community to break ground. If it was granted, then there was a good chance that the battle would go to court. Which would, in turn, mean more expenses for the eco people, not to mention the loss of time as their proposed site continues to degrade."

"And Jack was the eco-community's champion," Shana pointed out. "He was the point man with the legislators." She rubbed her belly. "And, of course, we were paying a lot of the group's expenses out of our pockets for them, too. Jack really cared about this initiative." Her voice sounded wistful. "He knew what a difference it could make for the future of the state. For our kids."

Even from across the coffee table, I could see her eyes getting misty. Time for a diversion, I realized.

"Let's get some air," I announced, standing up. "I believe a little birding might do the trick, don't you, Tom?"

With just a quick glance at Shana's trembling chin, Tom caught on to my ploy. "Who's driving?" he asked.

I clapped a hand on Alan's shoulder. "Alan is."

"I am?" the mighty Hawk choked.

"My car's in the shop, and Tom's shocks—or lack thereof—might be too hard on Shana," I explained. "Your Toyota's ride is smooth as butter, buddy. We can bird in style."

"But I don't bird," Alan tactfully reminded me. "I like spectator sports, preferably indoor and with a view from a hospitality suite."

"I can drive," Shana offered, pushing hard with her hands against the arms of the chair in order to get enough leverage to pull herself to her feet.

"No!" Tom, Alan, and I all said at the same time.

"Hey," Alan suddenly enthused, "I'd love to go birding! I bet it's just chock full of fun, right? Fresh air, nice trees, ah . . . all that good stuff. Can we make a pit stop in your room before we go, Bob?" he asked, turning towards me. "I'd like to clean up a little after making the drive down here." He grabbed my upper arm and dragged me out of the lobby into the hotel hallway. Behind us, I could hear Tom and Shana planning to meet us back in the lobby in another ten minutes.

"Gee, Alan, I'm so glad you've finally had a change of heart about my hobby," I told him as I slid the magnetic key card through my door lock. "Maybe I'll take back all those nasty things I told Lily about you."

We stepped into my room, and he closed the door quietly behind him.

"Do not even bring Lily into this," he told me sternly, "who, for the record, was absolutely right in being worried about you. Come on, Bob! What are you doing here? Practicing being a sitting duck? Somebody's got a death wish for you, and you're going birding? And as for the lovely, and exceptionally pregnant, Mrs. O'Keefe, are you sure you're just offering a shoulder here, and not wondering if a little detour down memory lane might lead to something special in the present?"

He tossed his hat on the bed. "Granted, that's a pretty big 'something special' with two babies on the way, and the woman has the most amazing green eyes I've ever seen, but, Bob, are you sure you know what you're doing here?"

I walked over to the room's oversized window and looked out. It was a beautiful day. Heck, it was still morning. The sky was a bright blue, a pair of Mourning Doves were perched in a tree outside the window, and a Killdeer was lightly running along the edge of the parking lot.

Did I know what I was doing?

Yes.

And no.

I turned back to face Alan. "You know, eighteen years ago, I thought Shana was the most beautiful, desirable woman in the world. She was smart. She was funny. She loved birding. When I was with her, I felt like I was on top of the world. As far as I was concerned, she was perfect." I shrugged my shoulders. "I was a kid."

Alan nodded, but didn't say anything.

"She's still all those things, Alan, but I'm not that kid anymore. I'm not interested in any trips down memory lane because memories can't come close to what I have with Luce now. No contest. There never was."

Even as I said it out loud, I knew it was the truth. Seeing Shana again had been an unexpected jolt to my memory banks, but as soon as the dust had settled, as soon as I saw the look that passed between her and Jack in the hotel lobby the night I checked in, I knew exactly what I was seeing and what I wanted.

A Bobwhite Killing

I saw the same electricity that arced between Luce and me every time we were together. And I knew I wanted it for the rest of my life, as soon as possible. If seeing Shana again made me regret anything, it was not being with Luce every moment I was breathing.

"Yeah, that's what I figured," Alan assured me. "You are just not that dumb, White-man. Any idiot can see that you and Luce belong together. Although, like I said, Shana does have the most amazing eyes I've ever seen. Really, really green. And she's got that whole Earth Mother thing going on, too, with being pregnant. It kind of brings out the protective side of a guy, you know?"

"Hey!" I barked at him. "You're marrying my sister. No looking at any other women. Pregnant or otherwise. I don't want to have to kill you."

He laughed and scraped his long black hair back from the sides of his face. "Are you kidding me? Your sister is all the woman I ever want to look at. Besides, she'd kill me long before you even got wind of it, anyway. Speaking of which," he suddenly sobered, "what are you doing about this death threat?"

This was the "no" part of my answer to the "did I know what I was doing?" question. I opened my mouth to tell him I felt safe as long as I wasn't walking alone in a state forest, when a screeching noise split the air.

A crash didn't follow it.

But two loud gunshots did.

CHAPTER
TWENTY

H oly crap!" I shouted, diving for the worn brown carpeting on the floor of my hotel room.

Almost simultaneously, I heard Alan hit the floor on the other side of the bed.

"Are you all right?" I yelled.

"Stay down!" he yelled back.

"I'm not getting up to wave a red flag, if that's what you're worrying about." I did, however, lift my head to see what damage had been done to the window.

None.

"What the hell?" I muttered, then slowly lifted my head and shoulders to carefully peer over the window sill.

There were no snipers posted in the parking lot. Of course, if there were really snipers, I probably wouldn't be able to see them anyway. From what I understood of that particular line of work, one didn't last long parading around in an open area with a rifle in your arms. Stealth was highly recommended as a character trait.

On the other hand, there was a jacked-up pickup truck parked at the far end of the lot. A couple of teenaged boys were sitting on the tailgate, laughing and pointing at the black rubber marks that now adorned the asphalt.

"Bob!" Alan yelled from his position on the floor. "What's happening?"

"I think," I said, "Mom and Dad went to church, and Junior's joyriding with his buddy."

"What?" Alan's head and shoulders popped up on the other side of the bed.

"They weren't gunshots, Alan. Just a truck backfiring. Maybe it's a Sunday morning ritual here in Spring Valley. The parents do doughnuts after church, and the kids do donuts in empty parking lots."

I stood up and brushed the carpet lint off my jeans.

"But you weren't taking any chances, were you?" Alan pointed out, likewise standing up. "You heard the shots, and you thought it came from a gun. A gun aiming for you. This is serious shit here, Bob."

A Bobwhite Killing

I sat on the end of the bed and looked at him over my shoulder. "Yeah, I know. Actually, I figured that out when my car brakes went out this morning, and Bernie ended up with a ride in an ambulance."

Alan sat down beside me.

"Someone wants to hurt me, and I don't have the slightest idea who or why," I admitted. "Yes, we have a note in Jack's handwriting that suggests I be killed. But Jack's dead, so he's not the one who cut my brake line. Shana thinks that Ben had the note. So let's pretend he cut my brake line as a favor to Jack. Why? I don't have a clue. I've never done anything to Jack or Ben that I know of to warrant even a verbal reprimand, let alone their killing me. I never even met Ben till yesterday. So I keep ending up in the same spot with all this speculation: nowhere."

"No," Alan corrected me. "You do end up somewhere—totally paranoid."

"Right," I said, "and I hate it. The view sucks. That's why I have to stick around, Alan. I have to find out why I'm someone's target, and then I have to figure out who that someone is."

"And somehow, this is all tied up with Jack and Shana," Alan added.

"That's my guess," I said. "Nobody was gunning for me back home. I come down here to bird, and bam! I'm a target."

"You must be trespassing, son," Alan said in a fake Southern drawl.

"I gave that up years ago."

That was the truth. Like almost every birder, I'd slipped around my share of fences and climbed over rails onto private property to chase down a bird, but I'd always been careful to leave nothing behind. No gum wrappers, water bottles, old tires, or cracked sinks. Actually, the only reason I'd finally sworn off doing that was the day a county sheriff met me back at my car after I'd been on a bird-finding mission behind an old sewage treatment plant. The plant's gate had big "No Trespassing" signs on it. I pretended they didn't apply to me. The sheriff thought otherwise and slapped me with a hefty citation. I would have thought he was being overly scrupulous, except for the fact that he'd already caught me there twice before and only given me warnings.

"You just don't listen, do you?" he'd said as he handed me the ticket. "You need to respect boundaries, Mr. Birdman."

Boundaries.

A couple of tumblers clicked into place in my head. I for sure hadn't trespassed on anyone's land, but there was something going on with boundaries in Fillmore County.

The boundary around Kami's sanctuary: someone kept trying to tear it down. I'd seen the evidence.

The boundary between Jack and Chuck and Ben: money was messing with their relationships. Stan and Shana had the proof.

The legal boundaries at the heart of the eco-communities' fight with the ATV lobbyists.

A chill ran up my spine. Thanks to my unplanned appearance on television last night, I'd been identified as a friend of Shana and Jack, the public face of the eco-communities. Had someone assumed I'd pick up where Jack left off in pushing for the rezoning and decided to cut me off at the pass—or rather send me off the bend in the road?

Quite a stretch, maybe?

Then again, it was awfully coincidental that the night after my television debut, my car's brake lines were cut.

And—another chill raced past the first one—that there was an ATV enthusiast right here at the hotel with us. One who, in fact, had a full set of mechanics tools with him in the parking lot last night. Now that I took a minute to think about the accident this morning, it suddenly seemed odd to me that Mac had so quickly known what had happened to my brakes.

"I think I've landed myself in the middle of a territorial dispute," I told Alan.

"Dispute? Looks more like a war to me," he said.

Shouting came from beyond my hotel room door.

"Sounds like one, too," Alan added.

It only took me a split-second to recognize the voices outside the door. Chuck was back, and he'd found Shana.

I yanked open the door to find the two of them yelling at each other just down the hall. Tom was there, too, trying to haul Chuck out of Shana's face, but not making much progress from what I could see. Chuck was on a rant, and he wasn't about to stop just because Tom was trying to run interference.

"You're a man-eater, you know that?" Chuck shouted at Shana. "It's what you do. Track down a rich old guy, turn on the charm and marry him. Then when you're through, just get rid of him."

"You have no idea what you're talking about!" Shana shouted back. "Get out, Chuck, and don't even think of speaking to me until you come to your senses."

"My senses? I'll tell you what my senses are telling me. Men take one look at you and they're falling at your feet. But if they're not pulling the strings on the family fortune, you kick them away. You've got a history, here, Mrs. O'Keefe," he practically snarled at her.

I grabbed Chuck's other arm, the one Tom didn't already have. "Okay, buddy, time to vacate," I told him.

He tried to wrench his arm out of my grip. "You think you're next, White? Sorry, buddy," he mimicked me. "You're not a money-bags. Shana only marries money. Don't you, Mom?"

He glared at her, and I noticed that Alan had slipped himself slightly in front of Shana, using his body as a shield for her bulging tummy. I realized that Chuck was too far gone to appreciate the precariousness of his own situation—if I'd had Alan facing me down in a brawl, I would have turned tail and run. Alan may be an easy-going guy, but you get him angry, and those gym-trained muscles of his could do some real damage.

"Come on, Chuck," I tried again, hoping to avoid having to make a second call for an ambulance in one morning.

"You don't know, do you?" he suddenly spun his body towards me. "She's got a history. Dad wasn't the first. Ask her about her first husband. Rich old guy in Costa Rica. Ended up dead within a year. Guess who got the money?"

I glanced at Shana.

She blanched and reached out a hand to brace herself against the wall of the hallway.

"Out, O'Keefe!" Tom pulled on Chuck's arm harder.

But Shana's stepson wasn't finished. "Yeah, White, that's right. She got the family fortune. Nice work if you can get it, don't you think? Oh, did I mention that the first husband was also shot? At close range? And nobody was ever arrested. Makes you wonder, doesn't it? You don't see a pattern here, do you?"

I couldn't help myself. My eyes sought out Shana's. She was leaning heavily against the wall and Alan had his arm around her, folding her against his side.

Or at least he was trying to.

It's kind of hard to fold in a pod of whales.

I turned back to Chuck. "You need to leave. Now."

He finally managed to shake off both Tom's and my hands. "All right. I'm going. For now. Besides, I see I upset the little woman. Excuse me—not so little anymore. Hey, Shana," he called to her. "Whose kids are you carrying, anyway? Dad was no spring chicken, after all. Is it this White guy?"

I didn't even think. My right fist shot out and slammed smack into Chuck's cheekbone. Chuck's head banged backward into the wall, and he went down like the proverbial sack of potatoes.

"Hash browns, anyone?" I asked, staring at an unconscious Chuck.

"I can't believe you did that," Alan said. He was staring at Chuck, too. "Nice right cross, White-man."

"I want to take a swing at him, too," Tom said. "Maybe I'll wake him up just so I can hit him. Before you got out here, he was accusing Shana of going behind Jack's back to audit the OK Industries' books."

"Somebody please call an ambulance," Shana whispered.

All three of us turned in alarm. "Are you in labor?" we asked her in unison.

"No," she sighed, color returning to her cheeks. "We just can't leave Chuck laying here in the hall. No matter how much I'd like to."

"Will he press charges?" Alan asked.

"He'll probably try," Shana guessed. "But I think Sheriff Paulsen has a soft spot for me, so maybe she'll just make this go away. You guys take off. Go birding. I can handle this."

"No way," Tom told her. "I'm staying. You guys go," he told me and Alan. "Find a rarity, Bob, and call us. We'll meet you there."

I started to protest about his driving Shana in his car, but he waved me off. "I'll drive Shana's car. No potholes. I promise."

"Go, Bob," Shana said.

I nodded and we left them in the hallway, Tom calling for an ambulance and Shana poking tentatively at Chuck's side with her foot. Her stepson was right about one thing, I had to admit: Shana always had men falling at her feet.

Not quite so literally as Chuck, maybe, but fall they did. In fact, I couldn't think of any man who wasn't charmed by Shana. Tom already seemed well past "smitten," and Alan had been prepared to play Sir Galahad. I'd seen Mac Ackerman sneak a few appraising looks her way during dinner last night, and the male deputies at the police station had fallen all over themselves to fetch water for her when we'd given statements yesterday morning.

Even Scary Stan was a member of the fan club.

A Bobwhite Killing

Of course, they were old friends, Shana had said. I hadn't known that. Then again, I hadn't known her marriage to Jack wasn't her first, either.

Come to think of it, Chuck had been a fountain of information before I knocked him out. I spun through the other things I'd just learned about Shana. One: Not only had she been previously married, but that husband had also been rich—and older—and likewise ended up with a bullet in his body. Two: When that husband died, Shana had inherited a Costa Rican fortune; widowed again, her net worth was probably going to double thanks to OK holdings.

Then I remembered something else I'd learned about Shana. Right before Alan showed up in the lobby, she told Tom and me that she and Jack had gone to a shooting range for some target practice.

Which meant that the lady knew her way around a gun.

As I walked out of the hotel with Alan, I wondered uneasily what else I didn't know about Shana O'Keefe.

CHAPTER
TWENTY-ONE

So where are we headed, exactly?"

Alan was behind the wheel of his Camry hybrid, heading north and east of Spring Valley. I wanted to have another go at the Green Hills youth camp where we'd found Jack's body yesterday morning. The camp had a variety of habitats and I was pretty sure we could find an Eastern Phoebe and an Eastern Wood-Pewee somewhere on the property.

I also hoped that focusing on something other than Shana, Jack, Billy, and a death threat would give me the chance to clear my head so I could start thinking logically again. Nailing Chuck O'Keefe without a moment's premeditation wasn't exactly the kind of habit I wanted to . . . well . . . get in the habit of. I was a trained counselor, for crying out loud. I was the person who was supposed to take the objective perspective in emotionally charged situations. Punching someone out was not part of the protocol.

No matter how good it felt.

And, man, it had felt good.

Two swallows swept across the road ahead of us and I pointed them out to Alan. "Cliff Swallow and Barn Swallow."

"How can you tell the difference? They just look like little dark birds to me. Heck, even 'swallow' is way out of my league."

I smiled and shook my head. "Listen and learn, oh mighty Hawk. One of the ways to identify birds is by their flight patterns. You see a big V of birds in the sky in the fall and you know they're geese. You see a spiral of big white birds in the spring and you're looking at American White Pelicans. You see sleek small birds diving and swooping over fields and you've got swallows."

"The geese I can do," Alan nodded in agreement. "And the pelicans—maybe. Guess I'd have to be looking up, huh?"

"Yeah, that would help."

"So how can you tell one swallow from another then? It's not like they're flying slowly by, flashing their little birdie IDs at you."

"It's the flight profile, Alan," I explained. "You're right—they're usually too fast to really note their markings. Instead, I look for the outline they make against the sky. Watch a minute—we'll see more and I'll show you what I mean."

Sure enough, more swallows dipped over the farm fields beside the road as we drove. "Look at the tails," I told Alan.

"Whoa! You're right, they've got tails. I can see that."

"Very funny. I mean look at the outline of the tails. The Barn Swallow has a deeply forked tail. The Cliff Swallow has a square tail. There must be a lot of old bridges and buildings in this part of the county, because that's where Cliff Swallows nest."

"Then why are they Cliff Swallows and not Bridge Swallows?"

"Because in a natural habitat, they prefer cliffs. But they've learned to be flexible, obviously. I guess they take advantage of what's available."

Kind of like Big Ben, I thought. Once Jack stopped funding him, he found another source of payments: Chuck. Which had to mean that Chuck knew about the conflict between his dad and Ben over the eco-community, but it didn't stop him from supporting Ben. He'd chosen the mayor over his dad. Drawing on my experience with high school kids, I could think of two reasons Chuck might make that choice: he was funding Ben to spite his father as payback for some perceived injury, or he was personally putting his money, albeit the family's money, where he thought it would do him the most financial good.

So either Chuck was angry at his dad for . . . what? Deserting him to marry Shana? Abandoning OK Industries to devote himself to the eco-community project, to which he'd been recruited by his lovely young wife?

Or was Chuck involved in some secret business deal with Ben that he hadn't shared with his dad? A business that his dad wouldn't condone because it flew in the face of what he was trying to accomplish with the eco-communities?

"Tell me about the ATV group," I told Alan. "The one you mentioned earlier—the one seeking the injunction against the eco-community project."

"Aflac," Alan quacked.

I raised an eyebrow at him. "I beg your pardon?"

"Aflac," he repeated. "You know, like the commercial on the television. My American government students were talking about the injunction one day before school let out for the summer, and one of the students kept saying 'Mac Ack' like he was impersonating a duck, and pretty soon, all the kids were doing the 'Aflac' quacking."

Another swallow zipped past the car and I pointed it out to Alan. "That one's a Northern Rough-winged Swallow. Its wingbeats are a little quicker, and it's all brown on top. So what does your students' quacking have to do with the injunction?"

"It was the name of the chief lobbyist—Mac Ackerman. Now, thanks to my students, every time I think of the controversy about the eco-communities, I think 'Aflac.'"

I stared at Alan. "Come again?"

"Mac Ackerman is the name of the guy leading the charge against the eco-communities." He glanced my way for a second. "What? You know the name?"

"Well, yeah," I replied. "He's one of the birders on this trip."

"Really? I don't think I would have pegged him for a bird lover judging from the comments he made in the press about the eco-communities. He was all about giving land to people to enjoy from the back of their ATVs and let the natural flora and fauna find somewhere else to . . . be flora and fauna."

"He also knows a lot about cars," I added. "In fact, he knew right away what had happened to my car when my brakes failed this morning. He was even right behind me on the road."

"No kidding?" Alan asked, then grew ominously quiet. "Are you saying he was involved in sabotaging your car?"

"I don't know," I admitted. "He was sure Johnny-on-the-spot. To be honest with you, I was already thinking he might have been behind it when I thought he was just another ATV fan, but now, knowing he's the head hauncho lobbyist, it really makes me wonder."

"Bob," Alan reminded me, "why would Mac Ackerman target you? You're not a player in the eco-communities."

"No, but remember that boundary thing I was talking about earlier? Maybe I've crossed some line in his head that makes me his enemy. Maybe he killed Jack to remove the opposition, and maybe he thinks I share Jack's mission to build the communities because I'm Shana's friend. Maybe he thinks he'll knock off all the conservation advocates in the state one at a time. I don't know!"

"Have you mentioned to anyone down here what your connection is to the eco-communities?"

"No!" I said, exasperated. "That's because I don't have any connection to the eco-communities! The only reason I'm involved with this mess this weekend is that I found Jack's body instead of a Yellow-billed Cuckoo, and I'm trying to be a friend to Shana in her hour of need."

"And you haven't given anyone a reason to think you're involved in the investigation of Jack's death?"

"No!"

Then I thought about it for a minute.

"Well, maybe," I corrected myself.

Alan spun his right hand in a circle. "Go on."

"I called the sheriff last night to tell her that Jack had recently ended a financial relationship with the mayor," I admitted, "and that she might want to check into it."

Alan turned onto the entrance road to Green Hills youth camp.

"So you told the sheriff to check out the mayor?"

"Yeah, I guess I did."

"I don't suppose you realize that sheriffs and mayors typically work pretty closely together in small towns?"

I shook my head. I was beginning to feel pretty stupid. "Never thought about it, no."

"You know what I think?" Alan asked as he pulled into an empty parking area near the camp headquarters. "I wouldn't be surprised if the sheriff, who has probably known the mayor a long time, went straight to him with your information. And I would guess, then, that the same mayor wasn't overly pleased to learn that the sheriff now was also privy to that information."

I stared out the windshield. "No, I would guess not."

But even as I mentally slapped myself for calling Sheriff Paulsen, another tumbler in my head clicked into place.

"That's how Chuck knew that Shana had the books audited!" I turned in my seat to face Alan. "Back at the hotel, Tom said that Chuck had accused Shana of having the books audited behind Jack's back. So Chuck knew someone had been through the books and caught him. I couldn't figure out how he'd found out so fast, since Stan just called me last night with the information for Shana. So Chuck must have heard it from Big Ben, after he heard it from the sheriff."

Alan nodded along with my reasoning. "Sounds possible. But how do you connect Mac Ack to it?"

Good question. Before I'd figured out the leak from Sheriff Paulsen to Big Ben, I'd just about convinced myself that Mac had ruined my brakes for some crazy reason having to do with the eco-communities. He did, after all, have a whole box of tools in the parking lot last night, and he knew right away what had happened when I'd spun out with Bernie. Now I wondered if Chuck was to blame. Could he have made a late night visit to the Inn & Suites to cut my brake line as payback for ratting out his buddy the mayor to the sheriff? I'd seen the possibility of a soured financial arrangement as a motive for murder, so I had to assume that the sheriff would see it that way, too. That was the reason I had called her last night—to make sure she didn't overlook the mayor as a suspect for Jack's murder.

Then again, maybe Chuck had a more personal reason to get rid of me. For all I knew, my phone call to the sheriff inadvertently opened a can of worms that may have begun with Jack and Ben's failed financial relationship, but actually bode much worse for the OK heir. Which begged the question: exactly what was Chuck's financial arrangement with Ben?

"Let's look for a bird," I told Alan, pushing my car door open. "I need some air."

Alan got out on his side of the Camry and looked towards the woods that spread out beyond the covered wagon at the base of the hill.

The covered wagon where I'd found Jack, just over twenty-four hours ago.

"Don't I need binoculars or something like that?" Alan asked.

I handed him the pair that was hanging around my neck. "Use mine. I'll bird by ear."

"Hey, isn't this the place where you found Jack O'Keefe yesterday? I saw the news last night with Lily, you know. I recognize the covered wagon."

I nodded.

"Okay, White-man. Lead the way. Just go light on the bodies. It's bad enough that you found one here, but if you find two, and I'm a part of the posse, my blushing bride-to-be will kill us both. I'm supposed to be pulling you out of this mess, not making it worse."

Worse? How could it get worse than it already was? I now had two good candidates for trying to put me into an ambulance, a handwritten death threat that I still couldn't account for, a very probable assault and battery charge looming in the very near future, a mayor who most likely wanted me out of the county for the rest of my natural life, and so far, not even a hint for finding a Northern Bobwhite.

Beside me, Alan thrashed through some bushes, scattering every bird within a half-mile.

Oh yeah, it could get worse.

I could have Alan birding with me.

I stifled a groan and headed off for the trees.

CHAPTER
TWENTY-TWO

Are you sure that Pewee bird is around here?" Alan asked, dropping onto a boulder to sit near the edge of a stream.

"It's here," I said. "This is exactly the habitat it likes—plenty of deciduous and mixed woods. And there's ample food source with all the little flies and gnats around here. I bet if we just sit here quietly for a few minutes, I'll hear it calling."

"Whatever you say, Bob. I'm just along for the ride. No, make that I'm along as the driver. You think they can fix your car first thing in the morning?"

"Yes," I whispered, giving him a pointed look.

He pulled off his felt cowboy hat and ran his hand through his hair. "Oh, right," he whispered back, loudly. "Time to be quiet."

I paced a few steps away from Alan and studied the branches overhead. High above me, I could make out a little movement as a small bird walked along a limb. Its underparts were a plain buffy color, and when it tilted its head, I could just make out a dark eye stripe.

I soundlessly reached my hand back towards Alan and hissed, "Binoculars!" while keeping my eye on the bird. Alan placed the binos in my hand and I brought them up to my eyes.

The bird's head was unmistakably striped with tan and black feathers, and its bill was too slender for a sparrow.

"A Worm-eating Warbler," I whispered in awe. I motioned to Alan to join me quietly and a moment later, I pointed out the bird to him. He looked through the binos and grunted.

"I know you don't appreciate what you're seeing, Alan," I excused him. "But that's a rare bird in your sights. I know a lot of birders who would give their right arm to see that bird here in Minnesota."

"Many are called, but few are chosen, huh?"

I could feel a smile tugging at the corners of my mouth. "Yeah, something like that, I guess."

"You should call Luce," Alan suggested, returning the binos to me.

I put the glasses back up to my eyes and watched the warbler hop along the branch. "She'd be thrilled to see it, for sure," I said, "but I can't guarantee we could spot it again by the time she got here."

"Bob," Alan said. "I'm not talking about the bird, I'm talking about Luce. You should call her. Lily's afraid she might have seen that television clip of you with Shana last night and jumped to the wrong conclusion. The reporters were sure making innuendos about you and the Widow O'Keefe."

I moved the binos away from my eyes and turned to my best friend. "Come on, Alan. You know how I feel about Luce. So does she. I can't imagine she's going to be upset by a television spot. She knows me better than that."

"That's what I told Lily, but she's still worried. She really likes Luce. They're pretty tight friends, you know."

I knew. I wasn't always happy about it, but I was well aware that my sister and my girlfriend were confidantes. So far, they hadn't ganged up on me too much. Of course, once Alan married my sister, I would definitely have the odds stacked against me for winning any argument with Lily.

"You know, Alan, I've been wanting to ask you—are you really sure about marrying Lily? I mean," I explained, spreading my hands out to include the forest, "we're out here all alone, and I'm your best friend, so you can tell me the truth. Don't you think you're rushing into this marriage just a little bit? I mean, you just started dating last month. Three weeks later, you're getting measured for a tux."

Alan pulled his hat off his head and slapped it against his thigh. Then he looked me right in the eye and said, "Not at all. I wish I'd married her the very first time I laid eyes on her when I came home with you from college that first midterm break we had. What was that, sixteen years ago now? Of course, I was young and stupid then, and she wouldn't give me the time of day, but I wish I'd had all those years between then and now with her. I'm just grateful we're getting married as soon as we are. If she hadn't wanted the big wedding event, we'd already be married. A justice of the peace would've worked just fine for me."

For a minute, I didn't say a word. I actually felt a lump in my throat listening to Alan's declaration of love for Lily. I guess I'd wanted him to express some hesitations or doubts—maybe the same hesitations and doubts I felt when I thought about proposing to Luce. I mean, I loved Luce, and I wanted to marry her, but the actual proposing part continued to escape me.

"Okay," I finally said to Alan, my voice sounding pretty normal again, "good to know."

"Jump in, White-man," Alan said, grinning. "The water's great."

"You hope so," I said.

"I know so," he replied.

"Tell you what, Hawk," I bargained. "Since you're willing to bird with me today, I'm willing to give engagement a try. You find that Pewee and I'll offer Luce a ring."

Alan laughed, and the Worm-eating Warbler took off through the trees. "Well, that's a safe bet for you, I'd say. Poor Luce—she's going to be an old woman before she gets to say her 'I do.'"

"Maybe. Maybe not," I said. "If there's one thing I've learned in all my years of birding, it's that the unexpected can unexpectedly happen."

My cell phone rang in my pocket.

"Just like that," I said, pulling the phone out and flipping it open.

"Ben's payments from Chuck," Stan's voice said in my ear. "They were funneled. In and out of Ben's account. Destination: ATV lobbyists."

"So Chuck was funding the opposition to his father's project," I concluded. "Not very conducive to happy family dinners, I'd say."

"There's more," Stan added. "Ben's got an account. Off-shore. Very tidy sum. I'm still tracking it."

"Should I tell Shana?"

"Your choice. I'm calling in help."

"Stan—don't hang up."

For a split-second, I debated sharing my find with him, but I couldn't resist. Locating an uncommon bird is always a thrill, but telling my rival I'd scored one on him was just too much to pass up. Besides, for everything he was doing to help Shana untangle the mess she'd landed in, I figured giving him the heads-up for his own bird chase was a small way to thank him. "I just found a Worm-eating Warbler. Here at Green Hills."

There was a moment of silence on the phone.

"I'm on my way."

Another silence.

"Thanks."

"You're welcome," I said, but he had already cut the connection.

Alan tucked his hat back on his head and gave me a questioning look.

"I thought Scary Stan was your long-time birding rival," he said.

I stuffed the phone back into my pocket and adjusted the bino strap around my neck. "He is. But I wanted to thank him for helping Shana, and I couldn't think of a better way than to tell him where he can find a rare bird."

"Worm-catching warblers aren't usually around here?"

"Worm-*eating* Warblers, Alan, and no," I said, leading the way back along the trail. "They're not normally here. A few years ago, someone supposedly saw one in Mystery Cave State Park, but it was never substantiated. From what I heard yesterday at the police station from a couple of deputies, Fillmore County saw more traffic that summer than it usually does in two whole years, thanks to all the birders showing up. I guess the sheriff got a first-hand education about all the hidden birding hotspots—the deputies said their revenue from traffic violations set a record that year."

Alan laughed again, sending more birds scattering.

"So, did you get enough air, Bob?" he asked as we walked through the old woods. "Did the birding clear out the cobwebs in that cluttered head of yours?"

"It's getting better," I reported. Stan's latest bit of news seemed to confirm my earlier suspicion that Chuck had more riding on the line with his payments to Ben than just funding his father's old friend. Obviously, Chuck and Ben had some kind of deal going—Ben was moving money along to the ATV group for Chuck. Ben was also getting a cut on the deal—enough to keep himself financially comfortable, according to what Shana had said—but what was in it for Chuck wasn't clear. It also made the death threat note even more confusing: based on what I now knew about the estrangement between Jack and Ben, it seemed highly unlikely that Jack would have charged the mayor with any task at all, let alone the task of killing me.

Yet someone had cut my brake line.

A furious Chuck?

A deranged Mac?

A vengeful Big Ben?

As I stepped over some exposed tree roots on the trail, I realized that the only way I was going to find out who had sabotaged my car was to figure out why I was a threat to someone.

A threat that was strong enough to cause someone to want to kill me.

Alan's hand suddenly shot out and grabbed my elbow, pulling me to an abrupt stop. "Look!" he said, pointing ahead.

Seated cross-legged on an enormous fallen log off the path, her very short silver hair glinting in the sunlight that streamed through an opening in the branches overheard, was a small woman. She was dressed entirely in green and blended in so well with the forest around her, I doubted I would have noticed her until I'd almost pulled level with her on the trail. She was motionless, staring at Alan and me.

"It's a wood sprite," Alan whispered.

"I don't think so," I said. "Birding is magical, but not that magical, Alan."

"Hello, Bob White," the little woman said.

"I knew it," Alan whispered again. "She's a sprite. How else would she know your name?"

I rolled my eyes in Alan's general direction. "Yeah, right." Although, to be honest, I had no idea who this woman was, how she knew me, or even how she managed to be on our trail.

"I'm sorry," I said, advancing toward the woman, who still sat in that pixie-like pose on the log. "Have we met?"

Her light-blue eyes speared mine. "Only in a dream, Mr. White."

Okay. I'd found a crazy woman in the woods. Happens all the time. Right?

Wrong.

Caution! Caution! went the bells in my head. Did she have a knife in her lap? A blowgun with a poison dart? A snare set in the earth in front of my feet? Was this tiny woman stalking me? I froze in place, trying to recall what I'd learned in grad school about handling people in the midst of a psychotic episode.

Actually, we never covered that in grad school.

Memo to me: on the next alumni survey, I should mention that.

"That's usually a conversation stopper," the woman observed. "Actually, Eddie Edvarg described you to me so accurately, I couldn't mistake you for anyone else. I'm Kami Marsden."

She smiled then and stood up, holding her hand out for me to shake. "I'd hoped to meet you yesterday when Eddie and I stopped by at the hotel, but you weren't around. And for the record, I did see you in a dream. It's a little habit I have—random flashes of precognition. Not that it's been very useful so far—I still haven't won the lottery like Eddie did."

"I'm Alan Thunderhawk," Alan said, taking Kami's hand after I had released it. "You made quite a picture on the log there. I was ready to chase you down and ask for three wishes."

Kami laughed. "It's the haircut, I know. That and my size. I could probably pose for Pixies R Us. When we were kids, Jack called me his leprechaun, and I'm not even Irish."

She folded her arms over her chest and planted herself on the trail in front of us. "You found Jack," she said to me.

"I did," I agreed.

"I didn't kill him," she said, "but I can make a couple guesses as to who did."

CHAPTER
TWENTY-THREE

A couple guesses?" Alan asked.

"That's why I'm here at Green Hills," Kami explained. "I was hoping my little habit of precognition might kick in and help me narrow the field of suspects. Sometimes I pick up impressions of people from a place if I can just tune in. I know it sounds crazy, but you go with what you've got, right?"

Yup—it definitely sounded crazy. Another memo to me for that alumni survey: add "dealing with psychics" to graduate instruction for counselors.

I took another look at the petite woman in front of me. Now that I was within arm's reach of her, she didn't look so much like a wood sprite, but more like a woman who had been raised outdoors. She had a healthy tan and the crow's feet around her eyes testified to a lot of smiling or squinting in the sunshine. Her bare arms looked lean and muscular, and her cargo shorts revealed well-toned legs. All in all, she didn't look particularly crazy.

Then again, she cared for a Bengal tiger on her private sanctuary of land in southeastern Minnesota. Nigel, her tiger, had to outweigh her by at least five hundred and fifty pounds, yet she cared enough for the big cat to jump through all the hoops to provide it a safe home.

In my book, that still made her crazy. Crazy and determined.

Kind of like a lot of birders I know.

"So who's on your suspect list?" I asked.

She looked me in the eye. "Chuck. Billy."

"Billy? Billy worked for Jack," I said. "And Chuck is his son. I understand that Jack and Chuck had problems, but were they that bad that you could honestly suspect Chuck of killing his own father?"

"Money is a powerful motive when you're talking about hundreds of thousands of dollars, Bob."

"Chuck siphoned off that much to Ben?"

Kami looked confused. *Well, duh*, I told myself. She hadn't had a phone call from Stan in the last hour like I had. Of course she wouldn't know about the money game at OK.

"I don't know anything about money going to Ben," she said. "I'm talking about the hundreds of thousands of dollars Chuck stood to gain if the eco-community got killed and the ATV park was developed in its place."

"ATV park?"

I looked at Alan, but he shrugged his shoulders. Apparently, his students hadn't reported anything about this little wrinkle in the zoning battle.

"That's the scuttlebutt. There's a big ATV manufacturer looking to set up shop here in Fillmore County," Kami informed us. "And that's not the extent of it, either. The word is that the manufacturer wants to develop a whole driving range through different habitats adjacent to the facility for both test driving vehicles and public usage. For a fee, of course."

"An ATV wonderland," Alan murmured.

"That's right," Kami agreed.

"And Chuck fits into this . . . how?" I asked.

Kami raked her slim fingers through her cropped silver hair. "He owns the land the manufacturer wants." She looked from me to Alan and then back again to fix her pale-blue stare on my eyes.

"It's a legacy from his mother—Jack's first wife. It's also the land where Jack wants to build the eco-community. And to top it all off, it's the land right next to mine. I don't expect you know this, but Jack's first wife was my sister."

"Jack is your brother-in-law," I said, trying to reconfigure relationships in my head.

"It generally works that way," Kami said.

I rubbed my hand over my eyes. "Give me a minute here. I need to get this straight." I made a chart in my head of all the players in the Fillmore drama. Jack and Shana were married. Jack's first wife was Kami's sister. Chuck was Jack's son and Kami's nephew. "So Shana knows who you are, right? That you're Jack's sister-in-law?"

"Of course," Kami said. "But I think she's not too comfortable with me. Not only do I look an awful lot like my sister Char—Jack's first wife—but Jack and I have a history that goes way back. We were high school sweethearts. Char was three years younger than me, and she and Jack didn't get together until after I'd gone to Texas for college and vet school. Jack stayed in state. Anyway, I think Shana feels a little left out when Jack and I start reminiscing."

"I think she feels more than left out," I pointed out. "She thought you and Jack were having an affair."

Kami's mouth dropped open. "You have got to be kidding me. Jack is so totally in love with Shana, he can hardly talk about anything else."

"Hormones," Alan announced. "Shana's pregnant. With twins. She's probably got so many hormones flooding her brain, she can't think straight. I had a cousin who swore she saw aliens in her backyard when she was pregnant. She refused to leave the house even when she went into labor. It was pure luck that the paramedics got there when they did to help her deliver the baby in her front hallway."

For a moment, neither Kami nor I said a word.

"Aliens?" Kami repeated.

I socked Alan in the shoulder. "Thanks so much for that little anecdote, Hawk. I'll be sure to share it with Shana. She'll probably kill you."

I started walking on the trail, and Kami fell in beside me. I told her what Stan had found out about the money from Chuck that ended up in the ATV lobby group's coffers after it had passed through Ben's hands.

"So Chuck was passing money along to the lobby to fund their zoning fight against the eco-community, but he didn't want his dad to know," she concluded.

"That's what I figure," I said.

"And Ben was the middleman."

"Yup."

"That bastard," Kami muttered.

"You mean Chuck?" I recalled that Shana had used the same euphemism for her stepson. Now Kami, Chuck's aunt, was using it. I began to wonder if it was, after all, some sort of family endearment.

"Not Chuck," Kami clarified for me. "Ben."

Okay, I could accept that, too. Ben, the longtime family friend, was obviously playing father and son against each other and coming out with a fistful of dollars, according to Stan's latest investigation update. I suddenly wondered if Kami was aware that Ben had publicly fed the rumor that she and Jack had been lovers. If she was already ticked off at him, I couldn't imagine it would improve her opinion.

But hey, I decided it might be fun to find out.

Especially since the guy had been carrying around a note to kill me.

"So, Kami, I understand that Big Ben assumed you and Jack were involved, too. At least that's what he suggested to the media yesterday afternoon at the hotel."

She pulled up short.

No pun intended.

She turned those blue eyes on me like fine-tuned lasers. "He said what?"

Oh, yes. Big Ben was in trouble now. I mean, here was a woman with a tiger. Literally. I sure wouldn't want to be on her bad side the next time I was anywhere near her property.

She repeated her new favorite name for Ben.

Twice.

At which point, Alan remembered a piece of our earlier conversation in my hotel room about a certain type of dart. "So you're a veterinarian. And I bet you have darts for tranquilizing animals, too."

Kami turned her attention to Alan. "Yes, I do. I use them on occasion in my practice, and I've had to use them with Nigel a few times as well. Mostly for traveling purposes. Why?"

Alan and I exchanged a look. Kami obviously hadn't heard from the sheriff, yet, about the dart in Billy's neck.

The tranquilizer dart.

I changed the subject.

"Before you said that Chuck was on your list of murder suspects, you mentioned Billy. Why was that? Especially since he turned up dead yesterday, too."

Kami walked a few more paces up the trail, then stopped, her back to both Alan and I. Surrounded by the greenery of the forest, her slight figure almost seemed to blend in with the woods. For a split-second, I had the eerie feeling she was going to disappear right before my eyes.

Then she turned, a frown on her pixie face.

"Billy was spying on Jack for Ben. He was Jack's assistant, but Jack and I figured out that Billy was feeding information about our progress with the eco-community to Ben, and Ben was passing it along to the ATV lobby. They always seemed to know exactly what our next move would be in the zoning process, and they were always there to block it."

She stared down at the trail for another minute, then raised her eyes to mine.

"I'm not especially proud of this, and it's probably illegal, but I had your friend Eddie put a tracking device on Billy's car when he arrived at the hotel in Spring Valley on Friday afternoon. Jack and I had decided it was the only way to see if Billy was meeting with Ben on the sly."

She dug her heel into the dirt. "I followed Billy. Sure enough, he and Ben had a cozy little chat at the trailhead to Mystery Cave State Park."

"Where Billy's body was found yesterday afternoon?"

"Yes, in that same area. But after midnight on Friday," she paused to heave a weary sigh, "Eddie tracked Billy from my house to Green Hills. Here—the youth camp."

Where I found Jack with two bullet holes in his chest early the next morning.

"Son-of-a-bitch," Alan whispered.

Chapter
Twenty-Four

We climbed up the rest of the trail in silence and found ourselves back in the small meadow just below the covered wagon that was still draped with yellow crime scene tape.

"You've got to tell Sheriff Paulsen," I told Kami, "about Billy being at Green Hills early Saturday morning. It places him at the scene of Jack's murder. Did Eddie get a time on Billy?"

Kami nodded. "Oh, yeah. Billy was definitely there within the window of probability of when Jack was shot." She lifted a hand to shade her eyes as she looked toward the wagon and its yellow ribbons. "So, what do you suggest I say to Paulsen? 'Hey, I know Billy's whereabouts for the twenty-four hours before he was killed because I was illegally monitoring him.' I figure I'd be arrested for stalking, at least, if not for Billy's murder."

The tranquilizer dart popped back into my head again.

"Well, see, I think the sheriff kind of already has that idea," I hedged, not wanting to tell her the piece about the dart in Billy's back. For a split-second, I wondered if it was confidential information. Would I be in trouble with the law—Sheriff Paulsen, to be exact—if I told Kami what I'd learned from Shana and Tom?

Alan, however, didn't have any problem with sharing.

"They found a tranquilizer dart in Billy's body," he explained to Kami. "Last we heard, the sheriff was on her way to ask you about it. So, yeah, I can see where you might not want to mention to her about tracking Billy's car. It's a no-brainer that if she knew about the tracking, she'd slap some cuffs on you. I hope you can think of someone else who might have tranquilizer darts. Otherwise, you'd better have a good lawyer in mind."

Geez, Alan, way to be sensitive and helpful.

Kami didn't seem especially rattled, though. Then again, like I already said, this was a lady with a tiger. I expect if you share your property with a megafauna like Nigel, it takes more than the threat of handcuffs to throw you for a loop. Instead of getting flustered or defensive, Kami became really still. I could almost see the wheels turning inside her head.

"That bastard," she whispered one more time.

"Are we still talking Ben here?" I asked, wanting to be sure I was still on the same train of thought with her.

"Oh, yeah," she replied. "We're talking Ben here."

"What does Ben have to do with the dart?" Alan wanted to know.

Kami looked from Alan to me. She was definitely considering telling us something, but hesitating for some reason.

"What?" I pressed her.

I could see her jaws tighten in silent anger.

"Ben would have had access to my darts."

Before I could even formulate the next question, she answered it for me. "Ben has a key to my home. We have an on-again, off-again relationship. It's been that way for almost twenty years. He knows where I keep my vet supplies, so it wouldn't take him more than a minute to pull one out of the cabinet and stuff it in a pocket."

Kami looked up into the treetops around us, pausing to collect her thoughts. "He's pulled some pretty low stunts over the years, but this . . . this would be a new low. I don't even want to think about the possibility he could have killed Billy, but how can I not? I saw them together on Friday in the same place where Billy was found dead the next day. Who else would know the place? I just can't believe it."

She lowered her eyes to the ground and dug her heel into the dirt. "And what reason would he have to kill Billy? Billy was working for him, spying on Jack and me."

"Maybe Ben decided that wasn't such a good idea, anymore," Alan theorized. "Maybe Ben wanted, or needed, to get rid of the messenger to protect himself from being exposed?"

"And then he tells the media I was sleeping with Jack? That bastard!" She looked up at me and Alan, her voice a choked whisper. "I'm going to kill him."

"I'd recommend you not mention that to the sheriff at this point," Alan suggested. "She might be a little overly sensitive to people announcing their plans to kill other people right now."

"He set me up!" she suddenly shouted. "He wanted me out of the way! Oh, my God, I get it now!" Kami slapped her palms against her temples and spun in a circle.

Clang! Clang! went the warning bells in my brain. Female meltdown coming up! Stand clear!

I grabbed Alan's arm and moved him back a few paces from where Kami's fury was beginning to send smoke out of her ears.

"Get what?" I carefully asked.

"What he was up to these last few months!" Kami hissed through her clenched teeth. "Here he's been Mr. Romance, telling me he's thinking maybe we should finally tie the knot, and I kept saying I had to think it over. It's the land! He wants my sister's property for the damn ATV project! How could I have been so stupid?"

She'd stopped spinning around and was now stomping the ground as hard as she could. "That jerk! I was actually starting to believe him! He was funneling the money to the lobbyists for Chuck, and I bet you my last dollar the lobbyists were paying him off big-time, too. He kept saying, 'Come on, Kami honey, forget the eco-community. We don't want that next door.' He wanted me to desert Jack and the project. That lying scum! For all I know, he made a deal with the ATVers that he'd get my property for them, too! That's Ben, all right, always thinking of the big score."

She pounded her heel into the ground, then stared at the dirt between her feet. "And then what? When I kept putting him off and continued making plans with Jack, he decided he needed more drastic measures to get what he wanted?"

Alan and I stood there, afraid to make any sudden moves. Kami stopped ranting for a moment, her eyes getting even larger in her small face as she made the obvious leap of deduction.

"No," she insisted, shaking her head. "No way. Ben could not kill Jack. They've been friends forever. Not even a fortune would make Ben do that."

"But it might convince Ben to frame you for a murder?" Alan quietly questioned.

She glared at Alan. "Ben knows I wouldn't kill Jack, but it would sure cause trouble for me and Nigel if I was drawn into a murder investigation. Putting pressure on me would only make Ben's job easier—no way would the county rezone the land next to me for an eco-community if there were doubts about my integrity, or about Nigel's security. Talk about lawsuits just waiting to happen!"

"Who is Nigel?" Alan asked.

"My tiger," Kami said.

"Her tiger," I said at the same time.

"You have a tiger?" Alan asked.

"Yes!" I said in exasperation. "Kami has a wildlife sanctuary. She has a tiger named Nigel." I looked pointedly at Kami. "And that's why someone's been wrecking your fence and trying to let Nigel loose, isn't it? Someone wants to prevent the eco-community from getting the zoning changed to allow them to build the project because that same someone desperately wants the ATV park to go in there instead. Could that someone be Ben?"

She shook her head in denial. "He wouldn't do that. Kill Jack, I mean."

"But he might sabotage your fence?"

Kami didn't respond.

"Or maybe he'd ask someone to do it for him? Someone from the ATV lobby?"

Someone like Mac Ack? I knew for a fact that the Ackermans had checked in ahead of me on Friday. I'd seen Tom briefly before hitting the sack and he'd given me a rundown on the birders attending the weekend. So if Mac had a little errand to run late Friday night for Big Ben, who was to know?

An awful scenario started to form in my head.

"What if Ben asked someone to pull the fence Friday night, Jack caught the guy in the act after he left Kami's place, and the guy shot Jack in a panic?"

Kami's face went white.

"Maybe you should sit down," Alan said, reaching for her arm as she seemed to wobble on her feet.

"That bastard!" she cried, flinging off Alan's arm. "That lying, cheating scum of the earth!"

I missed the next few names she came up with because my cell phone vibrated in my pocket. I pulled it out and saw Lily's name.

No way was I answering it. Instead, I handed the phone to Alan. "You talk to her. I can only deal with one screaming female at a time."

"Hi, sweetheart," he said after he flipped the phone open. "Yes, he's right here, but he's got his hands full . . . birding."

I rolled my eyes at him, and he walked away from me to finish his conversation with my sister. I looked back at Kami, who was transitioning from cursing Ben to plotting her revenge.

"I don't care if the sheriff does throw me in jail for Billy's murder, I'm going to tell her everything. How Ben has funneled money. How he wants my land. How he's in bed with the ATV lobby. How he met with Billy at Mystery Cave on Friday. How he got my darts! I am going to ruin that lying bastard!"

"Go for it," I cheered her on, grateful to see that she was making a quick recovery from her meltdown. In counseling circles, we call it "making an action plan," and it's a first step towards dealing constructively with the irritating agent. Of course, the action plans I usually see developing don't include drawing and quartering ex-lovers or ruining the career of the local mayor, but I'm always open to new ideas. The day you stop learning is the day you die, right?

Speaking of which, I had another question for Kami.

"Amidst all this other stuff that you're figuring out about Big Ben," I interrupted her ongoing tirade, "did he ever happen to mention that he and Jack wanted to kill me?"

Kami gave me an incredulous look. "What?"

I told her about the note that Shana had found, written in Jack's handwriting, and that we'd realized it had come from Big Ben's coat.

Kami rubbed her hand over her eyes. "I never heard a word about you, Bob. Not until Eddie told me he'd run into you yesterday afternoon. As for the note, I think I saw Jack jot something down on a piece of paper while we were talking late Friday night about the odds of the eco project succeeding. But I can't imagine it was a death threat, or that Jack saw Ben after he left my place. Then again," she added, her features darkening, "there are obviously a lot of things I never could have imagined, aren't there? It seems my little gift of precognition is vastly overrated."

Alan returned my phone to me. "Lily's happy . . . for now. But if I don't bring you home by noon tomorrow, we are both in very deep yogurt with your sister."

"Thanks, Alan. You're still my best friend, you know. Even if you are making the mistake of the century by marrying Lily." My eyes drifted towards the old covered wagon and its drape of yellow tape.

And then I had one of those stabs of realization that came zipping right out of my left brain.

Or maybe it's the right.

Wherever it came from, I realized with a jolt that there was a big flaw in my imagined scenario of Jack surprising his killer.

Jack wasn't found dead in the meadow with the downed fencing. He was sitting right there behind the covered wagon. If he'd been shot in the meadow, how had his killer moved him here without smearing blood all over Jack's body, not to mention driving Jack's car here? As I recalled, Jack's bullet holes had actually looked rather neat, and his clothes were blood-soaked only around those holes, which meant Jack had been killed right here, not in the meadow and then transported.

Jack had come here for a reason before he was killed. Since we didn't have after-midnight owling on the agenda for the birding trip, I had to assume he had another compelling reason to visit Green Hills camp in the pre-dawn hours.

I knew it in my gut: Jack came here to meet someone.

Someone he knew.

I turned back to Kami to share my revelation with her, but I was too late.

The pixie had disappeared.

CHAPTER
TWENTY-FIVE

Where'd she go?" I asked Alan.

He shrugged in reply. "She was right here a minute ago. Then poof! She's gone. Pretty spooky, if you ask me." He pulled his hat from his head and tapped it twice against his leg. "And I'm not so sure the lady doesn't have a couple of little-bitty screws loose, Bob. I mean, come on! She thinks she can pick up 'impressions' from places, and she lives with a tiger."

"To each her own," I muttered. Frankly, I wasn't quite sure what to make of Kami Marsden myself. The woman was undoubtedly elusive and eccentric, but I didn't get the sense she was a killer or a liar. Big Ben, on the other hand, seemed to be fitting the bill for both.

"If I were the mayor, I'd stay far away from Kami," Alan commented. "Like they say, 'Hell hath no fury like a woman scorned.' And that woman is past scorned, if you ask me."

"I was just thinking the same thing," I said. "Not only does she have the rage to fuel a full-scale campaign to trash Big Ben, but she also has plenty of circumstantial evidence that links him to Billy's murder, and maybe even to Jack's death, too."

Which meant that the sheriff would have to reconsider her conclusion that Billy had killed Jack. Or at least, that Billy had acted alone. Combined with Shana's protest that Billy didn't even know how to use a gun, it seemed to me that naming Billy as the killer was looking more premature than ever.

Rushed, even.

Can you spell "cover-up"?

We started up the slope past the wagon and headed for the parking lot where we'd left Alan's car. I could hear an Indigo Bunting and a Mourning Dove calling from beyond the lot, where the trees crowded in around the gravel area. On a normal weekend, the youth camp would have been a great spot for birding with all its different habitat areas: meadow, old-wood forest, stream, and wetlands. This weekend, though, it had proven to be a spot for murder and mystery.

Yup, you never know what you're going to get on a birding weekend.

Just as we stepped into the lot, a boy hopped out of the driver's seat of the car parked next to Alan's. I could have sworn he looked familiar, but there was no way one of my students from Savage was going to turn up here in Fillmore County on a Sunday morning.

"Excuse me," the boy said, "aren't you Bob White?"

I looked him over. He was probably about sixteen and maybe all of five feet tall.

"Yes."

He stuck his hand out to shake mine. "I'm Skip Swenson, and I'd like to interview you."

Alan turned to me with a smile. "Your reputation precedes you, Whiteman."

"The question is *which* reputation," I replied, dreading the answer. I took the boy's hand and gave it a brief shake. "Interview me about what?"

"About the murder of Jack O'Keefe," he announced, puffing up a bit like a male bird on display for a female. It didn't make him any taller, though. Or older. Or more commanding.

Skip Swenson was just a kid.

"And why is that?" I prodded.

"I saw you in the diner with Mrs. O'Keefe last night, and then on the nine o'clock news. I want to be a journalist, and I thought if I could land an exclusive interview with you, maybe it would get me an internship this summer with a TV crew."

That explained where I'd seen Skip before—he'd been one of the kids working at the A&W the previous evening. No surprise that he'd noticed Shana, since he was alive and breathing. The fact that he'd also noted who her companions were, though, was a little more impressive—Skip was obviously an observant young man. That's always a good skill in a high school student. I probably spend half the time in my counseling office at Savage High School telling kids to pay attention to what's going on in the front of the classroom instead of what's on their phone's text message window. Realizing that Skip had also taken his observation and turned it into a possible job opportunity bumped my estimation of him to even a notch higher. The kid was smart, and he had nerve.

Too bad he was wasting it on me.

"No comment," I told him.

"How did you find us?" Alan asked.

Yeah, that was a good question. I gave Skip a stern glance. "Are you stalking me?"

"No!" he cried in alarm, raising his hands to his shoulders.

"You can put your hands down, Skip. This isn't a stick-up."

The boy blushed a bright crimson and dropped his hands. "I know that," he mumbled.

I couldn't help myself. I was starting to like Skip. He may have been intruding into my life, but he was doing it so awkwardly that it made me smile. "So how did you know I would be here?"

He glanced up at me from under a long fringe of blond hair. He had that bowl cut thing going on with his mop of hair, like his mom had simply placed a bowl over his head and trimmed right around it. I guessed that Skip was definitely not the school GQ icon.

"This morning I drove over to the hotel to see if I could talk with you, and just when I got there, I saw you getting in the car with your friend." Skip pointed to Alan. "Then I followed you guys here, but I didn't turn in to the parking lot right behind you. I didn't want you to 'make' me, you know?"

"Make you?" Alan asked.

"Yeah, like on the cop shows. Identify the car following you. I wanted to see where you were going, then I doubled back and parked here after you had gone. I figured I'd catch you when you got back."

"Good thinking," I said. I glanced at Alan. "We didn't 'make' you at all, Skip."

He seemed to puff up a little again.

"So what kind of interview were you thinking about?"

Skip's face lit up. "Oh, man, that would be so great if you would let me ask you a few questions! I've even got a minicam in my car to film you."

"Bob," Alan warned.

"It's all right," I reassured him. I nodded at Skip. "Let's see what you've got, Jimmy Olsen."

"It's Skip," he corrected me. "Skip Swenson."

"I know. I was making a joke," I explained. "Jimmy Olsen, cub reporter, like with Superman and Lois Lane? Mr. White, the editor of the *Daily Planet*?

Skip just stared at me. He didn't get it.

"Never mind. Get the camera."

Alan snickered beside me.

Our eager journalist-to-be pulled his car door open and grabbed a small video camera off the passenger seat. "Could you hold it for me while I interview Mr. White?" he asked Alan.

"Sure. Show me how to run it. My name's Alan Thunderhawk, by the way." He paused for a beat. "Jimmy."

"It's Skip," he said again. I noted a hint of irritation in his voice. He was probably thinking that not only were Alan and I old guys, but hard-of-hearing as well. He gave Alan a few brief instructions, then came to stand next to me. A little more puffing, and he was ready to go. "Roll it," he told Alan.

"I'm here with Bob White, the mystery man who's been at the side of Shana O'Keefe since her husband's murder yesterday morning. Can you tell us, Mr. White, what your involvement is with Mrs. O'Keefe?"

"We're old friends, Skip," I told him, feeling relieved to have the chance to set the record straight. "Mrs. O'Keefe and I used to go birding together almost twenty years ago when I was about your age. I'm here this weekend because I was birding with her husband Jack's weekend birding group. In the light of what's happened, I know she appreciates having friends around her during this awful ordeal."

Skip brushed his bangs out of his eyes and crossed his arms over his thin chest. "And how is she reacting to the very real possibility that not only her husband has met his death this weekend, but that Bobwhite might also be killed in the process?"

Say what?

Actually, for a moment or two, or three, I couldn't say a thing. My heart felt like it had slammed into my chest.

"What did you say?" Alan asked, lowering the camera.

"Keep it rolling, Mr. Thunderhawk," Skip motioned with his hand for Alan to raise the camera back up again.

I put my hand on Skip's shoulder and locked my eyes on his. "What are you talking about?" I carefully enunciated each word.

Skip looked confused, and his eyes darted from mine to Alan's face and back again to mine. "The eco-community," he said. "I'm asking if Mrs. O'-Keefe is upset that the eco-community might lose its battle with the zoning council because of Mr. O'Keefe's murder."

"No," Alan corrected him. "You said something about killing Bob White."

"That's right," Skip agreed. "Bobwhite is the name of the eco-community." He paused for a minute, checking out the dumbfounded expressions on Alan's and my faces. "You didn't know that?"

I walked over to lean against Alan's car. I rubbed my hand over my chin, aware of a huge wave of relief washing over me even as I was busy mentally reassembling what had happened since I'd found Jack's body yesterday morning. Jack's note wasn't about me. It was about the eco-community's possible fate if the zoning didn't get approved. I wasn't on somebody's hit list.

Good to know.

Really good to know.

But before I could enjoy the full range of that feeling, a little fact jumped front and center into my consciousness to spoil the moment.

Someone had still cut my brake line and put Bernie into the hospital. Not what I would call a random act of the universe.

Around me, birds were singing. Automatically, I began to list their names in my head: Yellow-billed Cuckoo, Blue Jay, Eastern Phoebe.

"You didn't know that," Skip said, only this time it was a statement of fact, not a question. "Oh, I get it! You thought I was saying that you were getting killed, Mr. White. Bobwhite. Bob White. Got it. What I was talking about was the eco-community. The project's called 'Bobwhite Acres.' And the trail park the ATV lobby wants to build instead is called 'Ride on the Wild Side.' It's supposed to be huge and generate a whole lot of income for the county."

"Yeah, I think I heard that," I responded half-heartedly. "I'm just having a . . . moment . . . of . . . mental reconfiguration here, Skip."

Our cub reporter brushed his bangs out of his eyes again and gave me a careful once-over.

"Is there something else going on here?" he asked.

"Hey, Skip, I think we're done filming for now," Alan piped up. "Maybe we can do some more later." He handed the camera back to the boy and then came to lean against the car next to me.

"The news is both good and bad, isn't it?" he said.

"Yeah," I agreed.

"Can I talk to you later, Mr. White?" Skip asked. "Maybe I can do a written interview and email it to a station?"

"Sounds like a plan, Skip," I said, but without much enthusiasm.

He climbed into his car and left the lot.

"What are you thinking?" Alan asked.

I looked up into the trees that rimmed the parking area. "Oh, that I'm glad Jack and Ben weren't plotting my murder. Wondering who is. And why."

Alan took off his hat and wiped his arm across his forehead. "We're going to find out, Bob. You and me. And then we'll put the son-of-a-bitch in jail."

Alan suddenly went tense beside me.

"Did you hear that?" he whispered.

"What?"

"That bird call. It sounded like 'pee-oo-wee.' Is that what a Pewee sounds like?"

I stared at Alan, then tuned my ears to listen for the bird.

I didn't hear anything.

"Funny, Alan," I said, shaking my head. "Nice try, but no cigar."

"No, wait. Just be quiet," Alan insisted.

I listened again.

And then it came. The clear song of the Eastern Wood-Pewee.

"I'll be damned," I said in total amazement. "You got the bird, Alan."

He grinned at me.

"And you're going to get a fiancée."

I looked at him blankly.

"Our bet? You said if I found the Pewee, you'd ask Luce to marry you."

I felt the blood drain from my head.

"I did say that, didn't I?"

"Yes, White-man, you did."

Holy crap.

"Which gives us one more reason to find your car saboteur and get him put away as quickly as possible," Alan continued. "We don't want to keep Luce waiting any longer than she has to for you to put that diamond on her finger now, do we, White-man? Hey, maybe we could have a quadruple-ring ceremony. You know, we could all get married at the same time? Two-for-one? I bet it would save us a bundle on the reception, at least."

I could barely hear what Alan was saying over the roaring in my ears.

No, not roaring. Ringing.

Quadruple-ring.

Something clicked together in my head then, and I forgot all about proposing to Luce.

"Not a quadruple-ring, Alan," I said, the words tumbling out almost as rapidly as they were falling into place in my head. "A three-ring! A three-ring circus!"

"Please don't even suggest that phrase to Lily," Alan sternly warned me. "She'll never forgive you if you refer to her wedding as a three-ring circus. Even if you're right," he added.

"I'm not talking about the wedding!" I almost shouted at him. "I just realized why the ATV lobby might want that particular piece of land desperately enough to kill the opposition," I told Alan, pulling open the passenger door to his Camry. "Get in and drive. There's another birding spot we've got to look at."

"What do you mean? I got the Pewee, didn't I?"

"Yes, you did. But you didn't get a Bobwhite, and that's the reason I came to Fillmore this weekend in the first place. Jack promised us a Bobwhite, and I think I just figured out where at least one is. Drive, Alan."

CHAPTER
TWENTY-SIX

Alan's hybrid quietly came to life and rolled silently out of the Green Hills parking area. After about ten minutes, I noticed he kept looking in his rear-view mirror every few seconds. Since traffic was pretty non-existent on the county road, I finally craned my neck around to see what he was watching behind us.

Skip Swenson waved to me from behind the wheel of his car.

"Jimmy Olsen has us tagged," Alan announced.

"I see that," I said. "The kid is persistent, I have to give him credit for that."

"And he's obviously not worried about us 'making' him, either," Alan added, sticking his hand out the window to wave back at Skip. "He must have been pulled off into one of those driveways I passed right when I exited the camp, and because there was so much forest and winding roads, I didn't see him until now. He thinks you're going to give him his shot at that internship, Bob."

I leaned my arm on the open window frame and watched the forest turn into rolling hills. "Maybe I'll do just that."

"Uh oh," he said. "I'm not sure I like the sound of that. You know something I don't?"

"Maybe. Maybe not. That's why I want to see the ATV track again."

"I thought we were going Bobwhite hunting."

"We are," I assured him. "Turn left at the next road."

While Alan drove, I reviewed the pieces of information that had just assembled themselves into a partial picture in my head. The land that Chuck owned abutted Kami's land, making a big piece of real estate when combined—certainly large enough to accommodate both a manufacturing plant and a testing ground for ATVs. For whatever reasons—personal or professional—Chuck opposed the eco-community's bid for his land, and was secretly funding the recreational lobbyists to block the development. Ben, the middle man for the funds, had, meanwhile, pressured Kami to withdraw her support for the eco-community project, which would presumably remove an obstacle for the lobbyists. Failing to get Kami's compliance, though, Ben had—according to Kami—plotted to get control of her land by marrying her.

Yet that ploy hadn't worked for Ben, either, nor did it explain why he would be so quick to identify Kami as a leading suspect in Jack's death.

Unless he wanted Kami herself removed from the property and into a jail cell, leaving behind a choice piece of real estate already eyed by an ATV company, who would be happy to build next to a tract of land that was already popular with ATV riders.

And as for Nigel . . . that's where the three-ring circus came in.

"Ride on the Wild Side," Skip had said.

Couldn't get much wilder than a full-grown tiger, could it? I happened to know from very recent experience what a rush of adrenaline one got when face to face with a cat that big. Combine that up-close thrill with a challenging trail, and I bet you'd have the entire American population of ATV riders flocking into town.

Talk about a cash cow.

Or cash tiger.

That was what Ben really wanted from Kami—her property *and* Nigel. For all I knew, maybe the mayor was even planning to bring in some other exotic animals to place along the ATV trail. If, as I suspected, Kami's land sat next to the wasted prairie Tom and I had seen yesterday while looking for Bobwhites, then it would be a simple job for Ben to run that same ATV trail right along Kami's property line. Nigel would hear the noise of the ATVs, come to investigate, and pace behind the electronic fence. Maybe he'd do some roaring, or sprint along the fence. I could imagine how that would play in marketing the ATV park—"Race with the tiger at Ride on the Wild Side!"

Poor Nigel. All Kami wanted to do was give the big cat a sanctuary, but Big Ben was ready to turn him into an ATV side-show.

For a price, of course. And according to Stan's snooping, it was a pretty nice price sitting in that off-shore account that belonged to Big Ben. My guess was that the mayor had a back-room deal going with the ATV manufacturer to deliver both Kami's property and Nigel for use in developing the biggest ATV manufacturing facility/recreational park imaginable.

"Pull in over there," I instructed Alan as we approached the turn-off by the ruined grassland.

He put the car into park and stared out the front windshield. "There are Bobwhites here? You're kidding me, right? This looks like the setting for a post-apocalypse movie, not a birdie heaven."

I popped open the door and pointed towards some wire fencing stretched between trees about two hundred yards away on the edge of what was left of the prairie. "I saw that fencing yesterday when Tom and I were here, but it didn't mean anything to me at the time. I want to see if it's electrified."

"Electrified?"

"Because if it is, I bet you dollars to doughnuts that it's Kami's fence, which means this is the piece of land that her sister owned. That Chuck now owns. That the ATV manufacturer wants. That Jack wanted to build the eco-community on."

"This is the house that Jack built," Alan recited. "This is the malt that lay in the house that Jack built. This is the mouse that . . ."

I got out of the car and slammed the door behind me. "This is Bobwhite Acres, Alan. This is the Bobwhite that Jack was afraid that Ben was trying to kill."

Alan came around the car to join me and surveyed the scarred acres in front of us. "I think he was too late. This land looks pretty dead already."

"That's why he wanted it," I suddenly realized. "He wanted to use this property as a showcase for what the eco-community project could do: recover and revitalize ruined land. He knew this used to be a healthy habitat for all kinds of birds—including Bobwhites—and he had a vision to restore it. Maybe knowing it was his first wife's land made it all the more critical to him that this was the spot the eco-project could salvage. Maybe that's why he kept so much of it a secret from Shana, because he knew how she felt threatened by his memories of his first wife. Kami said that Shana seemed uncomfortable around her, so who knows?"

I scrambled down the little slope that led towards the old fencing. "I've got to see if it's electric."

"Mr. White!"

I turned to see Alan and Skip following me down the incline. I'd forgotten about our intrepid reporter tailing us.

"Mr. White, where are you going?"

"I'm taking a hike, Skip." I got within five feet of the fence before I saw the little warning tag tacked on it that read "No trespassing. Electrified fence."

I stooped and picked up a stick laying in the dirt by my feet and tossed it at the fence.

Nothing. No sizzle.

The fence was dead.

"This is the other side of Kami's land," I confirmed. "So this must be the property that her sister inherited and passed along to Chuck. The land everybody wants." I turned around to face Skip and Alan who had come to a stop just behind me. "Am I right, Skip? Is this the site the eco-community wants for Bobwhite Acres? The same place the ATV company wants for its manufacturing facility and test site?"

Instead of answering me, though, Skip went white.

So did Alan.

Then I noticed they were both looking past my shoulder.

I spun around in time to see Nigel come sprinting out of the trees to make a flying leap towards us.

I raised my hand and shouted "Stop!"

The big cat fell to the ground in a heap just inside the fencing.

I turned back to look at Skip and Alan, neither of whom, of course, knew about Eddie's electronic fence set inside the wire fencing perimeter. Their eyes were bugging out of their heads, their open mouths frozen in shock.

Alan was the first to recover and looked at me in awe. "Shit, White-man, I knew you were in tune with nature, but that was unbelievable."

Skip, on the other hand, managed to get his mouth closed just before his eyes rolled back into his head and he toppled over in a dead faint.

"Too much excitement for the boy reporter," Alan commented. "Maybe he should stick to restaurant reviews instead of investigative journalism."

We both knelt in the dirt to lift Skip up to a sitting position while he regained consciousness.

"Skip!" I patted his cheeks briskly. "You with us?"

After a moment or two, his eyes focused on mine. "Did I just see what I thought I saw? You stopped a full-grown tiger with a hand signal?"

Alan's gaze settled on my face, too. "Yeah, nature boy, tell us how you pulled that one off."

"What can I say?" I grinned, shrugging my shoulders. "I've got skills."

"Nobody has that kind of skill," Alan pointed out. "Something else is going on here, and you're not talking. Spill it, buddy."

I helped Skip stand back up and pointed to the fence and the groggy tiger beyond it. "There's an electronic fence inside the wire one. A friend of mine installed it for Kami to ensure Nigel doesn't get loose. He crosses the line, he gets a zap strong enough to bring him down. It doesn't last long and it doesn't really hurt him. Mostly it protects him, because if he did get loose, no doubt someone would take aim at him and shoot to kill."

A loud crack filled the air and a bullet hit the dirt in front of my feet. I immediately pushed Skip back down to the ground and covered his body with my own. Alan hit the dirt, too, rolling away from me towards a small dip in the earth.

"Don't make a move!" a woman's voice rang out.

I lifted my head very slowly to see Kami Marsden running towards me on the other side of the wire fencing.

She had a gun in one hand and a rifle in the other.

Which made me the proverbial sitting duck.

Quack.

CHAPTER
TWENTY-SEVEN

But since Kami didn't immediately line me up in her sights, I figured I wasn't duck stew just yet.

Instead, she tucked the gun in her shorts and aimed the rifle at Nigel. A dart zipped out of the barrel and imbedded itself in the big cat's haunch.

"That should knock him out for a while," Kami called to me. "The shock wears off pretty quick, and I want to be sure you all are gone before he wakes back up, or he'll think you want to play a game of predator and prey with him. If he only sees me, he'll follow me back to the house."

I sat up in the dust and pulled Skip up, too. "But you've got your electronic fence to keep him in. It worked great. He got the buzz when he crossed the perimeter, didn't he?"

Kami reached up and tugged the dead electric fencing down low enough to step over it so she could stand next to me. She held out her hand for me to see the small transmitter in it. "I used this, Bob. The remote. The electronic fence isn't finished on this side of the property yet."

I opened my mouth to comment, but nothing came out.

"The electronic fence isn't working?" Skip asked, his eyes wide. "You mean, if you hadn't used that remote control, the tiger would have landed on Mr. White here?"

Kami turned her pixie smile on the boy. "Maybe," she said. "That would have been a surprise, huh?"

Holy shit.

I waited for my head to stop spinning and my lungs to drag in some air before I could ask Kami the next question. "If the electronic fence isn't working on this side of your land, what is Nigel doing over here?"

Kami traced a small circle in the ground with the tip of the rifle and then glanced over at me. "Good question. Especially since he was securely contained this morning when I left for the youth camp. After I saw you there a little while ago, I came home to find his tracking signal was outside the electronic perimeter, so I hustled out here to locate him and herd him back home. Obviously," she said, jamming the rifle into the ground, "someone's messing with my fence."

"While you were at the youth camp," I added. "Someone who knew you weren't home shut down your system."

"That's what I figured," she agreed.

It suddenly dawned on me that Alan wasn't participating in this conversation. I looked around for him, but couldn't see him anywhere. "Alan?"

"I thought I saw him roll in that direction," Kami said, pointing off to my left.

Skip and I stood up and walked towards the small dip in the ground.

Only now, the small dip wasn't so small anymore.

Actually, it was more like a fissure. A fissure about five feet deep.

Alan was sitting at the bottom of it, his elbows propped against his knees. I squatted down on the edge of the rough earth and sent a little cascade of rocks skittering down to Alan.

"Weirdest thing," he said. "I dove into that little dip and the whole thing gave way right under me."

"Get him out," Kami whispered urgently in my ear. "Alan, stand up slowly," she told him.

Alan looked up at Kami, who had retreated a few steps back from the lip of the fissure. "This is karst country, isn't it?"

She nodded.

"Karst?" I asked. "What's karst?"

"It's a region where the land has been shaped by layers of limestone that have been dissolved over the course of time," Skip explained. "Underneath are caves. There's a lot of karst country in Fillmore County. We learn about it in school," he added.

"The little dip that was there when I hit the ground just sort of opened up beneath me," Alan said. "I figure it might have been an old sinkhole that just gave way a little more."

"I hope that's all it was," Kami said, continuing to wave Alan up out of the fissure. "Because if it wasn't, it could mean you're standing on top of a cavern roof that's just about to collapse."

Definitely not what I wanted to hear. How in the world was I going to explain to Lily that I lost her groom-to-be when he fell through a hole in a wasted prairie and ended up somewhere in the middle of the earth?

I reached my hand out to Alan. "Just put her there, buddy. No spelunking for you."

He grasped my hand and braced his foot against the crumbly side of the hole while I tugged him up and over the rim. All four of us backed away from the edge of the fissure.

"Does that happen a lot around here?" Alan asked Kami. "Holes suddenly opening up?"

She shook her head. "Not that I've heard, but Jack had a theory that all the ATV traffic on this piece of land might be damaging more than just the earth's surface right here. Depending on how many caverns are below us, and how extensive or fragile they are, the vibrations of the ATVs could be weakening those formations. It was one more reason we really want to reclaim this land for an eco-community—the surface development would actually help protect what's underneath."

"Well, duh!" Skip exclaimed.

The three of us turned to Jimmy Olsen.

"Duh what?" I asked.

"That's the story I need to land my internship—how tigers are once again finding a home in southeastern Minnesota, but this time, they're involved in preservation, not predation!"

"Come again?" Alan asked.

I smacked my forehead with the heel of my hand. "The saber-tooth cat skull they found. It was in this area, a place called Tyson Spring Cave. It's part of a huge network of underground caves in Fillmore County."

"That's right," Kami said. "It was just a few years ago. A couple of cavers were exploring one of the streambeds that flowed through the caverns and stumbled on the skull. It brought a deluge of natural history buffs down here. I guess it really shook up everyone's idea of what Minnesota was like thousands of years ago."

Now that my memory had been jogged, I recalled reading several articles about the discovery in newspapers and the journal published by the state Department of Natural Resources. Since Minnesota had been mostly covered by glaciers in the last ice age, no one expected to find many traces of Pleistocene creatures like the extinct stag-moose or the saber-tooth cat—species which preferred drier, ice-less environments—in southeastern Minnesota. Yet bones of both were unearthed in Tyson Spring Cave after the cavers reported their find, which meant that even more ancient animal skeletons might be waiting for explorers deep in the limestone tunnels that riddled the county. As a birder who regularly sought out the unusual and rare when I indulged in my hobby, I could only imagine the excitement and thrill of paleontologists when an unexpected ice age animal artifact turned up in a place no one had thought to investigate.

Did paleontologists report their finds on a list serve the way birders did?

"Jenny and I were scuba-diving through flooded narrow crevices about a hundred feet below the surface of the earth when my headlamp happened to catch the glint of a prehistoric snail shell embedded in the wall. We think it's a discus macclintocki, but I wasn't able to get a photo of it. It should be there a while, maybe another couple thousand years, if you want to try and see it. The dive wasn't too bad, unless you have trouble with the completely mind-bending darkness we had when my headlamp went out. Jenny only screamed for about two minutes, though. Good luck."

Skip, meanwhile, was outlining how he'd put his story together to connect the ancient saber-tooth cat with Kami's Nigel.

"They're both megafauna," he reminded us. "Both big cats. How cool is that? One is extinct and played a role in the eco-system here twenty-two thousand years ago, and now Nigel is here, a walking symbol of ecological preservation, right next to where they want to build Minnesota's first eco-community. I think this story could really rock."

"It would certainly rock the plans of the ATV manufacturer," Alan observed. "You start promoting this site as a possible prehistoric find, and there's no way the council is going to rezone it for commercial use, let alone give anyone permission to develop an ATV riding park here. Soil erosion is already a huge problem for the state's engineers, and they sure aren't going to want to encourage more of that happening here, especially if it threatens a natural history goldmine."

Goldmine.

Renee's words from last night came slamming back into my head.

"He kept telling us that one day he was going to find a goldmine in Fillmore."

I turned to Kami. "Does Ben know about the caves? I mean, the caves that might be under your property?"

She drew her handgun out of her shorts and slid it neatly into the holster strapped to her leg. She noticed me watching her, and smiled that pixie smile of hers. "When Nigel's loose, I bring both kinds of ammunition. I don't want to hurt him, but if he's a danger to somebody, I won't have a choice." She tapped the butt of the gun. "It's also useful in getting a person's attention."

"Worked for me," I said.

"Sure, Ben knows about the caverns around here," she replied in answer to my previous question. "Like your young friend here explained, the kids learn about it in school. It's a great opportunity to learn about earth science when your backyards are sitting on top of unusual geological formations. All the kids around here go exploring at some point. I know we did, when we were growing up." She shrugged. "Not a whole lot else to do when you're a kid in Fillmore County."

"But I mean about your property in particular, Kami. Do you know for a fact that there are caverns beneath it?"

"I've never been in any, if that's what you're asking."

"Has Ben?"

Kami tipped her head to the side and considered my question. She tapped the rifle tip on the ground a few times, frowned, then suddenly froze.

"Yes. Now that you mention it, he has. I'd forgotten about it. When we were about—oh, I don't know—maybe fourteen, he told me that he'd found a cave entrance near the seepage meadow on the other side of my parents' property. He wanted me to go in the cave with him, but I wouldn't do it." She glanced at Nigel, who was beginning to stir. "I hate bats," she said. "I was afraid there would be bats in the cave."

"Man, I hate bats, too," Alan agreed. "There was this old house Bob and I roomed in our senior year in college, and we could hear the bats flying around in the attic on some nights. Creeped me out. One night I opened the closet door in my bedroom, and this bat comes whipping out of there. I almost had a heart attack. I don't think I opened that door again the whole time we lived there."

"You didn't," I reminded him, "because the next morning, you took all your stuff out of the closet and taped all around the edges of the door with duct tape. Triple-taped it as I recall. In fact, by the time you were done, nobody could tell there was even a door underneath all the tape."

"It worked, didn't it? I didn't have any more bats in my room the rest of the year."

I rolled my eyes and caught a glimpse of Nigel shaking his head.

"The seepage meadow," I asked Kami, "is it where I ran into Eddie yesterday?"

She nodded in agreement, walking back towards the wire fencing where she'd pulled it low. She stepped over it back onto her property, then turned and stretched the fencing up as high as she could reach. "You guys need to go. I don't want to give Nigel another dose of sedative."

I watched the tiger blink sleepily as Kami approached him, crooning his name. He was a beauty, his coat shiny and thick, his orange and black stripes vivid against the green backdrop of the woods that bordered the wasted prairie. Living in southeastern Minnesota, at least half a world away from his native land, obviously agreed with Nigel. With Kami as his keeper, he was living the good life, safe from big-game hunters and poachers. I wondered how he'd match up in size to the saber-tooth cats that had preceded him in this area twenty-two thousand years ago. Maybe Skip really did have a tiger by the tail—figuratively speaking, of course—with this article he was talking about writing. I knew that the idea of huge cats stalking prey sure changed how I viewed Minnesota's distant past. When I was a kid, the big prehistoric hits at the Science Museum in St. Paul were the giant beaver skeleton and the claw from an enormous ground sloth. I think there might also have been some bones from musk oxen and maybe even a woolly mammoth or two. Large lumbering herbivores, every one of them.

Not exactly fodder for exciting boyhood fantasies. As far as I know, no film director has been inspired to produce a sci-fi thriller called "Sloth Park." Watching slow-moving beasts shuffle across the big screen didn't sound especially compelling, if you ask me. But a saber-tooth cat? Now, that was cool. I had to believe that Skip would be able to catch some editor's eye with a piece about a prehistoric predator and its contemporary descendent.

As I climbed back into Alan's car, though, I began to wonder about another, entirely different type of predator.

One who might be preying on Kami in order to gain access to a subterranean goldmine . . . of fossils.

CHAPTER
TWENTY-EIGHT

S o what do you know about the fossil trade?" I asked Alan as he followed my directions to the seepage meadow where I'd first made Nigel's acquaintance yesterday.

"Only the little I gleaned from a program on the History Channel," he replied.

No surprise there. The History Channel was another one of Alan's favorite pasttimes. Even when we roomed together in college, I'd find him up late into the night, glued to shows about naval battles during World War II, or the training of Japanese samurai, or secrets from Confederate army diaries. Those shows put me to sleep in the first ten minutes of the telecast, but for Alan, they acted like prescription-strength stimulants.

I hoped Lily was ready for a lifetime of boring documentaries.

Then again, not everyone is crazy about my hobby, either. When I was in high school, my buddies called me the Bird Nerd. It wasn't till I was in college that my pals came to appreciate the extent of my ornithological expertise: I can't remember how many times our team squeaked out a win for the free pitcher of beer at the local bar on Trivia Night because I was the only person in the place who knew the Latin name of the American Robin. Believe me, my buddies developed a whole new respect for my chosen avocation.

"And what does the History Channel say?" I asked Alan.

"Apparently, fossils are big business," he replied. "And there's a brisk commercial trade for them, too, which has opened more than one can of worms. On the one hand, you've got the scientists—the paleontologists—trying to preserve collection sites because so much of what they can learn about the fossils and the animals they once were depends on the little details they find around them."

"You mean like nesting materials, or prehistoric dunghills," I prompted him.

"Exactly. The site of a fossil find is critical to understanding the fossils themselves. So the paleontologists want all that preserved. Most of the commercial collectors, on the other hand, don't give a rip about the integrity of the sites because all they want to do is cash in on selling the fossils to everyone from tourist gift shops to fancy interior decorating firms to museum curators looking for rare display pieces. And since some of the best fossil finds—especially dinosaurs—seem to be in North America, international buyers, both museums and private collectors, are ready to shell out big bucks to buy American."

"And the government doesn't have a problem with that?" For all the other facets of life that our politicians wanted to control, I found it hard to believe that this particular industry was escaping regulation.

"America is wide open for business when it comes to fossil sales, Bob," Alan reported. "Other countries have laws about the export of fossils, but not the United States. As a result, any private individual who owns the land can legally sell what he finds on it. Or underneath it. And that's just the legal market we're talking about. I have to believe there's an illegal market as well."

"The black market for bones," I observed.

"Yup." He made the right hand turn off the main road towards the meadow along Rice Creek, just as Tom had done the day before. His car navigated the rutted road a whole lot better than Tom's old beast, though. I didn't get my head bounced against the ceiling even once.

"What exactly are we looking for here?" Alan asked, easing the hybrid over the bumps in the track. "For some reason, I get the distinct impression that this stop isn't about adding to my very short list of birds for the day."

"Very astute, professor. We're trading in our binoculars for caving equipment."

Alan shot me a look of panic. "You have got to be kidding me. No way am I looking for a cave. Bats, remember?"

I socked him lightly on his right shoulder. "Gotcha, didn't I?"

"Not funny," he answered. "It also wasn't especially funny when I felt the ground give way beneath me back in that prairie, Bob. I didn't see my life flash before my eyes, but I did think about Lily."

"So did I. I thought she'd kill me if you disappeared from the face of the earth, especially if it was during my watch."

Alan laughed. "Your sister is a marshmallow. You have no idea."

"You're right," I said. "I have no idea. And I never will. She lives to boss me around. I was kind of hoping maybe she'd direct some of that bossing around at you, now, and that she'd give me the break I so richly deserve."

"You marry Luce, and I'm sure Lily will let up. She'll just pass the torch to her."

"Luce doesn't boss me around. Luce is the easiest person in the world to live with."

"So why aren't you living with her?"

That made me pause. Why wasn't I living with her?

"I guess I'm just an old-fashioned kind of guy," I finally said. "Besides, the point is now moot, isn't it? I lost the bet. I'm going to propose to Luce, get married and live happily ever after with her."

Even as the words left my mouth, I felt stunned by how right they felt to say. I was going to spend the rest of my days and nights happy with Luce.

The earth moved beneath me in revelation.

"Geez!" Alan hissed as we heard a rock scrape the car's undercarriage.

Oops. My mistake: it wasn't a revelation after all, just the car jolting over the lousy road.

"I'm going to end up with some damage thanks to this track," Alan groused. "You'd have to have a car built like a tank to get in and out of here to avoid any repair bills."

"Just pull into the grass and park," I told him. "We're going to be walking all around the meadow, so you might as well get off the road."

"Gladly." Alan glided a few feet into the meadow and switched off the engine. Silence filled the afternoon.

I got out of the car and surveyed the meadow. To one side, Kami's wire fencing stretched along the grasses; the big hole in the fence that had tempted Nigel was still there, though the torn wire had been cleared away. Walking closer to the fence, I tossed a stick at the wires to gauge if it was electrified. As Eddie had said, it wasn't, and the stick fell to the ground without striking a spark.

"And that was supposed to make me feel more secure in case Nigel shows up?" Alan asked from behind me. "Knowing that this little old wire fence is absolutely useless in defending itself against a stick, let alone a full-grown tiger?"

I pointed at the fence in front of me and repeated to Alan what Eddie had explained to me. "None of this is electrified anymore, Alan. It's to keep people off Kami's property, not to secure Nigel inside it. The fence to keep Nigel in is invisible, and it's set up about ten feet inside of this one that you see. The wire fencing might give you some peace of mind, but it's the invisible one that does the job, and as long as it's operating, Nigel's not leaving the farm."

"Plus he has that collar that Kami used to zap him, right?"

"Right. It gives her a back-up for restraining him. And it's got a tracking device so she can check on his location anytime. That's how she knew he was by the ATV track."

"Slick. Though I guess you want the slickest system you can find if you're going to be keeping a tiger on your property." He squinted into the sun beating down on the meadow. "Of course, that system is only good as long as it's not compromised, which seems to beg the question of who else has access to Kami's control center?"

"That is the question, all right," I agreed. "I know that Eddie upgraded it because he said that he designed the new invisible fencing system, but other than the company that helped him install it, I don't know who else might even know about it."

Alan squinted my way. "Ben?"

"Good chance, I'd say. If he had a key to the house, I'd expect he'd know about the security system. At the very least, we know that whoever could access it to turn it off today also knew that Kami wasn't at home, or at least, came calling and found she was gone, leaving the perfect opportunity to sabotage another piece of the fence. Wait a minute," I interrupted myself. "If someone came to Kami's house this morning, there might be a record of it."

I pulled out my cell phone to place a call. "If Eddie's monitors caught Jack and Billy's cars at Kami's place on Friday night, then that means there are mounted cameras somewhere near her house. As long as those cameras were running this morning, they would have captured any visitors." I tapped in Eddie's number and after a short conversation with him, ended the call.

"He says the cameras are motion activated," I told Alan, "so if someone parked near the house, it will be on the surveillance loop."

"And then you'll have a suspect. At least for sabotaging Kami's fence."

"Right." I waved my hand out at the meadow. "And, if I'm not mistaken, I think we're going to find the motive for Jack's death right here in this meadow. Start looking for water trails, Alan. One of them is going to lead us to that cave Ben wanted to show Kami decades ago."

"A cave filled with prehistoric fossil specimens?"

"Either that, or it's the entrance to a network of caverns. My guess is that the caverns lead under Kami's property—that would explain Ben's sudden urge to marry Kami now after all these years. He'd get joint title to the property and would own whatever he found. This seepage meadow isn't part of Kami's parcel—it's state land, and no one can claim any fossils found on it, or underneath it. But Kami's land is privately owned, which means whoever lives upstairs can legally explore the basement."

I shaded my eyes with my hand from the glaring sunlight, straining to see if I could spot some creeks sparkling in the meadow, and another piece of the Ben puzzle fell into place.

"That's why Ben hasn't publicly supported the ATV manufacturer and the recreational vehicle park," I realized. "He doesn't want them to have the land any more than he wants an eco-community built on it. He's hoping the whole conflict will come to a stalemate with the zoning council, and then, Chuck's property, which is already trashed, won't be worth anything to anyone else. He'll be able to snap it up at a bargain, combine it with Kami's place, and bingo! He's sitting on top of his personal, prehistoric goldmine."

"Assuming Kami marries him, which I think is looking pretty doubtful given her rather distraught reaction to your comments this morning, Bob," Alan reminded me. "And even if she did, that still doesn't guarantee the council is going to stall out on making a decision favoring either of the other two parties—the ATV gang or the eco-community group. Typically, in local cases like this, one or the other party will get the nod. That's still a hurdle if Ben wants ownership of the land."

I ran my hand through my hair. "No, it's not, Alan. Ben might be taking a low profile in this debate, but the fact is, he has a lot of pull in this county. Ask anyone. Big Ben plays the fiddle down here and everybody dances. Besides, as a local boy, he's probably got long histories with enough council members to guarantee that nobody gets the nod to develop that property unless he says so. As for the ATV people, they must think he's working behind the scenes to help them out, especially since he's funneling Chuck's money into their lobbying group."

"But you think he's playing them for fools, using them to stonewall the eco-community while he manipulates the zoning council to shut both groups out."

"That's exactly what I think," I assured him. "If nobody can get the zoning they need, the land can't be developed, which means the buyers go away, and the property continues to sit and deteriorate."

"Which drives the price of the land even further down."

"Absolutely. Then Ben, Chuck's good old family friend, offers to take the property off his hands at a bargain price. Chuck can say 'good riddance' to a painful reminder of his quarrel with his father, and Ben gets legal rights—at a cut-rate price—to whatever he finds underground, maximizing his bone-selling profits."

I scanned the meadow again and caught some sun reflecting off the surface of a stream that meandered through the sedge. "I'm starting with that one," I said, striding towards the little ribbon of water. "Don't fall through the earth again, Alan. Or if you do, yell really loud so I can hear you."

"This is crazy!" he called after me. "We don't know anything about finding caves."

"You're never too old to learn, Hawk," I shouted back to him. "Don't you have some secret Lakota trick for finding water?"

"Yeah," he yelled to me. "It's called 'look for a faucet,' White-man."

I could feel a grin pulling at my mouth. Maybe having my best friend as my brother-in-law was going to be all right after all.

CHAPTER
TWENTY-NINE

Two hours later, though, neither I nor my sister's fiancé had found anything remotely resembling an entrance to an underground network of caverns. Even though I was convinced that the seepage meadow was hiding something, I hadn't been able to locate it. Defeated and hungry, we decided to take a break for lunch and drove back to Spring Valley and the A&W. Along the way, I tried the phone number that Eddie had given me for Kami Marsden. I wanted her to check her surveillance records for any cars that had visited her place in her absence that morning. Unfortunately, I only got her voice mail. I left a message explaining what I was looking for and asked her to let me know as soon as she could.

We'd just sat down with our menus when Jimmy Olsen showed up at our table.

"Hey, Mr. White! Mr. Thunderhawk," Skip greeted us, his brown and orange cook's apron reaching almost to his knees. "You fall into any more holes?"

Alan shook his head. "Nope. The earth has been steady under my feet, Skip. How about you?"

Our junior reporter tipped his head toward the grill behind the front counter. "I'm on shift till five. But then I'm working on my article about the big cats. Gotta run—my manager's giving me the evil eye."

As he scurried back to the kitchen, the front door of the restaurant opened and in walked Shana and Tom. I waved them over to our table.

They looked miffed.

"Bad morning with Chuckie?" I asked.

"Yes, you could say that," Shana answered, a hint of irritation in her tone. "You could also say that the only thing standing between you and a jail cell for assault is one very kind and understanding sheriff who has taken pity on me for being both widowed and pregnant," she added. "Frankly, I think the sooner we all get out of town, the happier Sheriff Paulsen will be. My ongoing drama with Chuck isn't helping her focus on solving Billy's murder."

"So she's closing the book on Jack's murder?"

Tom shrugged. "She's got the gun that killed him, and it was in Billy's car. That's good enough for her, I guess."

Alan and I exchanged a glance.

"It may not be once Kami comes to town," Alan noted.

"What about Kami?" Tom asked.

I filled him in on our morning's conversation with the tiger lady. When I finished, Shana groaned.

"Are you all right?" three male voices—Alan's, Tom's, and mine—nervously inquired.

Shana shook her head, her gaze fixed on the table in front of her. "It can't be Ben. He couldn't have killed Jack. They've been friends forever."

This was starting to sound like a Greek chorus. First Kami, now Shana.

"Money—lots of money—can make people do crazy things, Shana," I pointed out. "Even old friends."

"So what happened to Chuck?" Alan tactfully changed the subject.

"The sheriff basically told Chuck to go home to Minneapolis and let her do her job," Tom replied.

"Although she didn't say it quite that nicely," Shana reminded him.

"From my few interactions with the man, I doubt if anyone says things very nicely to him," I commented. "He doesn't exactly invite warm fuzzies, if you know what I mean."

Shana took a menu from the table and sighed. "Regardless, he was always a good son to Jack. All those years, it was just the two of them after Char died. I really don't know who was more dependent on the other—Jack on Chuck, or Chuck on Jack." She glanced at the menu briefly and laid it back down on the tabletop. "Even when I'm furious with Chuck, I can't ignore who he is and the importance of his relationship with Jack."

She gently stroked her belly as it nudged against the edge of the table. "Or his relationship with these babies. He's their big brother."

I kept my mouth shut, as did Alan and Tom. I wanted to remind her what an ass Chuck had been to her both yesterday and today, but I figured this was one of those misty-eyed pregnant-woman moments that I better not crush with cold, hard facts. The guy was a jerk. No question. But if Shana wanted to defend him and find some good in the bum, that was entirely her business. Secretly, I hoped that his new baby siblings threw up on him at every opportunity.

"You never know," Tom comforted Shana. "Maybe things will change when your babies come. Maybe he'll change."

Now I wanted to throw up. I know I'm usually Mr. Sensitivity, but I just couldn't get to that point when it had to do with Chuck O'Keefe. I kicked Tom's shin under the table.

"Ow! Actually," Tom added, throwing me a pointed look, "Sheriff Paulsen told us we all had till sundown to get out of her hair or she'll lock us up for obstructing her investigation."

"That's a little extreme, wouldn't you say?" Alan asked. "It's not like you guys are telling her what to do or compromising evidence, right?" He turned towards me and threw me the same pointed look I'd just gotten from Tom. "Right?"

I braced my hands on the table and tipped my chair back on its rear legs. "Why is everyone giving me that look? I'm not telling the sheriff how to do her job. I'm not contaminating evidence. I sure didn't sabotage my own car."

"Let's just say she wants a clear field, Bob," Shana said. "Without us around, she's got fewer people to distract her. I can't imagine having two murders in her county on the same day has made her happy. Especially when she's got two major buyers looking at property in her jurisdiction. Unsolved crimes aren't exactly the best publicity for attracting new investors into an area."

I dropped my chair back onto the floor. "Okay. I get your point. But I still have to wait on my car. It won't be repaired until tomorrow."

I looked out the front window of the diner just in time to see my car being driven into the lot at the Inn & Suites. A man got out from behind the wheel, went inside the lobby briefly, then came back through the hotel door to climb into the passenger seat of a tow truck marked "Don's Towing" that pulled up behind my car. Then the truck left the parking lot.

"I guess you don't have to wait after all," Alan said, watching the tow truck drive away. "Somebody must like you enough to make sure your car gets fixed even when the shop is closed."

At which point, Big Ben walked into the A&W, spotted us at our table, waved, and came over to join us. He gave Shana a light kiss on her temple and a squeeze of her shoulder. "How are you holding up, honey?" he asked her, concern evident in his voice.

"I'm okay, Ben. Thanks for asking. Did you get the auto shop to open and repair Bob's car?"

Ben smiled and gave us all a conspiratorial wink. "Sure did. Doesn't hurt to have a little pull with the local merchants now and then. I know you folks want to get home."

Not to mention off your back, too, I thought. Out of the corner of my eye, I caught Skip watching us intently from his post near the grill. Was he putting two and two together the way I had and coming up with Big Ben the Fossil Guy?

Speaking of which, I figured there was no time like the present to confirm a theory.

"Do you go caving around here?" I asked the mayor.

For just a second, the pupils in his eyes dilated.

Bull's-eye.

Score one for the birder.

"Sure I do," he casually answered. "Me and lots of folks in Fillmore. Why?"

"Just curious," Alan assured him. "We ran into Kami Marsden this morning while we were hunting for Bobwhites. It appears she's got some caves under her land."

Ben blanched. "Did she say that?"

"Not in so many words," I said. "But she thinks there's a good chance of it. Lots of karst country around here, right?"

"You could probably ask her yourself, Mayor," Alan suggested. "I think she was on her way into town to talk with the sheriff about a few things. What was that she told us, Bob? Something about a meeting on Friday?"

Ben's skin color drained another hue or two.

"Are you all right?" Shana asked him.

He rested his hand on her shoulder. "I'm fine. Just worn out is all." He turned back towards me. "So did you find your Bobwhite?"

"One of them," I said.

Shana and Tom both gave me incredulous stares.

"You did?" Tom asked.

"You didn't call us?"

I answered Shana first. "I didn't call because it wasn't a bird. It was a piece of property. Bobwhite Acres. The spot for the eco-community."

Now it was Shana's turn to go pale. "Bobwhite Acres?" she echoed.

"Yeah. A little birdie told us that was the name proposed for the community," Alan explained. "I'm guessing you didn't know that?"

Shana said nothing, just shook her head.

"He was naming it for you, Shana," Ben softly said. "He told me you said that Bobwhites were your favorite birds, ever since you fell in love with them one summer while you were still in college."

That was news to me. I'd always remembered that Shana loved eagles, just like I do. It was one of the things we'd had in common when we birded together.

I glanced at Shana's face then, and our eyes connected. And it hit me like the proverbial ton of bricks.

I wasn't the only one with a summer crush eighteen years ago.

Holy shit.

CHAPTER
THIRTY

Somewhere beyond the roaring in my ears I heard Tom's voice rising in excitement.

"You found a Worm-eating Warbler?"

I finally pulled my eyes away from Shana's and looked over to see Tom and Alan in animated conversation.

"Yeah, that's it. Worm-eating. Not worm-finding. I knew it was worm something."

"And you didn't call us?"

"We got sidetracked," I said, knowing that any birder worth his birdseed wouldn't take that lame excuse for an answer. I nodded slightly in Big Ben's direction, hoping that Tom would pick up my cue and not say anything about those sidetracks we'd filled him in on before the mayor's arrival.

Fortunately, Big Ben decided at that moment that it was time for his exit. He gave Shana another fatherly kiss on the top of her head and said he'd be in touch, then left the diner.

"He doesn't look like a killer," Tom commented as he watched the mayor go out the door.

"I don't think killers wear nametags identifying themselves as such," Alan responded. "It would be self-limiting in their line of work."

"He's not a killer," Shana insisted, staring at her menu. "Would everyone please stop saying that? He's Jack's oldest friend. He's hurting, too. Can we just get something to eat?"

I noticed she was avoiding making eye contact with me again. Or maybe it was just my imagination. Actually, I didn't really want to make eye contact with her again right now, either. At some point, I realized, we were going to have to talk about . . . Bobwhites.

And a summer I'd never forgotten.

I waved at Skip in the kitchen and he scooted out to our table. "Could you get a waitress over here?" I asked him.

"Sure thing," he said. "Coming right up. I didn't know you knew the mayor, Mr. White. He comes in here all the time. Usually he just gets a root beer float to go, but on Friday night he was in here really late with that guy from Canada."

"Canada?"

Skip turned to Shana. "I knew he was Canadian because he had that accent. You know, he said 'eh' a lot. Like 'oh, I'll have the onion rings, eh?' And he left some Canadian quarters in the tip money, too."

"Did you say Friday night?" I asked Skip.

"That's right."

I remembered the way Big Ben had reacted when Alan mentioned that Kami knew something about a Friday meeting, and was on her way to share it with the sheriff. Alan had been referring to Ben's afternoon meeting with Billy that Kami had secretly observed, but Ben didn't know that. On the other hand, if Ben had a meeting on Friday night with an out-of-towner in the diner, he'd have to reason that there was a good chance Skip wasn't the only person in town to note it, which meant it could have gotten back to Kami, which obviously had unsettled Ben badly. The question now was: how much of a nose for news did our intrepid cub reporter wanna-be really have?

"So, Skip," I said, "who was the Canadian?"

He flashed me a grin. "His name is Kurt Deregneur, and he owns a collections agency."

I caught the bemused look that Alan threw at Skip.

"He left his business card with the tip," Skip defended himself. "He wrote 'The onion rings were good' on the back of it."

"Collections? Like financial debts?" I knew that Ben was handling money for Chuck and the ATV group, and Stan had reported a big sum in the mayor's off-shore account. It didn't appear that Ben was hurting for cash, yet why else would he be involved with a collections agency?

"Not money," Skip clarified. "Collections like in museums. I looked his company up on the Internet. He specializes in representing collectors from Asia."

"Why would Ben . . ." Shana began to say, then stopped short as she obviously connected the same dots I'd used earlier to draw a possible picture of Ben's real motives in the eco-community versus ATV manufacturer controversy.

"He's planning to sell fossils," she concluded. "He's not working for Chuck, or the ATV lobby, or the eco-community. He's working for himself, and it's not even the land he's interested in—it's what's *underneath* it."

"Give the lady a cigar," I said. I glanced at Shana's tummy. "On second thought, bring her a big glass of milk," I told Skip. "We want those babies healthy."

"I'm not hungry anymore," Shana informed me. "I want to go to the hospital. The one where they took Bernie."

"Right now? I'm sure Bernie will call us when she's ready to be picked up."

"Yes, I know she will, but Bernie's not why I need to go to the hospital. My water just broke."

My eyes automatically dropped to her water glass on the table. It looked perfectly fine to me. No cracks. No cascading flood. "What are you talking about?" I asked, oblivious to Tom rising from his chair next to me.

"The babies," he calmly announced. "Shana's in labor, Bob."

"That can't be right," I inanely argued with him, even as I saw Alan pull out his cell phone to dial 911. "She told me she wasn't due for another two months."

"I lied."

"What?"

"I'm due in five weeks. But twins sometimes come early," Shana explained, breathing deeply as she pushed back from the table.

"They *usually* come early," Tom corrected her. "Just keep breathing nice and deep, Shana," he instructed her. "That's the way."

"Your ride will be here in a minute," Alan assured her. "Can you walk to the door?"

"I think so."

"Are you nuts?" I spit at Alan. "The woman's about to birth whales and you want her to walk?"

To my surprise, Shana laughed. Right there in the Spring Valley A&W, like she didn't have a care in the world, she laughed. "I can walk, Bob. Just help me up."

She started to stand, and Tom and I each took one of her arms to give her support. Alan was already at the diner's door, holding it open, and scanning the street for the ambulance he'd called.

"I don't know how to deliver babies," I told Shana. "You have to wait for the paramedics."

"I'm a trained paramedic," Tom said.

I gave him a panicked look, then refocused on Shana. "You have to wait for the other paramedics!" I commanded her.

"Bob, I've got some time here," she reassured me. "I only had the one contraction so far."

"That's one too many."

"My doctor said this could happen and it might still be hours before I deliver. And I'll probably end up with a C-section anyway."

Thank you, God, I prayed. But just in case . . .

"Where's the ambulance?" I shouted at Alan.

The sound of the siren cut through the afternoon air, and mere seconds later, Alan was waving the EMTs in our direction. A minute later, Shana was being escorted out the diner's door by two paramedics, one of whom looked back at Tom and me, obviously not sure which of us to address. "You want to come along, Dad?" he finally said to both of us.

"I'll go," Tom immediately responded and hustled out after them. I was rooted to the spot, still shaken from being called 'Dad.' It dawned on me that if my life had been different, if Shana hadn't left that following summer, if we'd become a couple . . . if, if, if. But the truth was that none of those "ifs" had happened. Shana was carrying Jack O'Keefe's twins, and pretty soon, she was going to deliver them. And the best baby gift I could think of was to find out who had murdered their dad.

"We've got to find Kami Marsden," I told Alan as the paramedics slammed the ambulance door on Shana and Tom, "and find out if she's got surveillance on her property from this morning. I bet you if we can find out who let the cat out of the bag—or the fence, as it were—this morning at her place, we'll find Jack's killer."

"Because a loose tiger and a murdered eco-community supporter are the best ways to drive down the price of a piece of land no one else is going to want?"

I nodded. "Yeah, something like that." I headed for my car in the Valley Inn & Suites parking lot. "I'm driving."

"Watch out, Fillmore County's finest," Alan laughed. "The birdman is back on the road."

I took a hard right out of the parking lot and flew towards Kami's sanctuary.

CHAPTER
THIRTY-ONE

Y ou think we'll arrive alive?"

I took a quick glance at Alan in my passenger's seat. His right hand held a death grip on the bar that sat just above his side window. I checked my speedometer and eased up on the gas. "Sorry," I told him. "I forget you don't drive with me often."

"And there's a reason for that, White-man. You scare the crap out of me when you drive on county roads."

"I'm a good driver, Alan," I assured him. "I just speed a little when I'm focusing on other things."

"Such as?"

"Catching a killer."

"You think it's the mayor, don't you? That he offed his old friend to cinch a deal for himself."

"It looks that way to me," I said. "I think Billy called up Ben after he followed Jack to Kami's at Shana's request. Ben figured it was a perfect opportunity to ambush Jack and knock the eco-community group out of the picture, so he somehow got him to meet him at Green Hills."

"Where he shot him in the wee hours of the morning."

"Yes." Alan's recap of my reasoning only made me more certain I had Jack's murder solved. Big Ben had been playing the ATV and eco-community group against each other, secretly funneling Chuck's money to the lobbyists so it looked like he favored the ATV crowd, even while he wouldn't publicly support them. While the zoning council floundered, trying to make a decision, Ben had added fuel to the fire by tampering with Kami's fences to use Nigel as both a public relations nightmare and a choice bait: for the eco-community, Nigel's lack of containment was a serious problem, while for the ATV enthusiasts, he was a selling point for their playground. All along, though, Ben had just wanted the land to be ruled useless so its selling price would drop, at which point, he'd step in and snap it up, hoping to make his fortune from selling the fossils he knew were buried beneath it.

"What about Billy?" Alan asked.

"I think Billy knew too much about what Ben was really after, so Big Ben promised him a payoff at Mystery Cave, and instead, killed him, and then planted the gun that he used to shoot Jack in Billy's car."

"Too many loose strings in your theory, Sherlock," Alan said after a moment of silence. "For one thing—maybe the most important thing—Ben didn't need to knock the eco people out of the picture at all. In fact, he wanted the opposite. He wanted the group to keep butting heads with the ATV crowd so the whole mess would stay deadlocked while the land kept deteriorating and falling in value to anyone, except him. So killing Jack would have been a stupid move, since it might have caused the eco group to give up and pull out, leaving the property wide open for the ATV manufacturer."

Ahead of me, a Cliff Swallow dove across the road, then arced back up into the sky, where two more swallows were swooping through the air. Alan was right, Ben really didn't want a resolution to the zoning conflict for either party, so eliminating Jack would have been detrimental to Ben's grand scheme to acquire the land and its hidden fortune of fossils. To win the game he was secretly playing, Ben needed both Jack and the ATVers to stay up in the air.

"Loose string number two," Alan continued. "How could Ben convince Jack to meet him at an isolated spot in the middle of the night? Even if they were old friends, that's pushing it. And it's not like Ben could say, 'Hey, Jack, I know you're awake and driving out in the country at 3:00 a.m., so how about we split a really early beer at Green Hills?' Ben couldn't let Jack know he was tracking him through Billy."

Okay, that part bothered me, too. Especially if, as Shana had said, Jack had any reasons to suspect some dirty work from the ATV crowd. If he were being even remotely cautious, the last thing he would do was meet someone—best friend or not—alone in the middle of the night in an isolated birding spot.

But that's exactly what he had done.

"And as for killing Billy, because he knew Ben's big picture, that would be plain stupid, too" Alan concluded. "Billy worked for Ben. You've got to assume that he knew a lot of his boss's plans, in which case Ben trusted Billy not to betray him. Ben Graham isn't stupid, Bob," Alan said. "He'd be very careful about who was on his payroll. He'd make sure they were absolutely loyal to him one way or another."

"A bullet dead center ensures loyalty," I pointed out.

"Or at least silence," Alan added.

I watched the three swallows wheeling in the sky. Suddenly a Red-tailed Hawk sped past the swallows, making a steep dive at its next meal of some unfortunate rabbit or rodent scurrying across a field of young grasses. The three swallows quit their acrobatics, and peeled off in separate directions. Watching them gave me an idea.

"What if someone else got into the picture?" I wondered aloud. "Someone who wanted to force the zoning council into a decision for his own reasons and thought the way to do that would be to kill Jack?" I thought about the scattered swallows. "That would ruin Ben's plans, but it might be the solution to someone else's problem."

Alan let out a low whistle. "Someone who wanted the ATV project to get started."

"Maybe." I suddenly recalled seeing the back of Renee's sweatsuit last night as she returned to her room and realized what A-Man stood for. I thumped on the steering wheel.

"Ackerman! That's it! Secure A-Man is Ackerman!"

"Come again?"

My foot fell a little more heavily on the gas pedal. "I think the Ackermans own a company called Secure A-Man. A-Man: Ackerman." I threw Alan a quick glance to make sure he was following my train of thought. "Their company is the one that worked with Eddie last week to install Kami Marsden's new invisible fencing. Eddie said the owner was an old friend of Kami's, and Renee and Kami went to school together."

"So Kami gave a job to an old friend."

"Yes! And so guess who knows the security system that mysteriously keeps going down and letting Nigel out?"

"The same man who's the chief lobbyist for the ATV group," Alan replied.

"Yes! Also the same man who knew exactly what was wrong with my brakes."

"So you think Mac Ack killed Jack in hopes that the eco group would pack up and go home, leaving the ATV manufacturer he supported as the last man standing in the zoning dispute?"

"It fits," I insisted. "For all we know, Mac Ack might have a big juicy contract waiting with the ATV company to do all their security for the new facility and the park they want to build. If that's the case, Mac had a motive for killing Jack in order to speed up the project approval and get the construction started, so he could get some dollars pouring into his security company."

Up ahead along the road, I saw a mailbox marked "Marsden." I made a quick left, spinning my tires into the gravel that lined the driveway to Kami's place. Out of the corner of my eye, I saw Alan grab the window bar.

"But that doesn't give Mac a motive for killing you," Alan pointed out. "Unless he knew what a maniac you are behind the wheel and decided to do the rest of us a favor by getting you off the road permanently."

I hit a rut hard and we both bounced off our seats.

"I know, I know," I cut Alan off before he could say anything. "I'm slowing down. Really."

Once again, though, I had to admit Alan was right. Mac had no reason to want me dead. Now that I knew the note was about the eco-community's proposed Bobwhite Acres, I had no reason to think that Mac was in cahoots with Ben to murder me.

Someone else had wanted me out of the picture.

"And," Alan was saying, "Mac Ack has no motive to kill Billy that we can see. Not to mention that he was birding with you guys Saturday morning when the sheriff says Billy was killed. We're still missing something important, Bob."

I had to agree, which meant that Alan was right for a third time.

"Three strikes and I'm out," I muttered. "This is why I'm a counselor and not a detective."

"I thought it was because of the stellar pay we get at Savage High," Alan laughed. "That and the adoration of all the females in the student body."

"Please," I said. "I'm on vacation. Don't even think 'drama queen' around me."

The dirt driveway led to a paved apron in front of a small garage, which sat beside an old brick farmhouse. I parked the car behind a red pick-up truck. "I hope this means Kami is home," I said, nodding at the truck. "I want to see those surveillance tapes."

Just as I was going to push open my car door, though, Alan grabbed my shoulder and pulled me back against the seat.

"You don't want to do that right now," he warned me, pointing past me to a spot where trees edged the parking apron about fifteen feet from my side of the car. I followed his finger and saw the reason why.

Hello, Simba.

CHAPTER
THIRTY-TWO

Part of me wasn't surprised to see a full-grown lion crouching a few body lengths beyond my car. After all, Kami's place was an exotic animal sanctuary. It stood to reason that Nigel wasn't the only exotic animal on the property.

The other part of me, however, was busy wondering if that same full-grown lion could rip my car window out and drag me from my SUV for a late lunch. Suddenly, I could relate to every bunny or mouse that a Red-tailed Hawk had snatched for a meal. No one aspires to being an entrée.

"That is one big cat," Alan remarked as we both watched the lion approach the car. He ambled over—the lion, not Alan—and plunked himself down right outside my car door. I figured his face was a mere inches away from mine on the other side of the window.

"My, what big eyes you have," I told the lion. He gazed back at me, his amber eyes hypnotic.

"Nice mane," Alan added. "He's really got that natural look going for him."

"I hope Kami heard us drive up," I said, my eyes still locked on the lion. "Otherwise we're going to be sitting here a while, because Simba doesn't look like he's in a rush to go anywhere."

At which point, the lion heaved himself up from the ground and slowly strolled around the back of my SUV towards the farmhouse, where Kami was now standing on the front porch. She walked down the porch steps to meet the lion, who rammed his big nose into her stomach while she rubbed behind his velvety ears. She waved to us to come over.

I looked at Alan in my passenger seat. "What do you think, Hawk? Do you feel lucky?"

"Sure," he answered. "I've always imagined throwing myself to the lions. Besides, it can't be much worse than planning the wedding of the century, and so far, I've survived that, too."

We got out of the car—although I admit I was moving pretty slowly, just in case the lion didn't like sudden moves—and carefully approached Kami's porch.

"He won't hurt you," she assured us. "He's a sweetheart, along with being almost deaf. That's why he stays close to the house. It's familiar and safe for him." She patted the lion's big head. "He probably felt the vibration in the ground from your SUV and didn't recognize it—that's why he came over to check you out. His name is Claudius, by the way."

The big cat nuzzled Kami's shoulder. Being as tiny as she was, Kami barely stood a head taller than Claudius and had to brace herself against the step's railing so he wouldn't bowl her over. She made a circular motion with her hand and the lion turned around to face me.

"Let him sniff your hands," she told me and Alan. "Then he'll know you."

"You use hand signals with him," I commented, and she nodded. I reached out a palm for Claudius to smell. The lion's nose felt soft across my hand and I watched his big nostrils flare as he snuffled. "Yo, Claudius," I said.

"So what brings you out here?" Kami asked after Alan had likewise made the lion's acquaintance.

I lifted my eyes from Claudius's big muscular body and focused on Kami. "I want to see your surveillance tape from this morning to see if it caught whoever messed with your fence. Whoever did it would have had to come here to your farmhouse, wouldn't he? I'm thinking it might be the same person who killed Jack, someone who's apparently getting desperate for the eco-community to drop out and the ATV project to dig in."

Kami cocked her head to one side, apparently considering what I'd said, then pushed Claudius away from her shoulder. "Let's go take a look."

She turned on her heel and led us over to a side door into the garage. Claudius walked right behind her, as obedient as a trained dog. Once we were inside, she flipped a switch that lit up the small space outfitted with an array of state-of-the-art monitors and equipment. Various lights blinked while the soft hum of a generator made a soothing sound.

"Very cool," Alan offered appreciatively.

"Eddie Edvarg was definitely here," I said to no one in particular. My electronics whiz buddy had, as usual, spared no expense in setting up his client with a superior surveillance system. If anyone had set foot anywhere near Kami's farmhouse this morning, we were going to find it on a surveillance loop.

I felt a big furry head brush past my back and looked over my shoulder in time to see Kami leading Claudius back outside the small garage.

"Stay," she told him loudly, parking him next to her red truck. I could just catch her hand signal to the lion through the open garage door. Claudius dropped to the ground and sprawled out on the pavement. "Good Claudius," she practically shouted at him, patting his flank. The lion blinked and closed his eyes, and Kami rejoined us in front of the monitors.

"We'll just have to scan back through the tapes to this morning," she explained, punching a couple buttons on the control board.

"Did Mac Ackerman do your new fencing?" I asked while she continued to program the monitors.

"Yes, he did. I always hire people I know for jobs around the sanctuary, and Renee and I go way back."

"Yeah, she told me about it," I replied. "The Four Musketeers—you, Renee, Jack and Ben."

Kami gave me a confused look. "Only in her dreams."

My turn. I shot back an equally confused look at Kami. "What?"

"Renee was never close to Jack and Ben and me. She always wished she were, but it didn't happen. We were in the same class at school, that's all. In fact, in high school, I'm pretty sure she hated me, because Jack and I were a couple. She was crazy about Jack, and he wouldn't give her a second glance. Ben was always nice enough to her, but she was only interested in Jack."

"Wait a minute," I protested. All kinds of comments were rushing back into my head and I needed a moment to sort them all out.

"Renee was making eyes at Jack."

"All the girls were in love with him, including me."

"Renee knows the area. She's birded it with Jack."

"We waited a good half-hour for her to get back from that twenty-four-hour pharmacy with her allergy prescription. If it hadn't been for her, we could have gotten an earlier start on our birding. I mean, really, how could the woman forget her allergy medication at home when it's allergy season? Talk about being unprepared."

Rene Ackerman had been missing when we gathered to go birding yesterday morning. She'd had a teenage crush on Jack—a crush that may have survived well into adulthood, if Bernie's observation on Friday evening had been correct. She'd also seemed pleased to pass along the gossip that Jack was cheating on Shana with Kami, which might have explained that smug feeling I detected from her in the diner last night, but now I wondered if that gossip was a vengeful move against Shana and Kami both. Lord knows I'd seen that kind of behavior plenty of times from the teen girls I counseled at Savage High, especially when unrequited crushes came into the picture.

On top of that, Rene knew three things Jack's killer had to have known: one—Jack was in Fillmore County early Saturday morning (and a quick check of the hotel parking lot would have told her his car was gone); two—she knew the birding areas he knew because they'd birded together; and three—she had access to the plans for Kami's security system since her company had done the installation.

Had Rene decided to finally get even with Jack for his high school dismissal of her and called him to meet her for an unusual bird sighting at Green Hills, where she shot him? I'd figured that Jack had to know his killer, and Rene certainly fit that bill. And if Rene had also decided to make some long-anticipated payback to Kami for being Jack's high-school sweetheart, what better way than to sabotage the sanctuary fence and support a suspicion that Kami was a killer?

I watched the monitor as Kami manipulated the images to arrive at this morning's surveillance.

"Try mid-morning," I told her. "The time during which you were out at Green Hills."

She ran the recording further ahead. Now I expected to see Rene, not Mac, Ackerman drive up on the screen at any moment.

But what about Billy? I asked myself, my eyes fixed on Kami's monitor. How did he fit into a picture of Rene's plan for vengeance?

"I'm still missing something," I muttered. I turned to Alan who was hovering behind my left shoulder. "I can't make Jack's and Billy's murders hang together," I whispered, not wanting Kami to hear my speculation. "I think there's a chance that Rene killed Jack, but I can't figure out a connection to Billy."

Alan studied me for a moment or two. "One bird at a time, Bob, isn't that what you told me once?"

I wasn't sure what he meant.

"You know, when you're on the trail of a specific bird? You told me that you focus on one bird at a time, but if others show up, you'll be glad to spot them." He pointed to Kami's monitor. "Find Jack's killer first, and if along the way, you can find Billy's too, then you're ahead of the game. Right?"

"Yeah," I said, nodding at his advice. "One bird at a time."

"Here's a car!" Kami's voice was laced with excitement.

I looked back at the monitor's screen as a vehicle approached the sur-veillance camera.

But it wasn't Rene Ackerman behind the wheel.

It was Sheriff Paulsen.

Chapter
Thirty-Three

D arn it," I said. I'd forgotten that Shana had said the sheriff was going to come out to Kami's this morning, possibly to arrest her. Naturally we'd see her patrol car on the tape. "Any other cars?" I asked.

Kami shook her head. "That's it, Bob. But anyone who knows my security setup could conceivably manipulate it at some other point along the fence itself, I think." She looked up at me apologetically. "And whoever's been messing with my fence seems to know it well enough to do just that. Nice try, but we're not getting anything we don't already know from these recordings, I'm afraid."

"Although they're going to come in real handy when the prosecution builds its murder case against you, Kami."

The three of us spun around to find Sheriff Paulsen standing in the doorway of the garage. "Jack and Billy were both here late Saturday night. You've got the tapes to prove it. The same gun killed both of them, and Billy had a tranquilizer dart in his neck, a dart identical to the ones you use for your animals. You're the only one left, Kami. Simple arithmetic. Three minus two equals the killer. You're under arrest, Ms. Marsden, and anything you say or do will be held against you in a court of law."

"She has an alibi," I blurted out. "You can't arrest her."

The sheriff gave me a glare. "Are you her alibi, Mr. White?"

I shook my head. "No. But I can get you in touch with the man who is."

I pulled out my cell phone to find Eddie's number.

"Don't bother," Kami told me, her voice miserable. "Eddie can't vouch for me."

I looked at her in confusion.

"He was here on the property, but he was out camping. He can't swear to my whereabouts all of Saturday morning."

"What about Ben?" Alan asked. "Could he swear to it? Any of it?"

Kami threw him an angry glance, but said nothing.

"Could he?" I pressed her.

"Now that's an interesting question," Sheriff Paulsen observed, her voice sounding unnaturally tight. "Especially if this Ben you're talking about is Ben Graham. Is it?"

I looked from one woman to the other, and guessed that despite her earlier fury at the mayor, Kami hadn't gone to the sheriff with her suspicions and accusations about Ben's role in the property tug-of-war. For some reason, she was still protecting hers and Ben's privacy, or maybe, unlike Ben, she was too loyal to tip a murder rap in the direction of her lover. I guess love really is blind. Though if she and Ben had been together in the wee hours of Saturday morning, they'd be each other's alibi, effectively safeguarding them from prosecution.

At least, that's what I thought.

"Is it?" the sheriff repeated, her voice even more strained than before.

"Yes," Kami let out on a sigh of resignation.

For a moment or two, the sheriff just stared at Kami. "I'm still taking you in, Ms. Marsden. And as soon as I find Ben Graham, I'm bringing him in, too. He told me he was home alone on Friday night and I didn't question it. So who's lying here? You or him?"

I knew the answer to that one: Ben. According to Skip, Ben had been in the A&W late Friday night with the Canadian collections guy. Whether he'd moved along to Kami's after that, only she and Ben knew. And judging from Kami's reluctance, she wasn't happy about admitting it to the sheriff.

"Check the surveillance record," Alan proposed. "If Ben's car was here at the house early Saturday morning, you'll have your answer, Sheriff."

She turned to Kami. "I want to see it," she demanded. "Right now."

Kami punched more buttons on her control board until the recording on the monitor was dated for yesterday morning. We watched Jack's car back out and drive away, then Kami fast-forwarded the video to the time stamp of three in the morning. Sure enough, a nice looking Audi sedan came into the picture and parked. The big bear of a guy who exited the car and walked up to the front porch of Kami's home was, without a doubt, Ben Graham.

I slid a glance at the sheriff, her face suddenly suffused with heat.

"Not exactly the paragon of honesty you were hoping for in a mayor, I'm guessing," Alan observed.

"Not exactly," Sheriff Paulsen agreed through gritted teeth.

"He wants fossils," I informed her. "He's been playing the eco people and ATV lobby against each other to drive down the price of the land."

The sheriff latched her eyes on mine. "What are you talking about?"

I filled her in on the mayor's plan as Alan and I had assembled it, including Skip's report about the Friday meeting with the collections man. By the time I finished, the sheriff was moving rapidly into melt-down mode.

Clang! Clang!

Geez—first Kami at Green Hills, now the sheriff. Ben Graham seemed to have that effect on women down pat.

"So he's been using everyone and everything to get just what he wants," Sheriff Paulsen spit out.

"Looks like," I said, backing a little bit away from the irate lawwoman. I didn't want to get burned by the steam she was generating in the small space. "Though I guess the rule is still innocent until proven guilty, right?"

She threw me a scalding glance. "I know how to do my job, thanks."

"So Kami's off the suspect list?" Alan asked.

"No. And I want you two out of here, or I'll arrest you for the obstruction of justice. In fact, I want you to get out of the county before you totally screw up my investigation. Are you getting the message here?" She dropped her right hand to rest on the butt of the gun on her hip.

Great. Just because I'd stuck around to give Shana moral support, I was getting the boot from the law. I remembered that Tom had also said this morning that the sheriff wanted us all to go home, but she didn't have to get nasty about it.

I exchanged a look of frustration with Alan. I didn't want to leave, and I couldn't shake a bad feeling about the way the sheriff's investigation was going if she was planning to arrest Kami for Jack's and Billy's murders. It was like Sheriff Paulsen had already made up her mind about Kami's guilt, even after we'd shared with her all the information we'd collected about Ben. Actually, now that I thought about it, she seemed a lot more upset about Ben's potential fossil business than she did about the possibility that he might be involved in a double murder.

There was something odd about that.

But she was the law, and she was basically throwing us out of town. Being the good citizen that I am, I didn't see any alternative but to honor her wishes. Even if that still left me in the dark about who killed Jack O'Keefe and Billy Mason, not to mention who had sabotaged my car and in so doing, had sent Bernie to the hospital to get a plaster fashion statement cemented on her arm.

The hospital.

Shana was having the twins.

"Look," I said to the sheriff as the four of us exited the garage, "we'll leave Fillmore, but first I've got to stop at the hospital to see how Shana's doing. She was in labor when we came out here."

"She's having the babies?" Kami asked. "She's early. Jack said she had another five weeks to go."

"Twins usually come early," Alan advised her, "or so we hear."

"I want you to show me this fossil cave entrance that you say is in that meadow on the other side of Ms. Marsden's property," Sheriff Paulsen said, oblivious to our conversation about Shana's impending motherhood.

"I'll lead you to the meadow," I offered, "but Alan and I already searched for an entrance earlier today and we couldn't find it."

"I know where the meadow is," Sheriff Paulsen snapped. "It's the cave part I'm still not believing. Show me the cave, and then maybe we can make some sense of all this."

I'd already made sense of it, but I didn't want to point that out to her. She'd already snapped at me once, and I wasn't about to further upset a woman with a gun on her hip.

We walked past Claudius, who apparently hadn't moved since Kami had signaled him to lay down on the pavement. I guessed he hadn't been curious about the sheriff's car when it had come up the drive. He must have recognized it from this morning, when Sheriff Paulsen had first come to arrest Kami. I expected that Claudius could feel the vibrations of the damaged patrol car as it bounced into the parking area in front of the farmhouse. I remembered how yesterday morning, I was afraid the damaged shocks would send Shana into labor.

And that was when I thought she still had more than a month to go before her due date.

I walked over to my car while Sheriff Paulsen opened the back door of her cruiser for Kami to get in.

"I have to cuff you," I heard the sheriff tell Kami.

Adding insult to injury, I thought.

And I suddenly knew who had killed Jack O'Keefe.

CHAPTER
THIRTY-FOUR

I climbed in behind the wheel, stunned by my revelation, and just sat for a moment, trying to figure out my next move.

"Let's go, White-man," Alan said, snapping shut his seat belt.

I pulled out my cell phone and punched in a number.

"Where are you?" I asked Stan when he answered.

"Green Hills. Looking at a Worm-eating Warbler," he replied.

"I need back-up."

"Where?"

"At a seepage meadow on the west side of Kami Marsden's exotic animal sanctuary."

"Don't do anything stupid," he said. The dial tone buzzed in my ear.

"You want to tell me what's going on?" Alan asked as I backed up the SUV enough to turn it around.

"Sheriff Paulsen killed Jack O'Keefe."

"And you know this . . . how?"

I glanced at my future brother-in-law as I put the car in drive and took off down Kami's driveway to the main road. "You know how I'm always telling you that to be a really good birder, you have to be both observant and able to make fine distinctions? That two birds can look very similar, but if you know the one thing that distinguishes one from the other, you can correctly identify the bird?"

"Yeeaah," he said, drawing the word out.

I threw him another glance and noticed that he had grabbed the door handle again. I checked my speed and let up on the accelerator a little. There was, after all, a sheriff right behind me. Even if she was a murderess.

"Her anger about the fossils, Alan," I said. "That was the fine distinction that started everything else falling into place for me. And then I thought about how Claudius didn't seem interested in the sheriff's car—because it had been there earlier."

"She came for Kami. We knew that. We saw her on the surveillance tape getting out of the cruiser and then getting back in."

"But the tape didn't show us where she went," I persisted. "We assumed it was to the farmhouse, but the cameras didn't show that. I think she went into the garage and pulled the plug on Nigel's fencing, Alan. The time stamp on the video proved that Paulsen was right there during the exact time Kami figured someone shut down the fence."

"You're making a big assumption, Bob. She's the sheriff," he reminded me.

"She also knows where the meadow is, and when I rode in her cruiser yesterday morning with Shana, she told us she'd just damaged the car. You saw how bad those ruts into the meadow were. You drove especially carefully not to bang up the undercarriage of your hybrid."

"So her bumpy ride is why you think she killed Jack?"

"No," I explained, trying to make myself put it all in sequence for Alan, "I think Paulsen is the one who's been sabotaging Kami's fence as a favor to Ben. Either he asked her to do it, or she figured she'd score points with him for it because she thought he was supporting the ATV project behind the scenes."

I looked in my side mirror to see the sheriff's car following me by just a few car lengths.

"Eddie said the fence in the seepage meadow was malfunctioning after midnight on Friday," I continued. "Saturday morning, when Paulsen was driving Shana and me into town, she said she'd just recently damaged her car. I'm betting that happened when she was in the meadow pulling the fence, which places her on that road very early Saturday morning, which is the same time Jack and Billy were on that same road, coming back from Kami's. Three people on the same road at that time of night, two of them dead the next day. Coincidence? That's a mighty big stretch, if you ask me. Besides, did you catch what Paulsen said after we told her about Ben's fossil scheme? She said that Ben had been using everyone. Which sure sounded to me like she was including herself."

I turned out onto the main road and checked my rear view mirror. Sheriff Paulsen was right behind me, her eyes shaded by her standard-issue sunglasses.

"But why would the sheriff kill Jack, or Billy?" Alan persisted. "It's not a capital offense to be on a lonely country road in the middle of the night. You're missing a motive, Bob."

I was still working that out in my head. If Paulsen felt used by Ben, there had to be a reason.

A Bobwhite Killing

"She didn't know about the fossils," I reasoned, "but she was sabotaging the fence for Ben. I don't know—maybe he promised her a kickback from the ATV group when they got their project approved, or that he'd okay county funding for a new fleet of squad cars for the department if she'd help him squash the eco-community. Either way, she'd think she stood to benefit from doing his dirty work. That would be using her, for sure."

"You told me that everyone keeps saying that Ben is the big man in this county," Alan conceded. "He pulled strings to get your car fixed. Maybe he's got the sheriff in his pocket, too."

"Or in his bed," I said, surprising myself, then realizing that jealousy was exactly the vibe I'd picked up when Sheriff Paulsen had asked if the Ben about whom Alan questioned Kami was indeed Ben Graham. Believe me, I'm very familiar with that particular vibe after counseling high school drama queens for almost a decade. To be honest, I'd rather have a rattlesnake in my office than two jealous girls—at least with a rattler, you get some warning before the venom spews out. With hormone-driven teens—not so much. Counseling high school students isn't all fun and games, you know.

Nor was going on a birding weekend and ending up with a killer on my bumper.

"Okay, let's go with this," Alan said. "Ben says 'jump' and the sheriff says 'how high?' He doesn't share his fossil plan with her, but lets her think he's helping Chuck push the ATV park. She sabotages Kami's fence, thinking that'll move the ATV project forward and win her points from her lover. But then Jack catches her in the act Saturday morning on his way back from Kami's place, so she's got to get rid of him before he connects the dots to Ben and Chuck, and blows them all out of the water politically and professionally. Who knows? Maybe by that point, Paulsen figured that killing Jack was doing Ben a very special favor to move the ATV project forward."

"But now," I finished for him, "thanks to our filling her in on what's really going on with Ben, it turns out to be the wrong favor, since Ben didn't want the ATV project to succeed anyway."

My eyes flew to the rear view mirror again. The sheriff was almost in my back seat.

"I have a really bad feeling about this," I told Alan.

"Join the crowd," he said.

170

I put my foot down on the accelerator and my car surged forward, giving me breathing room ahead of the sheriff. Let her give me a ticket, I figured. If she pulled me over, I'd grab her through the window until Alan could jump out and put a headlock on her.

Of course, if all my suspicions were wrong, Alan and I would be sitting in jail before dinner time for assaulting an officer.

Where, at least, we'd be safe from Lily, who would undoubtedly want to kill us both.

This was one of the problems with my sister marrying my best friend—depending on the situation, Lily could now probably hit two birds with one stone: a Hawk and a Bob White.

And then it dawned on me how Ben Graham could have had a note about killing Bobwhite in his pocket on Saturday afternoon that Jack O'Keefe had written on Inn & Suites stationery on Friday night at Kami's place.

The police must have searched Jack's body and found the note and turned it over to Sheriff Paulsen for evidence. Seeing that it was about the eco-community, she passed it along to Ben so no one would make a connection between Jack's death and the zoning dispute. She was covering her tracks, in other words.

In my side view mirror, I could see that Paulsen was back on my bumper, and I knew in my gut that she was going to cover her tracks with us, too.

CHAPTER
THIRTY-FIVE

She's going to kill us at the seepage meadow," I told Alan.

"Yeah," he agreed, "I'm coming to that conclusion. How fast do you think Stan Miller drives?"

"I don't know." But I sure hoped he was as much of a speed demon as I was.

More of one, actually. I knew I would definitely feel better if I could be sure that Stan was already waiting for us at the meadow. Stan would have a gun.

Another two minutes of flying down the road and I took the bumpy path into the meadow.

Sheriff Paulsen was right behind me.

I scanned the edge of the forest as I slowly drove to the center of the clearing. A few Wilson's Snipes took flight from the open wetland in front of me.

No cars.

No Stan.

"Maybe we should call the police," Alan said.

"The police is the problem," I reminded him. "You call 911 and you're going to get Sheriff Paulsen. Newsflash: we've already got Sheriff Paulsen."

"Correction, White-man—she's got us."

I put the car in park and Paulsen pulled up next to my SUV. A moment later, she was standing about five feet away from my car door, telling us to show her the cave entrance.

"We didn't find one earlier," I reminded her.

"Let's all look," she insisted, waving us out of my car. "Except for Ms. Marsden. She can wait in my cruiser."

I got out of the car and started walking towards the right side of the clearing. "You take the left edge of the meadow," I told Alan over my shoulder.

"Oh no, I'd like us all to look together," Paulsen said. "That way, there's a better chance we'll find the entrance. You fellows lead." She pointed in the direction I'd headed.

I started walking towards the forest edge, with Alan beside me. The sun was warm on my arms and the back of my neck. From the other side of the meadow I could hear Horned Larks calling. Then I heard a slight sliding noise behind me and turned around to face the sheriff.

She had her gun aimed at the center of my chest.

"Oh for crying out loud," I said, figuring that my best chance at survival was to brazen it out. "We just started looking! Don't tell me you're going to shoot us because we haven't stumbled over the cave entrance in the first two minutes of searching for it."

Paulsen's hand was steady on her gun, and her voice was calm. "You're right. I'm not going to shoot you because you haven't found it yet. I'm going to shoot you after you find it, then dump your bodies in it, along with Ms. Marsden's. Then I'm going to find that lying, cheating, son-of-a-bitch Ben Graham and shoot him, too."

High time for a counseling intervention, I decided, my mouth going dry as I stared at the gun. Keep it conversational and non-threatening. Hopefully buy some time for my backup by the name of Stan to make a very welcome appearance, although I knew that Alan wasn't just standing there beside me, taking in the scenery. My best friend might be a pushover for my sister, but Alan backed into a corner was asking for trouble.

I just didn't want him asking for a bullet.

How was I going to explain that one to Lily?

"Sorry, Sis. He took a bullet a crooked sheriff meant for me. You know Alan—he's got that impulsive streak. Or at least, he did."

Shit.

"Okay," I agreed with Paulsen, praying that Alan would just hold off rushing the sheriff another minute or two while I formulated some kind of plan to save us. "I get the part about you being angry with the mayor, but what did the three of us do to get included in this plan of yours? Wrong place, wrong time? Bad karma? Bad breath?"

A tiny smile pulled at the corner of the sheriff's mouth. "You're an idiot, White."

"So I've been told," I assured her.

"You just didn't take the hint to get out of town, did you? After you called me last night with all that information about Ben's finances, I figured you were going to be a problem. You were too involved with Shana's situation to let it go. I've met enough birders in the last few years to know how obsessive and persistent you people can be when you set your sights on scoring a bird."

"The Worm-eating Warbler," I said, remembering how the deputies at the police station had complained about all the birders around Mystery Cave State Park a few years back. "You know all the birding spots."

I couldn't connect with her eyes through her sunglasses, but I didn't need to see the truth there as I realized she'd shot Billy, too.

"Why Billy?" I asked, unable to help myself.

"Why Billy?" she echoed. "Why aren't you asking 'why Jack,' or do you think that you've already figured that out?"

I could feel Alan shift slightly beside me.

"Don't even think about it," she warned him. "I'll put a bullet through both of your hearts before you even draw another breath. Conversation closed, boys. Find the cave."

I slowly turned back around and walked along the edge of the forest, wondering how long we had till Stan showed up. At the same time, I was beginning to question whether Stan's arrival was going to bail us out, since no matter which direction he approached us from, there was open meadow, which meant the sheriff would see him coming. Not even Scary Stan could cross that much open space without making a sound. Maybe instead of three bodies to stuff in the cave entrance, Paulsen would make it four.

And then I heard it. An almost imperceptible padding sound coming from the other side of the old fence.

Nigel was stalking us through the cover of trees.

My mind raced with possibility.

I quickly scanned the fence ahead, looking for the spot where the wire fence had been ripped out yesterday morning. Sure enough, the cut edges still framed a wide open gap from the meadow into the forest. The sheriff obviously knew about Kami's new electronic invisible fence on the far side of her property, but did she know there was a new invisible fence operating on this side as well? I had to assume she didn't, since she'd been cutting the old flimsy wire one early Saturday morning in hopes of wrecking more havoc around Kami's land. So the question was: if I could get Paulsen near enough to the gap, could I bluff her into believing the big cat had her in his sights long enough for Alan and I to disarm her?

Was this a pathetic plan or what?

Definitely pathetic.

But pathetic or not, it was all I had.

I edged closer to the gaping hole in the fence, pretending to study the ground for traces of a cave-in like the one Alan had fallen in earlier at the ATV wasteland, all the while trying to catch a glimpse of Nigel as he moved silently through the woods parallel to our path. I saw a glimmer of orange fur, which blended in perfectly with a shaft of sunlight cutting down through the trees.

"Look at this!" I said, especially loudly. I grabbed Alan's arm and pulled him next to me, pointing to a noticeable depression in the ground. Sheriff Paulsen kept her distance, her gun still trained on us. I kicked hard at the ground with my heel.

"It's loose! I bet the entrance is right around here. Alan, walk around this," I directed him with my hand. "You don't want to fall in like you did earlier today in that other spot. Sometimes these old entrances get covered with a thin coat of soil."

"You can both walk around to the other side," Paulsen said, pointing her gun to the place I'd indicated about fifteen feet from where we stood. "Let me take a look at this."

Alan and I slowly skirted the depression in the ground, walking in an arc away from the forest edge, while the sheriff came to stand in our place, her back practically framed by the gap in the wire fence. She kicked at the ground.

Nothing happened.

"I thought you said this soil was loose," she said to me. "It feels like solid rock."

Behind her, Nigel slunk out of the tree cover and silently positioned himself to leap at where she stood.

Poor cat. He was going to get a nasty shock when he crossed the line of the electronic fence. I guessed that Nigel wasn't a fast learner.

I opened my mouth to call the sheriff's attention to the tiger poised behind her, but Nigel beat me to the punch.

He let out a low growl.

Even from twenty feet away, I felt the hairs on my arm stand up from the sound.

The sheriff froze in place, and six hundred and fifty pounds of tiger launched itself into the air.

CHAPTER
THIRTY-SIX

Screaming in terror, Paulsen dove into the depression face first, her gun spinning off towards the forest.

Nigel, stunned by the electronic fence, landed in an unconscious heap right behind her. The momentum of his big body had carried him past the old wire fence line and into the meadow.

"Holy crap," I heard Alan breathe beside me.

"Go get Kami and bring her over here to take care of Nigel," I told him, hustling over to where Paulsen's gun had landed. "He'll be out for a little while, but I'd much rather she was right here when he does wake up." I snatched up the gun and aimed it at Paulsen, who seemed equally unconscious in the dirt.

"A pathetic plan, huh?" I congratulated myself, then studied the sleeping tiger. "Thanks, buddy. Anytime you want to take a flying leap, it's okay with me."

A moment later, Paulsen stirred as Alan and Kami came running back to meet me, Kami's hands still cuffed together. I handed the gun to Alan. "You cover her, Hawk. You know I hate guns."

Alan expertly drew a bead on the base of Paulsen's skull. "Sit up with your hands on your head," he told her. "I grew up shooting snakes on the reservation, and I'm not about to miss one now."

I looked at him in surprise. "Pretty intimidating for a high school history teacher, don't you think?"

He threw me a grin. "Man, I could get used to birding with you, Bob. It sure beats the hell out of watching C-SPAN."

Great. Alan the Six-shooting Birdwatcher.

"I'm positively underwhelmed," I told him, pulling out my cell phone.

"Who are you calling?" Kami asked, kneeling beside Nigel. I noticed her hands resting on the tiger's flank, rising and falling with his deep breathing.

"Stan Miller," I said, just as he picked up at his end. "Where are you? And why aren't you already here?"

"Flat. Had to fix it."

"You got a flat tire?" I almost laughed out loud. I'd always assumed real life didn't apply to Scary Stan.

He ignored my question and my tone, too. "Be there in five."

"No rush," I said. "We have the situation under control. But I don't know who to call when the sheriff is the one we want to arrest."

He let out a soft whistle. "In four," he replied. The phone went dead in my hand.

"Stan will know what to do," I told Kami and Alan, who had raised the gun to keep it level with Paulsen's head as she had lifted herself into a sitting position on the ground. She kept her back towards us, but took a look over her shoulder, probably just to make sure Alan really did have a gun on her.

"Why Billy?" I asked her again.

"Why Jack?" Kami added, her voice crackling with anger. "If it was Ben's idea, I swear to God I'll kill him myself."

Paulsen didn't say a word.

"I think it was the sheriff's idea," I explained to Kami. "A spur-of-the-moment one. I'm guessing Jack caught her tearing down the fence right over there on Friday night, and somehow she forced him over to Green Hills before she shot him. Then she figured she'd frame you for it, thereby eliminating you as an obstacle to what she thought Ben wanted: the ATV project. She killed Jack at the youth camp because she knew he'd be found faster there than here in this seepage meadow that only a few birders know about." I took a look at Paulsen's back, still stiffly erect. "Have I got it right, Sheriff?"

She didn't answer.

Not that I really expected her to.

But it would have been nice to have some affirmation of my guesswork.

Kami, however, began to fit together a few more pieces of the murder puzzle.

"Wait a minute," she whispered. "Remember I told you that Eddie and I started tracking Billy's car on Friday? Eddie told me on Saturday morning that Billy's car had made a brief stop not far from the turn-off to the meadow here after he left my place following Jack, but neither of us could figure out why Billy would do that. But he was following Jack, so he must have stopped because Jack stopped. And Jack must have stopped because he saw a car turning back onto the road from the meadow's turn-off and thought that was odd."

Kami's fists clenched on Nigel's fur. "Jack knew there was nothing down that road but the seepage meadow, so why would anyone be out there at two or three in the morning?"

"Unless that someone was messing with your fence?" Alan suggested.

"So Jack followed the car," Kami continued, conviction coloring her voice. "He had to have recognized it as the sheriff's patrol car and wanted to know what was going on in the seepage meadow that had caused her to come out there."

"Let me guess," I interrupted her, and looked at the sheriff, who still kept her back towards us. "You led him to Green Hills, because you knew it was deserted and a popular birding spot, pulled a gun on him when he got out of the car, walked him down the slope and shot him."

"And Billy, who was following far enough behind not to give himself away to Jack, showed up at Green Hills just in time to hear the gunshots," Alan concluded. "So Billy knew who killed Jack. Then, a few hours later, Billy, theoretically on his way to Mystery Cave, ends up with a dart in his neck and a bullet in his head."

Kami suddenly smacked her forehead with her shackled palms. "Of course! The county sheriff has access to tranquilizer darts to manage wildlife problems—Paulsen must have picked one up to use on Billy, which would also implicate me. But why Mystery Cave?"

"Ben," Stan said, suddenly materializing behind me.

I swear the man is half ghost.

"Where'd you come from?" Alan demanded, obviously rattled by Stan's silent approach. I, at least, was getting somewhat more accustomed to his sneaking up on me. Then again, I wasn't holding a gun on a murderer who happened to be an officer of the law, either. No wonder Alan was jumpy.

"Thief River Falls," Stan replied, his voice flat.

Alan looked even more confused. Thief River Falls was more than halfway across the state from Fillmore County.

"He means where did you come from right now, Stan," I clarified, "not where you grew up."

Stan gave me his usual empty-eye look. "Oh."

"What's Ben got to do with Billy's death?" Kami asked him, picking up on what Stan had said when he appeared.

"Traced Billy's phone calls. Ben was last." He held his hand out to Alan. "Gun."

Alan passed the gun to Stan, who slipped it into the back of his camou-flage pants. "Friends are on the way," he added.

"Care to elaborate?" I asked him.

He gave me another empty-eye look.

I shrugged. "Just thought I'd ask."

He turned his attention to Kami. "Billy called Ben yesterday morning. We're going to talk to Ben about it. My guess is that they set up a meeting for something, but only Ben walked away."

"The sheriff was the one who walked away," I corrected him.

"That right? Guess she took the meeting, then. Not Ben." He studied Paulsen's back. "We'll see." He glanced again at Kami and focused on her cuffed hands. "Let me get you out of those." He took two steps toward her, then froze as Nigel stirred beside her.

"It's okay," she assured him. "He's going to be unconscious a little bit yet." She held out her hands for Stan to release. He slipped a thin wire from one of his pants pockets and slid it into the cuffs, which sprang open. "Thanks," Kami smiled, watching Stan's fingers remove the cuffs from her wrists. He stuck them in the back of his camo pants, too.

"Are you always this well prepared?" I asked him.

"Apparently not," he replied, his voice a dull monotone. "Didn't expect a flat."

I looked over at Paulsen, who still wouldn't face us. "I didn't expect a crooked sheriff."

For a moment or two, we were all quiet, and then Kami spoke up. "I wonder where that cave entrance is," she mused. "If it's the real motive be-hind everything here, it's got to exist."

She pointed to the far side of the meadow that seemed to crest abruptly. "If I were hunting for a sinkhole or cave entrance in a hidden bluff, it might be over there. It looks like old karst territory."

I looked in the direction she pointed. It was beyond the area Alan and I had searched earlier and seemed to form a natural border to the seepage meadow's wetlands.

"Let's take a look," I said to Alan, striking off towards the opposite side of the meadow. At the same time, I heard cars approaching on the road. Stan's friends were about to show up. "Give him the whole story, Kami," I shouted back to her. "He really is one of the good guys."

A Bobwhite Killing

Ten minutes later, Alan and I were bending over, inspecting a wide dark mouth of a cave in the underside of the meadow's far crest.

"What do you think, Professor?" I asked Alan.

"A definite possibility," he replied. "It's big enough for a person to crawl into, and though I can't see very far into it, I don't see a back wall, either." He straightened up. "You want to go in and investigate?"

I took another look into the black maw. "Nah. I think I'll let the experts get swallowed into the depths of darkness where they are helpless prey to the whims of unstable geological formations."

Alan laughed. "I guess caves rate right up there for you where bats rate for me."

"You got that right."

We both looked into the cave entrance again. Near my feet a small wet trickle of water soaked into the ground. I looked at the brush and empty fields that spread away from the cave; it was actually a good habitat, sheltered and quiet, and chances were good there were some other hidden springs of water rising up through the karst land.

Someone whistled my name.

Bob-WHITE!

I grabbed Alan's arm and put my finger to my lips, cautioning him to be quiet and listen.

Very slowly I turned in the direction of the call.

A Northern Bobwhite was perched in a low branch of a sturdy shrub maybe twenty-four feet away on my right. It was a male, its white throat and eye line almost startling bright in the sunshine. Just below it, two more round reddish-brown quails foraged on the ground.

These were the Bobwhites Jack had promised us, tucked far away from the noise of the road and any ATV unsanctioned trails. I pointed them out to Alan, silently mouthing the birds' name.

"Are they rare?" Alan whispered.

"Pretty much," I whispered back. "They're considered extinct in the wild in Minnesota."

"They don't look extinct from here." He pinched my arm hard.

"Hey!"

Twenty feet away, the three Bobwhites took flight, leaving us alone on the edge of the field.

Alan feigned an innocent look. "Just checking. As long as this Bob White is alive and kicking, that's all I'm worried about."

"You just don't want to be alone on that altar when Lily comes marching down the aisle," I accused him.

"Damn straight," he agreed. "What's a best friend for, anyway?" He nodded towards the shrub that had held the calling Northern Bobwhite. "You going to tell your buddy Stan about the birds?"

I closed my eyes and rubbed my hand over my forehead. Stan had been a huge help in the last two days, trying to track down Ben's dealings to solve Jack's murder. For that and for Shana's sake, I was grateful.

He was, however, my longtime rival in the world of Minnesota birding, and I'd already handed one rare bird to him today.

"Sure," I said. "I'll tell Scary Stan." I paused a beat and grinned. "To-morrow."

Chapter
Thirty-Seven

John and Julianne O'Keefe looked impossibly small, their faces all scrunched up beneath little knit caps in their cribs in the hospital nursery.

"It's a good thing babies get better looking," I commented to Tom, who was standing at the big nursery window with me. "Those puffy eyelids look like they've been on a heck of a bender all night."

"You'd look that way too if you'd just spent nine months immersed in fluid," Tom replied. "And I don't recommend you give it a try, either." He nodded towards the twins. "They look great, especially considering they were about a month early. They don't even have to spend time in the preemie ward. These are a couple of healthy kids."

I watched John and Julianne continue to sleep in their twin cribs and wondered if either of them would have Shana's emerald eyes. Judging from the wisps of black hair escaping from under the little caps, the O'Keefe kids definitely had their mother's raven hair.

Bernie stood next to me, the middle of her body looking especially bulky thanks to the bandaging around her ribs beneath her shirt. "Have you seen Shana yet?"

I hadn't. After reporting back to Kami that Alan and I had located a probable cave entrance in the far side of the seepage meadow, we'd been swept up by Stan and his numerous friends from various law enforcement agencies to accompany them to the nearest police station. While we drank enough coffee to float a flotilla, we laid out everything we knew about Big Ben, Sheriff Paulsen, fossil finds, Jack, Billy, ATV manufacturers, and invisible fencing for exotic animal sanctuaries. Four hours later, Alan had headed home to his blushing bride-to-be, and I'd driven over to the hospital to see how Shana's labor was progressing.

Obviously, it had progressed very well. In fact, according to Tom, the ambulance had barely reached the ER before the twins made their grand entrance.

"I'm sure she'd like to see you," Bernie said. "Come on, I'll take you to her room."

We walked down the hall to a door that had two helium balloons—one pink, one blue—tied to the nameplate beside it. Just as Bernie reached for the door handle, though, it opened from the inside.

"Stan."

"White."

"Shana's not sleeping, is she?" Bernie asked. "I know she'd like to see Bob before he leaves for the Cities."

"She's awake," Stan said and walked away down the hall.

Bernie's eyes followed Stan past the nurses' station until he turned a corner and disappeared.

"Not exactly Mr. Conversation, is he?" she noted.

"Not exactly," I agreed. "But his actions definitely speak louder—and volumes more—than his words. If Stan hadn't been so quick to dig up information about Ben's questionable finances, I don't know if Sheriff Paulsen would be in custody right now for a double murder. I do know that without Stan and his friends, Alan, Kami, and I would probably still be sitting in the seepage meadow trying to figure out how to turn in a sheriff to her own police department."

"I heard the nurses say that Big Ben is in custody, too," Bernie said. When I gave her a startled look, she grinned. "News travels fast in a small town, Bob. Actually, I'm surprised the big city media hasn't shown up yet. They've got to have sources down here."

"Hey, Mr. White!"

Bernie and I both turned towards the end of the hall. Skip Swenson was waving at us, his forward progress blocked by two determined nurses.

"The press has arrived," I announced, waving back at Skip. "Wait here a minute. I'll go talk to him."

The nurses parted to let me through, and I took Skip by the shoulder, turning him around and leading him to a small waiting area at the end of the hallway where we could talk in private.

"What a story!" he gushed. "I called the hotline at two television stations in the Cities, and they're sending crews right away to cover the whole thing. If this doesn't get me an internship, I don't know what will."

"That's great, Skip. But do me one favor, okay?"

"What's that?"

"You tell the crews that Mrs. O'Keefe isn't talking with anyone for a day or two. She just had her babies, and that's what she needs to focus on right now. I'm sure she'll make a statement later, but for now, you keep the media clear of her. Can you do that for me?"

"I'll try, but some of these media people can be really persistent, you know?"

"Yeah, I know. Present company excepted, right?"

Skip blushed and ducked his head. "Yeah."

"And something else, Skip?" He looked back up at me. "Okay, it's two favors I need. Leave me and Mr. Thunderhawk out of it."

"But," he started to say as I cut him off with my hand.

"Skip, there are plenty of other people involved in this story, and I'm sure they'll be more than happy to talk with you and the media. More power to them. I just want to go home and forget about a really bad birding weekend. Do this for me," I added, sweetening the pot, "and I'll personally help you find an internship for next summer—in the Twin Cities."

I glanced down the hall at Bernie, who was waiting for me outside Shana's room. Even from down the hall, I could hear her making fussing noises to the nurses about Shana's care. The woman was an incorrigible mother hen. I smiled at Skip. "In fact, I may even know a sweet old lady who'd love to rent you a room in her house and mother you to death for the summer. Deal?"

Skip brushed his blonde bangs off his forehead, then held out his hand to shake mine. "Deal," he said, and we shook on it.

"Great. Now keep the press out of here when they show up, because I've already been on the nighttime news one more time than I ever wanted to be." I patted his shoulder a final time and went back to Bernie.

"Anyone else in there?" I asked, nodding towards Shana's open door.

"Nope. It's your turn, Bob." And with that, Bernie fluttered away to badger the nursing staff some more.

I knocked on the door frame and walked in.

"Hi," Shana said from her hospital bed. She had an IV dripping into one arm and wore a hospital gown covered in little angels.

She was also wearing a very pretty smile that lit up those emerald eyes of hers.

"Did you see them?" she asked, her voice tired but filled with unmistakable pride and joy.

I pulled a chair next to her bed and sat down. "They're beautiful, Shana. You do nice work."

She laughed and tears clouded her eyes. "Yeah, I do," she agreed. "Me and Jack. He would have been an extraordinary father, Bob."

I reached out and took her hand. "Absolutely."

She smiled and color rushed into her cheeks. "About Bobwhites—"

"It was a great summer, wasn't it?" I interrupted her. "You and I birding all over the Cities. Man, we were just kids, weren't we?"

"Yeah, we were." She smiled, and for a split-second, I could almost smell the White Shoulders perfume from that summer. "I had a huge crush on you, you know," she quietly admitted. "You were the first guy anywhere close to my own age I'd ever met who got as excited as I did to wade through a swamp just to see a bird."

I laughed, too, then patted her hand. "The feeling was mutual, Shana. I never thought I'd meet anyone else like you. When you left for grad school, you broke my heart. I didn't think I'd ever recover."

Her eyes met mine and she smiled. "But you did. And so did I. We birders are a very resilient species, aren't we?"

I returned her smile. "Yes, we are."

"And extremely clever, too, if half of what Stan told me is true about how you solved Jack's and Billy's murders."

"Depends on what he told you." Thinking of Stan, I couldn't help but add, "That's assuming he actually spoke to you in full sentences."

Shana laughed again. "Stan's a good man. A little verbally challenged at times, but a good man." She studied my hand over hers. "We worked together for a while."

"You were an accountant?"

Her eyes flew back to mine and her lips twitched in amusement. "No, I wasn't an accountant."

I opened my mouth to ask her what she meant, but then it hit me like a sudden downpour.

Shana had worked for the CIA.

"Costa Rica?" I asked, remembering Chuck's nasty accusations about Shana's first marriage and her murdered husband.

"After that, actually," she said. "My first husband—Dennis—unknowingly tripped across a smuggling ring in Nicaragua and was murdered. Stan was working the case and recruited me to help with the investigation, and then, for a couple years, I continued to do some jobs for the agency. Meeting Jack changed all that. I wanted to come home, settle down, have kids. Pretty dull, I know, but I'd had enough excitement in my life."

I squeezed her hand. "Newsflash, honey. The excitement isn't over yet, not by a long shot. You've got a couple of gorgeous kids to raise. And between Bernie, Tom, me, and everyone else who cares about you, you're going to have more help than you ever imagined. Maybe even Stan will help out—he could teach John and Julianne how to hold entire conversations using only one-word sentences."

Shana laughed. "Oh great. My kids will sound like teenage boys their whole lives."

"Hey, I was a teenage boy once."

"I know. And I was crazy about you, but you were still barely articulate."

I squeezed her hand again. "I don't have to take this kind of abuse from you. I've got a sister who dedicates herself to abusing me. I'm going home." I stood up and then leaned over to plant a kiss on her cheek. "Take care of yourself, Shana. Call me?"

She nodded. "Definitely. I want the twins to learn birding from only the best." She paused, her eyes misting. "Thanks, Bob, for everything."

I gave her a little salute and went out into the hall, where Tom and Bernie were waiting.

"Taking off?" Tom asked me.

"Yeah, I need to get back home. Are you two sticking around a while?"

"Just till Shana's folks get here," Bernie said. "Their flight should be landing in Rochester in the next hour."

"Good. She needs her family."

"Speaking of which, we just left Chuck O'Keefe in front of the nursery," Tom told me. "I got the distinct impression he plans to make amends with Shana. I told him good luck with that, but he seemed pretty intent on making things right between him and his new siblings."

"I hope she makes his life miserable," Bernie objected. "He deserves it for the way he's treated her, not to mention the scam he was pulling on his dad."

"Why, Bernie," I said, "I'm surprised. Here I thought you were such a sweetheart. No way I would have pegged you for a vengeful woman."

"I've got a cracked rib," she pointed out, "thanks to him."

I frowned. "Chuck cut my brake line? Who told you that?"

"Nobody. But I figure it's like that nursery rhyme, 'This is the house that Jack built.'"

"Come again?"

"'This is the house that Jack built.' One thing leads to another. If Chuck hadn't funded the ATV group against his dad's eco-community project, there wouldn't have been a zoning dispute which the sheriff was trying to force by cutting Kami's fences and Jack wouldn't have caught her in the act and gotten himself killed."

"And this has to do with my car . . . how?"

Bernie rubbed her bandaged side. "Well, I don't know exactly, but I'm sure it's connected somehow."

"You just want to blame Chuck because he was so mean to Shana," Tom said.

"Maybe I do. He's a poor excuse for a son-in-law."

Since I'd already made my feelings about Chuck O'Keefe abundantly clear when I'd decked him earlier in the day, I decided it was as good a time as any to make my exit.

"I'm out of here," I told them. "Call me if the sheriff breaks down and spills her guts to Stan and his friends. From what I overheard at the police station, they're going to need either a confession or some hard evidence to prove she's guilty. Everything else is just circumstantial."

Which, in the birding world, is all you need sometimes: the right circumstances conspiring together to help you find a bird—the right location, the right time of year, the right weather. Of course, dumb luck never hurts either. Just like the way Alan and I had stumbled on the Bobwhite this afternoon.

In the same way, I could only hope that all the right circumstances would come together for the detectives now investigating Jack's and Billy's deaths, and with any luck—dumb or otherwise—Sheriff Paulsen would be put away for a long, long time.

I drove out of the hospital parking lot and headed for home.

CHAPTER
THIRTY-EIGHT

I was almost home when my cell phone rang on the passenger seat beside me. I flipped it open and hit the loudspeaker key. "Hello?"

A stranger's voice came on. "I'm looking for a Bob White."

So was I, I thought, recalling how I'd turned around from the cave entrance that afternoon and seen a Northern Bobwhite in the branch of a shrub. And I found it, too, I congratulated myself.

"This is Bob."

"This is Detective Harriman in Fillmore County. Stan Miller asked me to call you and let you know we found evidence that Sheriff Paulsen was the one who cut your brake line. We found a tool in her squad car trunk with brake fluid on it. I understand that your vehicle is readily identified by your vanity plates, so that would explain how she knew which car was yours at the hotel lot on Saturday night."

No surprise there. It wasn't the first time my plates had given me away. Usually it was to the highway patrol when I was racking up speeding tickets. Tagging my car for sabotage was a novelty.

"We also know that you spoke with the sheriff Saturday night concerning your suspicions about Ben Graham. We're operating on the assumption that was her motive for cutting your brake line—she didn't want you nosing any further into his affairs, so she decided to make you feel unwelcome in town."

"That's putting it mildly," I noted. "Especially since it resulted in an accident that injured my friend. It could, conceivably, have been a lot worse, Detective. We could have been killed."

"That's why I'm calling. Do you want to press charges?"

I wasn't sure. Naturally, I wanted justice for Bernie and myself, but at the same time, I wasn't convinced I wanted to be a part of the media feeding frenzy that was bound to spring up around a sensational double murder case like this one. I'd already had a taste of sound-byte fame on television, and it sure hadn't left me with an appetite for more.

"Can I get back to you on that?"

"Your call, Mr. White. Oh, and Stan said I should tell you something else we found. The bug on Billy Mason's car not only broadcast location, but it was an amazing piece of hardware. It actually recorded conversations in the car—in particular, we got one side of a phone conversation that Billy had with Ben Graham after he'd witnessed Jack's murder. Billy told the mayor he had some information about the sheriff that could ruin them both and he set up a drop point for a blackmail payoff at Mystery Cave. We played the tape for Graham, and he admitted he'd called the sheriff about it. Apparently, they both decided that Paulsen should be the one to meet Billy. And the gun that shot O'Keefe? It turns out it was one that had gone missing from the evidence room at the police station."

"So you've got enough for a solid case against the sheriff?"

"I'd say so. The prosecutor in this case is going to have his pick of charges, for both the sheriff and the mayor. That little bug turned out to be a big break for us."

"Thank you, Eddie Edvarg," I said. Crazy Eddie's electronic wizardry had once again won one for the home team.

There was a momentary silence at the other end of the phone connection. "The name's Harriman," the detective reminded me, "but you're welcome anyway. Let me know what you decide about charges."

I closed the phone and turned into the driveway of my townhouse. The automatic garage door opener jammed and refused to raise the door, so I left my car outside and let myself in through the front door.

I wasn't alone.

Sprawled across my living room sofa was Luce, sound asleep. Her long blonde hair trailed over the cushions and her left hand hung off the couch, almost touching the floor rug. A couple of cartons from her favorite Chinese take-out place were sitting on the coffee table, empty, but still filling the room with a lingering aroma of lemon chicken.

I sat next to her hip and laid my hand on her shoulder.

"Luce. Wake up. I'm home."

She made some sleepy noises and blinked her eyes open.

"You're home."

"I know. Not that I'm not happy to see you, but what are you doing here? You knew I was gone."

She pulled herself up onto her elbows and yawned. "I'm in hiding."

"From?"

"Your sister. She's driving me crazy. I don't think I want to be a maid of honor anymore."

I traced my finger over her full lips and smiled. "Then how about being the bride instead?"

She rolled her beautiful blue eyes and groaned. "I don't want to marry Alan, Bob. I know he's your best friend, but he can't tell a Northern Cardinal from a Bluejay."

"I'm not so sure about that," I told her. "He was birding with me today, and I think he's salvageable." I pressed my lips against hers in a warm, soft kiss.

"I mean *my* bride, Luce," I said a minute later. "I love you. I want to spend the rest of my life with you. Will you marry me?"

For a few seconds, she didn't say a thing. She just stared at me.

And then, finally, she smiled.

"Yes."

BOB WHITE'S
"A BOBWHITE KILLING"
BIRD LIST

Yellow-billed Cuckoo
Red-shouldered Hawk
Upland Sandpiper
Eastern Meadowlark
Western Meadowlark
Bobolink
Horned Lark
Turkey Vulture
Acadian Flycatcher
Vesper Sparrow
Savannah Sparrow
Field Sparrow
Willow Flycatcher
Indigo Bunting
Great Horned Owl
Mourning Dove
Killdeer
Cliff Swallow
Barn Swallow
Northern Rough-winged Swallow
Worm-eating Warbler
Blue Jay
Eastern Phoebe
Eastern Wood-Pewee
Red-tailed Hawk
Northern Bobwhite

ACKNOWLEDGMENTS

Several years ago, I went on my first Minnesota Birding Weekend led by Kim Eckert. Our group didn't find any bodies, but we did see turtles, along with quite a few birds. That experience convinced me I had to set a Bob White Birder Murder on a weekend birding trip in order to take advantage of the wonderful repartee amongst a flock of seasoned birders. Thanks, Kim, for introducing me to that part of the birding life. I also want to express my appreciation to Karla Kinstler, Director of the Houston Nature Center, for allowing me to write her and Alice into Bob White's world. If you ever have the chance to attend the International Festival of Owls in Houston, Minnesota, in early March, it's well worth the trip—the whole town goes crazy over owls (think owl-face pancakes and a Great Gray mocha for breakfast), thanks to Karla's efforts.